Welcome to Land of Fright™!

Land of Fright™ is a world of spine-tingling short horror stories filled with the strange, the eerie, and the weird. The **Land of Fright™** series encompasses the vast expanse of time and space. You will visit the world of the Past in such places and eras as Ancient China, Medieval England, the old West, World War II, and other epochs and locations yet to be revealed. You will find many tales that exist right here in the Present, tales filled with modern lives that have taken a turn down a darker path. You will travel into the Future to tour strange new worlds and interact with alien societies, or to just take a disturbing peek at what tomorrow may bring.

Each **Land of Fright™** story exists in its own territory (which we like to call a **terrorstory**.) These terrorstories can be visited in any order you choose. Some of the story realms you visit will intrigue you. Some of them may unsettle you. Some of them may even titillate and amuse you. We hope many of them will give you delicious chills along your journey. And there are many new uncharted realms yet to be mapped, so keep checking back for new discoveries.

First, we need to check your ID. **Land of Fright™** is intended for mature audiences. You will experience adult language, graphic violence, and some explicit sex. Ready to enter? Good. We'll take that ticket now. **Land of Fright™** awaits. You can pass through the dark gates and—Step Into Fear!

Readers Love Land of Fright™!

"This is the first story I've read by this author and it blew me away! A gripping tale that kept me wondering until the end. Images from this will, I fear, haunt me at unexpected moments for many months to come. Readers, be warned! :)" – Amazon review for **Dung Beetles (Land of Fright™ #27 – in Collection III)**

"Some truly original stories. At last, a great collection of unique and different stories. Whilst this is billed as horror, the author managed to steer away from senseless violence and gratuitous gore and instead with artful story telling inspires you to use your own imagination. A great collection. Already looking for other collections… especially loved Kill the Queen (God Save the Queen)." – Amazon UK review for **Land of Fright™ Collection I**

"This was a great story. Even though it was short I still connected with the main character and was rooting for her. Once I read the twist I cheered her on. This was an enjoyable short story." – Amazon review for **Snowflakes (Land of Fright™ #3 – in Collection I)**

"Love the freaky tales from the Land of Fright. This one is particularly nasty and dark. A tale of double revenge unfolds in a graveyard where a perceived business betrayal causes the perceiver to enact an insidious plan to impose the ultimate suffering on his partner. The suffering takes an unexpected turn that I did not see coming." – Amazon review for **Cemetery Dance (Land of Fright™ #49 – in Collection V)**

"I absolutely loved the heck out of this story. The whole story was bizarre, and the end? Well, it was perfect!" – Amazon review for **The Throw-Aways (Land of Fright™ #31 – in Collection IV)**

"I like the idea of a malevolent dimension that finds a way to reach into our world… this was an entertaining read and can be read at lunch or as a palate cleanser between longer stories." – Amazon review for **Sparklers (Land of Fright™ #15 – in Collection II)**

"I enjoyed this quite a bit, but then I enjoy anything set in Pompeii. A horror story is a first, though, and well done. I'm become a fan of the author and so far have enjoyed several of his stories." – Amazon review for **Ghosts of Pompeii (Land of Fright™ #14 – in Collection II)**

"Fantastic science fiction short that has a surprising plot twist, great aliens, cool future tech and occurs in a remote lived-in future mining colony on a distant planet. This short hit all the marks I look for in science fiction stories. The alien creatures are truly alien and attack with a mindless ruthlessness. The desperate colonists defend themselves in a uniquely futuristic way. This work nails the art of the short story. Recommended." – Amazon review for **Out of Ink (Land of Fright™ #26 – in Collection III)**

"I am a fan of the Land of Fright series and have found the horror found in the stories diverse and delightfully bizarre. This tale amp's up the gritty to 11. The barbarian warrior king in this short story is a well written, fearsome, crude and believable beast of a man. This story is not for those offended by sex or violence. I was immersed and found it great escapism, exactly what I look for in recreational reading."- Amazon review for **The King Who Owned The World (Land of Fright™ #50 – in Collection V)**

"Another great story; I've become a fan of Mr. O'Donnell. Please keep them coming…" – Amazon review for **Sands of the Colosseum (Land of Fright™ #18 – in Collection II)**

"Perfect bite size weirdness. Land of Fright does it again with this Zone like short that has two creative plot twists that really caught me off guard. I know comparing this type of work to the Twilight Zone is overdone but it really is a high compliment that denotes original, well conceived and delightfully weird short fiction. Recommended." – Amazon review for **Flipbook (Land of Fright™ #19 – in Collection II)**

"An enjoyable story; refreshingly told from the point of view of the cat...definitely good suspense." – Amazon review for **Pharaoh's Cat (Land of Fright™ #30 – in Collection III)**

"A fun thrill-ride into the Mexican jungle, and another great Land of Fright tale. Not enough people have written horror stories or novels about Aztec sacrifices." -Amazon review for **Virgin Sacrifice (Land of Fright™ #42 – in Collection V)**

"This short has a cool premise and was very effective at quickly transporting me to the sands of the coliseum in ancient Rome. The images of dead and dying gladiators are detailed and vivid. There is a malevolent force that very much likes its job and is not about to give it up, ever. Recommended." – Amazon review for **Hammer of Charon (Land of Fright™ #29 - in Collection III)**

"The thing I like about the Land of Fright series of short stories is that they are so diverse yet share a common weird, unusual and original vibe. From horror to science fiction they are all powerful despite of their brevity. Another great addition to the Land of Fright festival of the odd." - Amazon review for **Snowflakes (Land of Fright™ #3 – in Collection I)**

Welcome to the **Land of Fright**™
A World of Spine Tingling Stories filled with the Strange, the Eerie, and the Weird

Land of Fright™

Collection IV

JACK O'DONNELL

DEDICATION

To everyone who likes to escape into a good story. Especially to those who hate coming back out of one...

LAND OF FRIGHT™
COLLECTION IV
CONTENTS

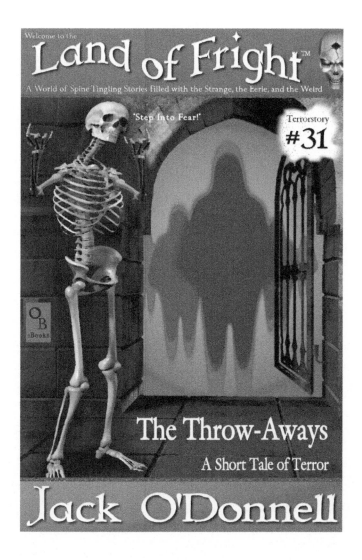

TERRORSTORY #31
THE THROW-AWAYS

Brock Magnuson stared at the shape of a shadowed human form standing still in his backyard. The moon was full in the night sky, looking like a glow-in-the-dark communion wafer. Layers of wispy clouds drifted by, obscuring the moon's wan light so its moonbeams only reached the Earth in pale streams of intermittent light. Brock was in his late forties, pale of skin, pale of hair, and pale of any desire to move from where he stood in his kitchen staring out the sliding glass door that led to his backyard.

An open bottle of rum rested on the kitchen table nearby, the spicy aroma permeating the entire area. Brock had mixed the first two glasses of the night with some generic cola, but now he just sipped the rum straight. He thought about calling up to his wife, who was sleeping in their bedroom upstairs, but he kept quiet. Anne was already pissed enough about his drinking, and getting her out of bed at three AM to ask her about his hallucination wouldn't go over very well.

His kids were fast asleep, so he didn't want to bother them either. He vaguely remembered that Trina had a test in Algebra, so he was not going to disturb his daughter's much needed sleep. *Or was that yesterday she had her test?* No matter. He wasn't going to wake her. Sammy was probably still out with his buddies somewhere. Brock never knew where that kid was. Ever since Sammy dropped out of college, the kid had just flitted about, working a job delivering pizzas for two weeks, getting fired, working another job making burgers for two weeks then quitting. Sometimes he didn't see his son for a week.

Brock took another drink of rum and the golden liquid burned his throat with a most welcome burn. He stared back at the shape standing in his backyard. Brock could now see the shape was clearly a man as a stream of moonlight revealed the shadowy figure more clearly. The man stood in the middle of his yard, right in the center of the circle of dirt where he was going to put in his new patio. They had taken down their above-ground pool the previous summer because the kids had outgrown it and never used it anymore. He wasn't going to work at maintaining a pool if no one was going to use the damn thing, so they tore it down. All that remained was a cut circle in the middle of the yard, dug out a foot or two into the ground, layered with sand. They still needed to level it and put the stones in to create the patio base, but they weren't planning on doing that until the weather warmed up. So there the man stood in the middle of the circle of sand, wearing a red shirt and dark pants, staring at the house. Staring at him.

Despite the murky moonlight shadowing the man's features, Brock knew who the man was. He could tell by the long black hair that curled around the man's broad shoulders. He couldn't see it because of the dim light, but Brock knew the man had a long jagged scar on his face, running from beneath his right eye down across his cheek and under the right side of his nose. The scar pulsed when the man was angry. Brock wondered if the man was angry right now. Then he realized that was a foolish thought. Of course he was angry. The man was always angry. *Isn't that what I had named him? The Angry Man?* Brock struggled to remember, but the fog of the rum and the lingering effects of too little sleep muddled his thoughts for a moment. *Yes, the Angry Man. That was it*, he thought. *That was the man's name. Angry Man.*

Brock glanced down at the tumbler in his hand. There were still a few fingers of rum left in the glass. He swirled the amber liquid absently, then took a sip. No sense wasting good rum, despite the hallucination it was causing him. He knew the man in his backyard wasn't real. He couldn't be. Brock had imagined him. He was just a character in one of his action thrillers. He was one of Brock's creations. He only existed for the sake of adding violence and death into the story.

The man was just a throw-away. A character he introduced so he could kill him off.

Brock looked back up at the man standing in his backyard. The moonlight seemed to have grown brighter because he could now see Angry Man more clearly. Angry Man was wearing a red shirt. Brock thought about that for a moment. A Red shirt. Red shirts were how fans referred to the characters on the classic Star Trek TV show who always died in the episodes. Wearing a red shirt on that show was a sure sign of imminent death. The color red was a running gag Brock used in most of his novels. He only mentioned it once per character. Sometimes it was a red shirt, or a red dress, or red shoes, or the character was holding something red. Some of his readers caught on to the gag, but not too many. The 'red' characters always died, no matter what. Sometimes he would tease the reader, letting them think a red character was going to live, but they never did.

And then Brock remembered Angry Man more clearly. He was from his novel *The Butcher's Boy*. Angry Man had died an ugly death. The hero of that book, Ignatius Quinn, had tracked down the main villain of *The Butcher's Boy* in the deserts of Arizona. Angry Man had been one of the villain's bodyguards, one of his top henchmen. The hero Quinn had taken Angry Man down with the arm of a cactus, putting a thousand tiny holes in Angry Man's flesh with the cactus's spines as he fought him in a duel to the death in the desert.

Brock stared out the window. He wondered why Angry Man. Why was he seeing him? Why was his brain conjuring him up? The character really hadn't made much of an impact on him. He had created

6

him, gave him a few paragraphs of back story, and then wasted him.

Brock took another sip of rum from his tumbler, then lowered his hand, holding the glass very loosely in his fingertips. He knew he should go to bed, but he also knew he wouldn't be able to sleep. He hadn't been sleeping well for weeks now. He was exhausted, but he still knew sleep would be difficult, if it came at all. The bouts of insomnia hit him a few times a year and this year had been no exception. He was smack dab in the middle of another bad one. Too many bills, too many family squabbles, too much yelling, too many bad reviews for his newest thriller, too many added pounds around his waist, too much social media negativity, too many Twitter rants about his misogynistic heroes. Too much graphic violence. Too much sex in his books. Too little sex in his own bedroom. Too few sales. That was the real kicker. Too few sales lately. *Maybe I should just throw in the towel,* he thought. *I had a good run for a few years, but the market is so saturated with ebooks now that it's difficult to break through all the clutter.*

Brock was tempted to throw open the sliding glass door and yell at Angry Man, but he was afraid Angry Man might yell back. Brock knew that would only prove to himself that he had gone insane. No, best to leave his hallucination alone. No sense in giving it a voice, too.

Brock glanced at a coffee-stained paperback on the table that he sometimes used as a coaster. It was one of his own books. A thin little WWII action ditty about a rogue private hunting down Mussolini's bastard son. The enemy bastard killed all the men in the private's squad with poison and the GI wanted revenge. Brock had knocked that sucker out in a few weeks. It barely reached 150 pages. ***Mussolini and the Mustard Gas Bastard.*** What a dumb title. But it still sold a few copies a day. He shrugged.

He read the name of the author he had invented for himself on the spine of the paperback. Brock Magnuson. Brock Magnuson, what a name. He quirked the corner of his lip up in a snide smile as he thought about the pen name. *That's not even my real name. Even I'm a character I just made up.*

What is your real name? Do you even remember? The little voice in his head goaded him with its mocking whisper. *Of course I remember. It's—* and then he had a moment of real panic. *What the fuck is my real name?* He felt his head start to swirl, his thoughts threatening to spin out of control. His breathing quickened. He forgot. He forgot his real name as easily as if he had forgotten where he had set down his car keys. *It'll come back to me.*

You're Brock. Brock Magnuson. It says so right there on that book you wrote. He forced himself to calm down, forced himself to take a slow breath, a gentle inhale and an easy exhale.

Then Brock noticed two more figures standing in his backyard. Young Boy and his Sister were holding hands. He hadn't seen them appear, but suddenly they were standing in the backyard near Angry Man. Neither one had much of a face, but Brock still immediately knew who they were. He hadn't bothered to give them much of a description in the book before sending them out into the middle of the street to get run over by a truck. From where he stood looking out into the backyard, all Brock could see was a dark patch where their eye sockets were supposed

8

to be and a crimson slash where their mouths were supposed to be. The Sister was wearing her My Little Pony pajamas, with a rainbow design running across the shirt behind the ponies that were on the front — that's where the hint of red came in, from the rainbow. Young Boy had his gym shorts on, the shorts lined with a red stripe running down the side, part of the color of his school gym uniform.

The two kids were from his action novel *The Sheik and the Suburban Hitmen*. Brock thought about the silly title and still couldn't decide whether he loved it or hated it. He took another sip from his tumbler of rum. The Sheik had sent two hitmen after a man who lived next door to Young Boy and his Sister. The two children had heard gunfire and shattering glass, and were afraid. Young Boy had grabbed Sister's hand and had raced away from the gunfire, dragging her along with him, thinking he was pulling her away to be somewhere safe. They had raced right into the path of an oncoming truck full of more hitmen and got crushed. Splat. Just like that they were dead, smeared across the cracked asphalt like a glob of cherry peach ice cream that had fallen off a sugar cone and flattened as it smacked against the ground.

Brock looked away from the two children.

There was now a woman sitting in one of the white plastic lounge chairs in his backyard. He immediately knew was Hooker. Brock actually felt a sense of relief at her presence. He always enjoyed bringing Hooker into a story. She titillated him just by thinking about how to use her in a story, about how to get her naked for the sake of the plot (yeah, right), and how to get her some of the cock she so loved to touch and suck and fuck. Brock looked at her fiery red hair, her long slender legs. She wore a tight-fitting white halter top and a short white skirt that barely had any material to it whatsoever. He knew she wasn't wearing any panties underneath the skirt. She never did. He could see the shimmer of her green eyes from where he stood. He felt a stirring in his loins, but he was too tired and too intoxicated for it to get much beyond a twitch. Brock used Hooker in nearly every book. Oh, he changed her name, gave her a new troubled background, gave her big tits, tiny tits, a big ass, a small ass, but she was really the same woman over and over again. Most of the time she died a gruesome death right after falling in love with the hero and his very skilled cock; he threw in other random deaths for Hooker in some books to kept it less predictable. He thought about letting her live in a few novels, but he never did. Her fiery red hair wouldn't allow it. That would break the rules he had set up for himself and his fictional universe. *Gotta be true to your own rules.*

Brock struggled to recall what had happened to Hooker in his latest book. Then he remembered and slowly nodded his head. The Butcher's Boy had carved her up like so much roast beef. He had even fed strips of her to his pit bulls. Brock shivered. That was a particularly nasty death for Hooker. Especially because she had still been alive and had to watch the Butcher's Boy feed her own flesh to his dogs.

He lifted the tumbler to his lips, but the glass was now empty. He grabbed the bottle of rum from the table nearby and poured a few more fingers of the amber liquid into the glass. Brock knew he should try and get some sleep, but he had a very pleasant buzz going on right now and he wanted to keep it going. And besides, he had guests. He looked back outside.

Hooker had removed her halter top and her beautiful breasts gleamed in the pale moonlight. She appeared to be moon bathing as she lounged in the chair, tilting her pretty face towards the light. *Ahh, Hooker,* Brock thought. *She never disappoints me.* She cupped her breasts and squeezed them, arching her back as her lips parted in a soft moan. He couldn't hear her from where he was standing, but Brock knew she was letting out a hot, throaty moan. Hooker loved to touch herself. She squeezed her tits some more, pinching at her erect nipples. She parted her legs wider, spreading her creamy thighs, giving him a glimpse of the glorious sight that had been hidden beneath her short skirt. Brock knew she was wet. Hooker was always wet, always ready. She slid her hands down to her thighs, rubbing her slender fingers up and down her flesh, teasing herself, teasing him. She looked up at him and Brock could see the obvious lust in her eyes, the aching desire for someone, anyone, to touch her and fuck her good. She moved one of her hands deeper between her legs, going for her pussy. She touched the edge of her cunt and rubbed her finger over the opening, then spread her lips wide with her fingers. *Jesus, she was a hot piece of ass.*

Brock felt more than a twitch between his legs now, but he was too tired to jerk off. He thought about going upstairs and waking up his wife by wagging his cock in her face, but he knew that wouldn't go over very well. *Oh, no. That wouldn't go over very well at all.* He mentally laughed at the thought of the extremely sour expression Anne would have on her face waking up with his dick dangling over her mouth. Hooker would love it, but his wife not so much. He took another sip of rum and continued to gaze out the window.

Young Boy and Sister stood at the edge of the circle of sand, still clutching hands. Young Boy darted his head this way and that, as if looking for somewhere to run but not knowing which direction to go. Sister looked up at Young Boy with her nearly non-existent eyes, obviously waiting for her brother to make a move that would bring them to safety. Angry Man hadn't moved at all. He continued to stare at the house. At Brock. Not surprisingly, Angry Man still looked mighty ticked off.

Brock looked away from Angry Man. He fought back the urge to go take a piss. The bathroom was barely a dozen feet away, but he knew once he broke the seal, he'd probably be pissing every two seconds.

Another man was visible in his backyard now. Brock knew who he was, too. It was Chef. He was wearing his white apron and his chef hat. He stood near the grill in Brock's backyard, which, of course, was the most obvious place for him to be standing. Chef had died in a gunfight in **Boobies and Bloodshed**. Brock had written that story in two weeks and spurt it up into KDP, selling the book on Amazon within hours after finishing it. There were still a bunch of typos in it, and he had even misspelled a character's name a few times, but his readers didn't seem to care. They all clamored for a sequel. Hell, he had even gotten a few good reviews for it. It was an erotica action story with a ton of explicit sex and rough violence that he wrote under one of his other pen names, Ginger Scarlucci. Erotica? Brock scoffed at himself. It was porn with Walther PPK's. Tits and bullets. He thought about emailing Amazon and telling them they needed to add another sub-category to their ebook classification system. Maybe breasts and bullets? Violence and vaginas? Booty and bazookas? He paused. *Booty and Bazookas. Shit, there's a story in that one somewhere. I'll have to remember that one. Ta-Ta's and Terrorists. Nut Sacks and Narcs. Beavers and Cleavers.* Brock glanced around for a notebook. *Shit, I need to write some of these down before I forget.* But he didn't see a notebook within easy reach, so he forgot just about all of those titles within a few seconds. He found himself looking back out the window, back out at his guests.

Brock's thoughts moved back to Chef and what had happened to the man in **Boobies and Bloodshed**. Chef hadn't even had a chance to turn around to see his killers. He was just an innocent victim in a Mafia turf war over prostitution. Chef had been tossing some vegetables in a skillet (red peppers, ha ha) in the kitchen of his posh restaurant when the bullets hit him in the back. One of the rounds knocked his white chef hat off his head and into the skillet first, seconds before the other barrage of bullets riddled Chef's back with a dozen slugs. Chef just grunted and slumped over. His face fell into the skillet where it started to sizzle. His blood mixed in with the olive oil, and the vegetables started to blacken along with his flesh. The gunfight continued on around Chef in the kitchen as the Mafiosos made their escape, and two sentences later Chef was a forgotten corpse.

Brock tilted the tumbler up against his lips and took another sip of rum. He smiled behind the glass.

This is kind of fun. Fucked up, but fun. He wondered if he was dreaming. This was just way too bizarre to be anything more than a dream. *I'm probably passed out on the kitchen floor,* he thought, *dreaming all this shit up in some kind of drunken stupor of a dream.* The rum was warm and delicious as it slid through his mouth, the bitter bite in the back of his throat calming him in a reassuring familiarity. He really did have to piss, but he pushed away the urge.

Another figure appeared out of the gloom. Brock recognized him immediately. It was Sissy Security Guard from **The Vault**, a heist story Brock had written years ago. Sissy Security Guard moved up next to Hooker, dressed in his dark blue security guard uniform. Sissy Security Guard paid no attention to Hooker as she continued to pleasure herself, but that didn't surprise Brock. Hooker wasn't his type. Sissy Security Guard was gay and he wore a tiny red jeweled earring in his right ear. He had a secret coke finger, just a slight extra tip of fingernail on his right pinkie finger. He kept a tiny pouch of blow in his pocket and dipped his pinkie into it when he needed a quick snort. The poor overworked guy needed it to stay awake on the night shift. The last guy who had the job fell asleep and got fired immediately. Sissy Security Guard needed the job, so he was willing to do anything to stay awake. Brock didn't know why he remembered those details in particular, he just did.

Of course, the coke kept Sissy Security Guard alive a little bit longer than the poor guy might have liked. The first bullet blew his pinkie finger right off, just as he was bringing a tiny scoop of white powder towards his nose for a third snort. The shit all happened to the poor guy at once. The gun firing, his pinkie finger

14

exploding, the footsteps racing towards him. Sissy Security Guard stared in shock at where his pinkie used to be on his hand; blood spurted out from the jagged rip in his hand where the digit used to be. The second and third bullets caught Sissy Security Guard on the shoulder, spinning him around to stare at more masked intruders racing towards him from the opposite direction. Little good his Kevlar vest did him. The bullets kept hitting Sissy Security Guard everywhere his vest wasn't. The fourth bullet put a hole in his throat and he gurgled like a baby spitting up baby food he didn't want, only Sissy Security Guard spit out blood not whipped carrots. The fifth bullet hit him right between his widening eyes. Sissy Security Guard couldn't see the image himself, but the reflection of the main villain was caught in his wide, dying eyes as the villain strolled passed him into the building to continue orchestrating the heist.

Brock looked closer at Sissy Security Guard. The bullet holes were visible on his body, little streams of blood dripping out from each one. They looked fake to Brock, like really bad squib effects in a very low budget movie. Brock scoffed at himself. *I can't even imagine realistic bullet holes in my own hallucination.*

A thick bank of clouds rolled past in the night sky above, completely obscuring the moon, plunging the backyard into total darkness. All of the figures vanished into the blackness. Brock just continued to stare into the darkness. He suddenly felt a wave of sadness and disappointment flood over him. He was kind of enjoying this. *Are you crazy? You're enjoying your own madness? You're enjoying this delusion?* He took another drink of rum. *Why, yes. Yes, I am. You need help.* And then the clouds cleared the moon and the pale light returned. Brock felt a sense of relief rushing through him. He put a mental gag over the cautionary voice inside his head.

They were all still there. All his throw-aways were alive and well and still kicking in his backyard.

And then another man appeared. Italian Soldier Number Two. Italian Soldier Number Two walked up out of the darkness to stand next to Chef. Brock knew Italian Soldier Number Two was from *Mussolini and the Mustard Gas Bastard*. He was one of the bastard's soldiers. Italian Soldier Number Two had black hair and a face darkly weathered by exposure to the elements. He wore a red scarf beneath his uniform, just a hint of the red silk visible near his neckline. Brock hadn't really named him Italian Soldier Number Two, but he could see the movie credits scroll through his mind and he knew that's exactly how the guy would be labeled. Plus, he forgot what he had named him. So Italian Soldier Number Two he was. Italian Soldier Number Two had been one of many in that endless string of sentries who never seem to be paying attention to their surroundings, even though that was their primary job. Brock knew it was an overused cliché, but he still used it anyway. It was a lazy shortcut, but he didn't care. The GI hero caught Italian Soldier Number Two jerking off to an American issue of Playboy and cut his throat just as he was ejaculating right onto the page. Nasty stuff. It was a waste of a really good issue with a really hot brunette centerfold. But, hey, it was war.

Brock stared at the — at the what? He didn't know what to call them. Were they ghosts? No, ghosts didn't seem appropriate. Visions? Phantoms?

16

Spooks? No, none of those seemed right. Apparitions? Yeah, that seemed right. Apparitions. They were his playthings. His pawns. His minions. His throw-aways. He could do whatever he wanted with them. Give them families, wives, friends, children. And he could take them away just as easily. He could make them feel pleasure. He could make them suffer pain. Brock took another sip of rum. Is that why he did it? To be the master of his own domain? To play God with them? He took a drink and smiled into his glass. It was all in good fun.

It was then that Brock noticed his own reflection in the glass of the patio door. It was then that he felt his balls shrivel in their sac. It was then that he felt his asshole pucker up tight. It was then that he felt a ghostly hand reach through his ribcage and squeeze his heart. It was then that he realized what he was wearing. They had come in the mail, addressed to him. He had thought they were just a gift from a fan. The lettering on the box had been very elegant, most certainly from a female fan. Brock was surprised how many women fans he had, what with all the violence and sex in his stories, but he knew he had quite a few ardent female followers. He often received such things in the mail. Only last month, he had received a box of frozen steaks from a fan who loved his thrillers, specifically *The Butcher's Boy*. He supposed that particular gift should have been disturbing, but the steaks had been delicious. It was fun getting gifts from fans. He never knew what to expect when a surprise box showed up, but he was rarely ever disappointed. This latest gift had been no exception. The pajamas in the box were quite classy. They even felt expensive, and their silken surface shimmered with obvious quality.

Brock glanced away from his reflection to see Angry Man staring right at him, standing right on the opposite side of the sliding glass door a mere few feet away. The scar on Angry Man's face pulsed furiously.

Brock felt a hot wetness blossom out from his groin and stream down his right leg. *I fucking pissed myself,* he thought. Yet, he couldn't look away from the apparitions standing nearly on top of him, only a thin sheet of glass separating them from him.

The faceless Young Boy and Sister stood next to Angry Man, looking at Brock with their dark eye sockets. They had no actual eyes, but somehow he knew they were still watching him. Their mouths weren't really mouths. They didn't even have two lips. Their mouths were just single red smears wiped across the lower parts of their faces, yet they now wriggled on their faces as if both were trying to speak but had no actual means of making words come out. The Young Boy twisted his head this way and that, as if still looking for some avenue of escape that wasn't there.

Italian Soldier Number Two had his dick out. He clutched his chubby cock in his hand as he obscenely licked his lips. He stroked his meat as he moved closer. Italian Soldier Number Two was quite obviously aroused by Hooker's presence as he stared lustfully at her.

Hooker pressed her big bare breasts up against the sliding glass door, flattening her tits against the glass. Her nipples were very pointed, very erect, threatening to poke holes in the glass. If Brock wasn't so terrified out of his mind, that display of flesh might have been really hot. The glass shook slightly under the pressure of her naked torso pressing against it. Brock thought about that for a moment. *Wait a minute. If she's just an apparition, then why is the glass moving?* He also noticed her short skirt was now missing and her red-haired bush was pressed up tightly against the patio door.

Chef stepped up next to Hooker, clutching a huge meat cleaver in his beefy hand. Beavers and Cleavers. The title flashed madly through Brock's head, but then was gone. The right side of Chef's face was a ragged mess, the skin shriveled and puckered and enflamed and blackened in an ugly blend of scarring and burns. His white chef hat was cocked slightly askew on his head, giving him a comedic appearance that was so out of place right about now.

Brock heard a clicking sound and looked down to see the sliding glass door opening. His tumbler dropped from his fingers, shattering against the kitchen floor as it struck the tiles. The little bit of rum that had been left in the glass mixed in with his spilled urine.

Brock again stared at his own reflection in the glass patio door, stared at the pajamas he was wearing, the luxurious silk pajamas.

The red silk pajamas.

Brock looked into Sissy Security Guard's glassy eyes and saw his own reflection staring back at him. Ted. His real name burst back into his mind. My name is Ted Hiller. I'm Ted Hiller. He took a fumbling step back away from the door, stepping in the pool of spilled rum and urine. "No," he muttered. "My name is Ted." *I'm not a throw-away.* "I have a real name." He snatched at the red silk pajama shirt, ripping at the buttons, desperate to get the red off of his body. "My name is Ted Hiller."

The sliding glass door opened wider.

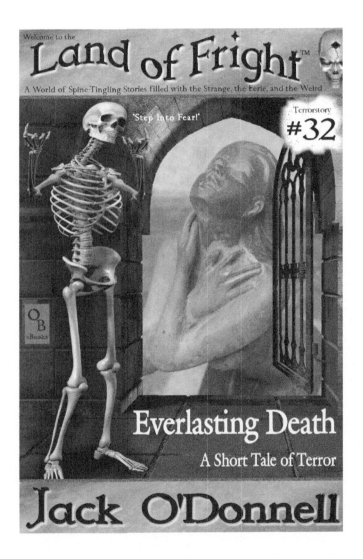

TERRORSTORY #32
EVERLASTING DEATH

I **maneuvered around the soulstone of Mrs. Roarke** as I walked down Main Street, making my rounds. She had died walking her dog when a stray bullet had struck her in the neck. Someone had cut the leash, so her little poodle was long gone, but Mrs. Roarke was still there, the empty leash just dangling from her soulstone fingers. She had a scowl on her face, as if she had been about to scold her little dog right before she died. Her soulstone was a very pale white, nearly translucent. That's what a soulstone looked like, a pale white sculpture. The soulstone took on the shape of the deceased, as if the newly dead had been posing for a sculpture at the exact moment of their death.

The first few months after the soulstones started appearing had been absolute madness. No one knew what was going on. No one knew how widespread it had become. It was mind-boggling how many people died every day, and the manner in which they died. Car crashes were common causes of death, but so were other accidents, and illnesses, and natural causes. Though I don't why they call them natural causes; there is nothing natural about death any more. People died stepping out of their bathtub. People died straining on the toilet. People died in their sleep. People died having sex. People died from disease. People died from gunshot wounds or stab wounds. People died from drug overdoses. People died from allergic reactions. People died from all manner of unpredictable accidents. And they died in every conceivable place. They died in their living rooms, ironic but true. They died on their stairs. They died in the streets. They died in their cars. They died in stores. They died in parks. They died in hospitals. They died on the ocean. They died in the air. It was like a twisted Dr. Seuss story from Hell come to life.

No one has figured out a way to move the soulstones, these perma-death statues, and I doubt they ever will. A tank can't move them. Explosives can't shatter them. Nothing can move them. People are truly permanently affixed to the spot where they died. Frozen in place forever. Nothing can destroy them. Nothing can budge their stone souls, not even a millimeter.

No one knows what the soulstone material is made of, either. It can't be chipped or broken or sanded or scoured away. It's the hardest material in the universe.

Now everyone is used to the soulstones, which is

sad, but that's just the way it is. You just do your best to avoid the soulstones as you go about your daily life. Accidental deaths still happen, of course. Even murders, but those are much more rare now. There is no way to stop all of the death from happening. You just do your best to avoid it, do your best to avoid putting yourself into any situation where you might die. And if you are getting on in years and even think you might be getting close to the end, please strongly heed this advice and stay away from the public toilets. You don't want your soulstone to end up eternally stationed in a public toilet stall, believe me. I've seen it happen, and it's not pretty. Forgive me for being crude, but keep the straining down to a minimum and push them out at home. Of course, if you really are getting close to the end of your life, your best solution is to seek out a Relocation Safety Unit member and get their assistance in transporting you to the RSU Island of your choice.

The first soulstone appeared on an isolated farm in Marendo, Illinois. The man involved happened to be a farmer, out inspecting his crop of corn. His name was Silas Eisen. Silas was a good man, a kind man. He loved his family, especially his grandson Nate. He doted on the boy, showering him with affection and smiles and the love of a proud grandfather. Silas loved showing Nate the big farm equipment because Nate was still young enough to think his grandpa was the coolest guy on the planet because he rode a giant harvester. Silas really liked being the coolest guy on the planet.

Silas was walking through the corn rows when the heart attack hit him. He didn't suffer long. The heart attack hit him hard and fast, the pain stabbing at his chest for but a moment, killing him within seconds. He was dead before he even hit the ground. But what was truly odd was the fact that he never did hit the ground.

Silas's daughter Evelyn was close nearby, walking in a nearby row with her son Nate, when she heard Silas cry out.

"That was Grandpa!" Nate said. He was still a young boy, just turned six, but he knew the sound of someone in agony.

Evelyn and Nate quickly pushed through the tall corn, racing through the neatly lined up rows of green stalks, but Silas was dead before they reached him, his body seeming to hang bizarrely in mid-fall. His knees had started to buckle and his head drooped as his torso started to fall forward, but that's where his body remained. Frozen in death. He looked like a distorted statue, his face frozen in a painful grimace, his eyes open, one hand clutching at his chest. It was almost a caricature of a heart attack victim. He may have died quickly, and without much prolonged pain, but it looked as if he was now suffering some eternal torment.

"Grandpa!" Nate shouted, racing to his grandfather's side.

Evelyn grabbed at her father, thinking he was still falling, but Silas didn't move when she gripped his arm. "Dad!" She didn't feel his weight pulling on her. Silas was stiff, solid, his body suddenly immobile, unmovable. His skin was still fleshy, but something had happened to him beneath his flesh, something

26

had changed inside of him.

Not soon after Silas's death, and the deaths of many others, it was discovered that it wasn't the flesh of the victim that transformed into something else. It was the person's very soul. The flesh still rotted and flaked away, but the soul remained beneath. The soul itself hardened, transforming into something like a pasty white marble. But it wasn't really marble. It was something else. Something never before seen. Someone somewhere called it soulstone. Soulstone. The name stuck and spread.

Evelyn and Nate screamed, but there was no one around for miles so their screams went unheard except by each other.

And so started the chain of events that is still being felt to this day.

The next soulstone occurrence happened on a busy road in Dallas, Texas. This was the first soulstone story that made the national news. A woman texting and driving didn't notice the light before her had turned yellow and she entered the intersection after the light had turned red. A truck coming from her left sped through the intersection, striking her small car right in the driver side door panel. The texting woman died instantly from a broken skull and massive internal injuries. Her soulstone formed instantaneously upon her death. The truck then hit her soulstone, slamming with great force into this immovable object, and the big rig collapsed like an accordion, killing the driver as slabs of metal penetrated him in a dozen places in his chest and legs. His soulstone formed instantaneously upon his death as well, and so his body remained frozen where it died. Yes, in mid-air. His soulstone is still floating half a dozen feet in the air in the middle of the intersection, at the height of where he had been sitting in his truck cab when he died.

Emergency rescue teams tried to move them both, but no one could budge the woman's soulstone or the man's soulstone. They could not move them even with a crane, or a bulldozer. Some military guys eventually even tried to blow them up with C2 explosive charges, but that just shredded what remained of their flesh. Their soulstones remained in place, affixed permanently in the exact spot where they died, in the exact position their bodies were in when they perished. Their forms were indestructible, their souls somehow transformed into the unbreakable soulstone material. They were like ghosts in one sense, their pale white soulstones haunting the area where they died, but these were not ghosts. They didn't wail. They didn't rattle chains. They didn't fade in and out. They just remained permanently attached to the spot where they died.

There flesh is long gone now, but their ghostly white soulstones remain. Nearly all of the metal debris that had been lodged in their bodies has been shorn away, some of it cut away with a metal saw when the emergency rescue teams first came on the scene, but there are still pieces of metal lodged in both the texting woman's soulstone and in the truck driver's soulstone. When a soulstone appears and solidifies, it somehow traps whatever is being held by the victim, like the leash Mrs. Roarke had been holding, or whatever might be inside the victim, like the accident debris in the case of the texting woman and the truck driver. Or a murder weapon, like a knife; there are plenty of soulstones with knife handles sticking out of them all across the world.

So the truck driver's soulstone is still there in the intersection, hanging in mid-air. The texting woman's soulstone is still there, too, the eternal ghostly memory of her corpse frozen in a seated position. You see, soulstones seem to have no weight to them. Gravity doesn't affect them. No one knows why or how this is, but then again no one has any idea at all what the soulstones are, or where they came from, or why they just started appearing.

The texting woman and the truck driver's tale may have been the first soulstone story to hit the headlines, but soon there were so many reports of similar occurrences happening all across the country, all across the world, that this story was lost in the chaotic shuffle of all the rest.

⁕⁕⁕⁕⁕

A terrorist killing in a mall in Nairobi left thirty-seven soulstones frozen in a grotesque tableau of death. A child lay dead in a frozen embrace in her mother's arms, both mother and child riddled with bullets. Another man's soulstone was frozen in a running position as he was shot in the back trying to flee the carnage. Four children huddled together near a fountain, their small bodies full of bullet holes, all permanently enjoined in their frozen eternal death.

A man died in a hospital emergency entrance doorway; his soulstone now blocks any stretchers from entering the hospital from that direction.

A woman had a heart attack and died in an elevator; her soulstone permanently prevents the elevator from ever being used again because even though the elevator cage can still move, her soulstone doesn't move.

A man cleaning leaves out of his gutter fell off his ladder and died; his soulstone now makes his driveway impassable to any vehicles.

And on and on and on.

People thought soulstones were jokes at first. Some kind of elaborate gags for some TV show. They posted pictures of them on Instagram, YouTube, Snapchat, Twitter. They wrote blog posts about them. A lot of people took selfies with soulstones, their stupid grins plastered on their faces right next to the distorted faces on the dead bodies. Some people even painted the soulstones, decorating them with gang symbols, or the colors of their local sports teams. Everyone thought the soulstones were fake, like crop circles or something.

For a while.

And then they started to believe. There were too many of them. And they were everywhere. More and more appeared every day, every hour, every minute, every second. The cities filled up first, of course. Then, the suburbs. Rural towns still aren't so bad, but more and more soulstones crowd the environment every single day, every hour.

It doesn't affect animals, just humans. In case you are curious about that. Dogs and cats still decompose into the dirt when they die. Speaking of dogs, it's still very upsetting for me to see a dog using a soulstone as a urinal. I saw a dog piss on Patrick Lanier's soulstone like it was pissing on a fire hydrant and I screamed at the dog and chased it away. Can you imagine your eternal soul getting pissed on? I don't even want to think about it.

Random observation: no one takes selfies with the soulstones anymore.

All over the world, the dead continue to take up space.

The ghostly white statues of the dead are all over the place now, soulstones filling up highways, streets, hospitals, homes. They are truly everywhere. No one drives much anymore. If they do, they drive very slowly, having to maneuver around the soulstones that are permanently clogging many of the roads, the eternal reminders of the dangers of driving.

Only the very foolhardy fly anymore, even though statistically it's still safer to fly than to drive. The man who had a heart attack and died mid-flight put an end to most air travel. His soulstone froze in place in the sky and the plane kept going, ripping a huge hole in the hull as the plane's momentum pushed it past the soulstone shape of the man. This caused a cascade of death in the sky as numerous other passengers were torn up by sharp debris, or suffered heart attacks of their own. There are over a hundred and fifty soulstones in scattered positions frozen in the sky near LAX airport. Some of the people survived the initial destruction of the plane and tumbled down out of the sky to land in various places across Los

Angeles. One man, still strapped to his chair, hit the roof of an apartment building and crashed through several floors before he died. His soulstone is still sitting in the middle of an apartment on the twenty-third floor of the apartment complex, frozen in the space right where he died.

Those dead passengers are all still frozen high up in the sky. Some people swear they can see them at night when the moonlight reflects off their soulstones.

A few more mid-air deaths put the fear in just about everyone that someone might die on their flight and kill them all. Now, it's mostly just unmanned drones in the skies. The only occupied planes in the sky now are small private jets, or small single-engine aircraft, or military planes. And even they have to be incredibly cautious to avoid any soul statues that are permanently obstructing the air lanes. Every pilot and all passengers must go through a rigorous physical exam before they are allowed to fly. Even now, the World Security Council is trying to ban all flights, decrying them as a hazard to everyone on the ground. Falling debris from earlier death events in the skies killed quite a few people on the ground.

The same rules apply to anyone using any type of public transportation where a large number of people are gathered together to use the same mode of transport. Everyone must show their proof of vigorous health card before boarding any bus, or Metra train.

Are you getting a clear picture now? I'm pretty

sure you are, yes? When someone dies, their body becomes permanently attached to the spot where they died. They don't fall. Their flesh decays, and may get eaten by parasites, so they still decompose in that sense, but their eternal soul remains behind. They just become some kind of eternal statue marking the exact position and spot where they died. It doesn't matter if they died in bed, died in a car accident, died in a plane. It doesn't matter if they died standing up or sitting down. It doesn't matter if they died in their bathtub, on a sidewalk, in the street, in the water, in the air. It doesn't matter. Wherever they die, however they die, whatever position they die in, that's where they still are. As far as I know, that's how they'll remain forever.

You just can't believe all the weird ways people die. Usually only ambulance crews, emergency crews, close family members, police officers, and crime scene investigators get to see the actual corpse in the place where the death event happened. But now... Now everyone can see how everyone else dies. In the beginning, Facebook and YouTube and Instagram and Twitter, and even Pinterest, were full of death photos, but that got old real quick. There were too many of them. Oh sure, the first videos were fascinating, and a few videos actually went viral like the one of the wing jumper who died when he smashed into a cliff wall; his soulstone just hung in midair, his one arm curled up, his other arm still spread wide like an eagle in flight. His GoPro camera caught it all right up to his death event when he smashed his head, and his camera, against the cliff wall.

Actually, his video didn't go viral. It was the

second guy's video. It was his wing-jumping buddy's video that went viral. The second guy caught it all from behind his friend, taping his friend smashing into the cliff wall, recording the formation of his friend's human flesh into a soulstone. It was very odd to watch the dead guy immediately undergo the transformation into the soulstone material. Even watching the video in slow motion didn't help much. The transformation happened instantly. One moment, there is a human body made of soft flesh hitting the cliff wall, the next moment there is a soulstone in its place, made of indestructible soul statue material. In one frame the soulstone wasn't there, then in the next frame it was there. Bits of broken bones and shattered skull fragments were trapped in the soulstone when it formed, so the wing jumper's body looked like it had weird spikes erupting out of it. The fragments of trapped bones extending out of the soulstone have probably decayed away by now, or have been gnawed away by birds.

There were other videos those first few days. Some with kids that I didn't have the stomach to watch. And I usually avoided all those terrorist beheadings and body burnings, but I had to watch the first one that happened after the soulstone events started. It was an HD video, professionally shot by someone who knew how to use a camera. The victim was a hostage from Sweden. I don't remember what he was doing in Syria. Probably on some humanitarian mission. Anyway, in the video the poor guy was naked on his knees, his blond hair all ragged and unkempt, his beard scraggly and wild. A terrorist stood behind the Swede, his face covered in a black hood, sword in hand. They were in the middle of an urban street, with some bombed-out building behind them to give it atmosphere. The burnt-out husk of a car was visible just off to the right, behind the terrorist. Other voices could be heard jabbering off screen, but no one else stepped into the camera's view.

The black-hooded terrorist swept the sword across the hostage's neck and severed his head with a very clean strike. But the Swede's severed head just hung there, frozen millimeters away from his neck. Blood pumped out of his body like lava erupting over the sides of an active volcano crater, but his head never fell. The terrorist just stared at the body, at the spewing blood, and you could tell he was having a hard time believing what he was seeing.

Another black-hooded terrorist move into the video from the left and pushed at the head, but that effort didn't budge it. The terrorist put both hands on the severed head, clearly straining to push it away from the body beneath it. He couldn't move it. He kicked at the head, trying to knock it away from the body, but that didn't do anything but smash the Swede's ear and tear it off. The terrorist kicked at the severed head again and again, his obvious frustration growing. This only caused more skin to slough off. Then the nose of the Swede went the way of his ear as the heavy blows from the terrorist's boot continued.

The terrorist continued to batter at the Swede. He got so enraged, he started clawing at the Swede, ripping off shreds of flesh and tossing them aside like he was peeling away the outer layers of an onion. He kicked and clawed and clawed and kicked, grabbing the poor Swede's cock and ripping it right off his corpse. I still cringe at the memory of that; that was just downright nasty to watch. Soon, there was nothing of the Swede's flesh left. All that remained was the ghostly stone statue of his human form. All that remained was his soulstone.

The Swede's soulstone is still in the middle of that street, blocking traffic until the end of time. But that's the least of their worries over there. There are so many soulstones littering the countryside that one man blocking a street means nothing anymore.

No one knows why this is happening. No one knows how. There is no plausible, rational explanation for it. Some say it was the meteor shower of Twenty-One, bringing some kind of cosmic bacteria to Earth, or some new chemical compound from the outer reaches of the universe, that causes the formation of the soulstones upon death. The Bible thumpers say there is no more room in Hell, so the dead are walking the Earth. But nobody dead is walking, so I don't put much stock in that theory. Others say the first manned mission to Mars brought back a plague, but that's similar to the cosmic bacteria theory so I kind of lump those two together as the *it came from outer space theory.*

No one can break off a sample of the death statues, so no one's been able to deeply analyze the composition of the soulstone material. Sure, they've brought equipment to the soulstone death scenes, but that hasn't revealed much except that no one knows what the fuck the material is.

But you know all this, don't you? If you are

reading this, you probably know all this. But maybe you don't. Maybe you are reading this hundreds of years from now and the soulstone effect has faded away and human bodies once again fully decompose and return to dust, taking their souls with them. Maybe the soul statues are gone from the planet, but the world is very empty and you want to know why.

You probably want me to tell you I finally figured out why this is happening. Guess what? I don't know why. Nobody fucking knows why. Oh, there are theories up the wazoo like I said, but no one really *knows*. You've got the Stoneys saying it's God's punishment for all the evil going on in the world. It's a sign that He exists. You've got the Hellions saying that there truly is no more room in Hell so the dead walk the earth. Except they don't really walk, like I said already. They just stand there, or sit there, or lie there, or stay in whatever position they died in. You can go looking for the answers from the Mystics in Myanmar. You can go chat with the Priests in Paduca. You can beg the Monks of Manilla to tell you the secret. You can take lunch with a Rabbi in Richmond. None of it will get you anywhere any time soon. Because there is no answer. There is no great secret to it all. It just fucking happens. That's it. No more. No less. Good people die. Bad people die. Caring people die. Indifferent people die. White people die. Black people die. Young people die. Old people die. Catholics die. Atheists die. Shy people die. Boisterous people die. Weak people die. Powerful people die.

All their souls turn to stone. All their souls turn into soulstone.

I can only imagine what the surface of the Earth will look like a hundred years from now when there will be billions of soulstones littering the planet. Yes, billions.

Of course, not too many people choose to have children any more. Some do, but not many.

⟋⟍⟍❀⟍⟋

Special groups were formed to deal with the soulstone crisis. I was chosen to lead one of them. Most of the doctors like me were chosen to spearhead the units. We were the most qualified to participate. Actually, the hospice workers and the EMT techs and hospital staff were the most qualified because they were the ones who actually saw more people die, but everyone just felt that doctors should lead the groups. Nobody argued that point, and so the groups were formed with doctors in command.

They eventually called us Death Squads, but I'm not too keen on that name. I prefer our official name. Relocation Safety Units. We transport those on the verge of death, the critically ill, the severely wounded, the aged, to the RSU islands. These RSU islands are man-made islands all over the world where bodies are taken to be stored before the perma-death strikes and a soulstone forms.

Wow. I just read what I wrote down and I had to stop. *Where bodies are taken to be stored.* I actually wrote that. *Where bodies are taken to be stored.* Even I've stopped looking at everyone as human beings. I've started to see people as things that are just an inevitable source of a possible future nuisance. Okay, well, it is what it is.

We have to err on the side of caution. If there is even the whiff of death coming from someone, they are immediately taken to one of the RSU islands. Some of those taken to the islands live for years. But once someone is brought to the islands, they are never allowed to leave. They are, in essence, sentenced to die. They are given accommodations, food, entertainment, drugs of all kinds, and they are taught to watch for the signs of their own deaths. Everyone is now taught to head for the zones if they feel the end is near, taught to find a space amidst all the other soulstones and just wait for their end to come, just wait to join the others in their eternal state of frozen death.

The zones are beautiful, filled with magnificent natural backgrounds, like open fields, forests, waterfalls, lakes, even facades of cities, or a suburban town. People get to choose the type of environment they like best, so it's not all that bad. Of course, some of the zones are already full, but more are being built all the time. Some creative types have even created zones that look like wild west towns, medieval castles, or futuristic or fantasy settings as the final resting places. Those imaginative zones fill up real fast.

Unfortunately, it didn't take long for fear and despair and hopelessness to give way to terror. It was bound to happen sooner or later. The suicide cells started to appear overseas first, but then quickly spread across the globe.

Suicide cells. They were reviled and feared. They knew they could cause chaos and permanently disrupt our way of life. They planned elaborate spectacular deaths for their groups, knowing full well that their bodies would be eternally frozen in place as soulstones. There's a group of bodies on the White House steps now. They all took fast-acting poison, then just laid down on the steps. And to think they used to be members of Congress. Makes my stomach turn in knots every time I think about them. I can't even remember which political party they were from. Doesn't matter much now.

There's a dozen soulstones blocking the entrance to the Lincoln Tunnel; you can only get through with a motorcycle now and some very careful maneuvering. There's a huge group of four hundred and forty soul statues completely blocking Interstate 90 in Illinois just outside of Chicago, making the highway inaccessible and unusable for a stretch of three miles.

It was now part of my job to stop the suicide cells before they struck, render them unconscious, and transport them to the Pits, where they would be dropped into a very deep hole and allowed to die in the dark depths. The Pits terrified even me. I hated getting anywhere near them. They were just massive holes dug deep into the ground, miles into the earth. A few of them were already filled, but they dug some newer Pits last year, digging them much, much deeper. How's that for an eternal resting place? How'd you like to stare into the darkness until the end of time? No, thanks. But that's what we do now with violent criminals or would-be suiciders. We throw them into the Pits. Some of them might even die with fright before they hit the bottom of those deep black holes, but we think most of them don't die until they hit the bottom or crash into another soulstone; no one's gone down into a Pit to check for sure. The Pits scared most sane people straight, but some people just didn't have their brains screwed on right.

So not only did I constantly have to be on the lookout for those who might be near death, now I had to be vigilant for those who might be planning their own deaths. Pretty big fucking task if you ask me. But nobody asked me. It just got added to the RSU's responsibility charts. We were the lookouts of death, trying to outwit the grim reaper in all his forms. It was absolutely fucking impossible to prevent most of the suicide cells from doing their deeds, but what were we supposed to do, not even try to stop them?

The problem is you can't just shoot the suiciders dead or they'll be frozen where they stand when their soulstones form. You have to knock these crazy suicide cell fucks unconscious first so they can be transported to the Pits. It's a damn tricky thing. All manner of new weapons have been developed, not to kill, but to paralyze or temporarily knock a person unconscious. I preferred the lighter paralyzers, but they were hard to come by and needed constant re-charging. The heavier brute force stunners held a longer charge and I could fit a few extra charge packs in my pockets.

I saw the suicide cell scouting their location on Tuesday morning. I had a feeling they wanted to make a splash at the old football stadium at Northcon University. No one played football anymore. The off chance of someone getting killed and permanently ruining the field was something no one wanted to risk, not after a player died in Soldier Field in Chicago right on the 50 yard line. His soulstone was still there, lying flat where he choked on his tongue after suffering a brutal blow as a defenseless receiver crossing the middle of the field going for a pass. They only used the Northcon field for folk music concerts now, some outdoor ballroom dance shows, even a flea market sometimes. It had become a gathering place for the townies. They held a community wide cookout in the stadium several times during the summer. It was a communal sanctuary. A place where people could gather in safety. Strict search rules were in place; everyone was frisked before they entered and Stunners patrolled the area as an extra safety precaution. No one had died in the stadium since the Everlasting Death began, and everyone felt it was a blessed place.

A perfect target for a suicide cell wanting to make an impact.

The suicide cell I saw was comprised of a group of five. Three men and two women, all of them older, probably mid-fifties or so. One of the men had grey hair, another was nearly completely bald. One of the women had a bad leg and she gimped around in her obese body with a perpetual grimace on her face. I didn't recognize them as townies. They were most likely Strangers kicked out of their own town for some reason. Or maybe they were just looking for the end and decided the stadium was going to be their final resting place for their eternal moment of glory.

They should've been stopped by security, but somehow they had made it through. I feared the worst. They might have already killed some of the security detail, especially if they were determined to do the deed today. I tried to call Addler on the radio, but he didn't respond. I didn't have time to try and track him down. Turns out they had killed Addler. Addler's soulstone is still near Gate 7, two knives stuck into his back.

I looked around for Phoebe and caught her eye. She was fourteen, just as beautiful as her mother. She usually liked to wear her black hair in a ponytail and today was no exception. My daughter was smart, too. She caught on to the suicide cell just as quickly as I had. I gave her a hand motion and she casually nodded back. She slowly started to make her way towards them, stopping to say hello to Bert Vicary and his two boys.

I looked back at the suicide cell. They didn't appear to be carrying any weapons, at least none that I could see. I couldn't tell if they were laced with explosives or not. They were wearing loose-fitting shirts, though, so they could easily have had something destructive hidden beneath their clothes.

They suddenly started to move for the center of the stadium. Their pace quickened and they kept their focus forward, not glancing around, not speaking to anyone as they moved with great deliberation.

Shit, they were going to execute their plan right now. I darted towards them as I saw Phoebe do the same. There were five of them and only two of us. I only hoped we could get our stunner shots off in time before one of them set off whatever the hell they had planned.

We didn't make it.

The explosions sent nails and ball bearings and jagged strips of metal flying in every direction. Two ball bearings and a nail ripped straight through my daughter's chest, bursting through her rib cage, puncturing her lungs, killing Phoebe instantly.

I didn't even see Phoebe die. When I turned to her, she was already frozen in place. She didn't even have time to register surprise. She had the same look of determination etched into her features that she always had before an important mission. Even in everlasting death, my daughter was strong.

I ignored the chaos and the screams going on all around me and moved closer to Phoebe. There were dozens more dead near her, all of them solidified in everlasting death. A piece of shrapnel had nicked my cheek, and a nail grazed my head, but I was otherwise unharmed.

There was one other person near me who got caught in the blast. She wasn't dead, but she was hit by the shrapnel. Janice. My pregnant wife.

Now, I'm just sitting next to Janice, waiting to die. What else would you have me do? Keep fighting the suicide cells? Why? So I can die somewhere far from my wife and from my daughter? No, I don't think so. I belong here, with them. At Janice's side. She'll be dead soon because of me. Our security safeguards failed. Safeguards I had been in charge of.

No one comes to the stadium much anymore. It's tainted grounds. Dozens of soulstones fill the field now. There is one man who visits his dead wife, but he never talks to me and I never talk to him. He just stands near his wife's soulstone for a while. I think he talks to her, but he's too far away on the other side of the field for me to hear him. I do think I see his lips move, though. One time he waved to me, but I didn't feel like waving back at the time, so now he doesn't bother, and I don't either.

I keep begging Janice to do it, but she won't. She won't shoot me. She can't bring herself to do it. I even put the gun in her hand, but she won't pull the trigger. She just can't do it. I suppose I could just do it myself, but I'm too chicken to do it. I'm too damn scared. Because maybe it will all just stop. Maybe I'll be the first to crumble back to the dust and not have a soulstone. That wouldn't be such a bad thing, would it? It's what's supposed to happen, isn't it? But it terrifies me.

So I wait. Hoping something will happen. Hoping the next day will bring something different.

Janice took a bit of shrapnel in her belly. Nothing major. I could sew it up. No big deal, right? Just take her to a hospital, you say. The problem is I couldn't sew up the baby that had been growing inside her. Our baby. Our second daughter. She's dead. She's dead inside my wife's body and now my wife can't move or the baby's soulstone will rip her insides to shreds. People wonder when human life starts? When the soul forms? I can tell you. The moment that little sperm hits that egg and buries into it. Bamm. Life begins. The embryo was only a few months old, but now it's a soulstone inside her. A hard lump of some indeterminate material that is permanently frozen in the spot where it died. Inside my wife's belly.

We discussed cutting her open and somehow maneuvering her body around the soulstone of our dead child, but Janice doesn't want to do it. She's too scared to do it. And the thought of slitting her pregnant belly open, and watching the soulstone of our baby ooze out of her as she contorts herself to escape that little body frozen in space inside of her, disgusts us both. But more than that, she's just too tired to do it. We're both so tired…

I hold her hand now. Day and night. I know her end is near. No one notices us. I keep quiet. I don't want any attention.

And then the end came. I grabbed her hand and held it tight, watching the last of her life ebb and fade away. And then I felt a tightening around my fingers as she grabbed hold of me with every ounce of life she had left.

I cannot move.

Her hand solidified around my fingers. That's another thing that surprised people when it happened. If you were holding someone who died, there was a chance you couldn't get free after your loved one suffered perma-death and their soulstone formed. It's why no one even held the hand of a seriously ill person anymore. You never knew when the end would come. You never knew if you would get trapped in a stone grip or locked in an eternal embrace of stone. It made the slow deaths of aging and illness so much worse, so much sadder, so much lonelier.

I could try to rip my hand out of hers, maybe chop my wrist off. Hell, I could even try to chew it off. But I'd probably bleed to death before I got free. So I'm stuck.

But you know what? That's okay. I'm with her and my daughters. Phoebe's soulstone is just visible over my wife's shoulder, so if I angle my head just right I can still see her, too. I'll just keep staring at Janice's face with a weird little tilt to my head. It's not a bad face to be stuck staring at for all eternity. I'll be with them forever. And that kind of makes me feel happy inside.

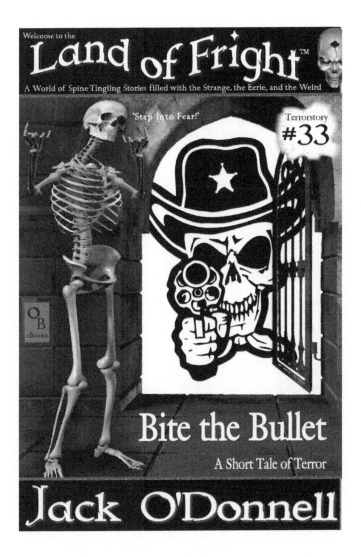

TERRORSTORY #33
BITE THE BULLET

"I got me a bullet with your name on it."

Alvin Chaddock stared at the bullet. His name *was* etched into the side. The five letters of his first name were tiny, crudely carved into the small cylinder, but it was his name sure enough.

Harvey Posson rolled the brass cylinder in his fingers.

The smug look on Harvey's face made Alvin want to plant a tightened fist seed into the fleshy soil of his cheek. Alvin also wanted to grab one of the long curls of Harvey's mustache and rip the waxed length of hair right off his self-satisfied face. "Where in fuck nation did you get that?" Alvin asked. Alvin was in his mid-twenties, slight of build with short brown hair.

His face was coarse with several days' growth of beard starting to shadow his freckles like tombstones shadowing their burial mounds.

Harvey smiled at him, his tobacco stained teeth looking like they were freshly smeared with horse dung. "Courtesy of that fine Gypsy woman who set up camp just outside of town." He hooted like an owl farting out the last remnants of a mouse it had devoured. "I put your name on it and she gave it a good ol' Gypsy blessing. Cost me a few gold nuggets." He paused to roll the bullet between his stubby fingers. "But it was worth every ounce of it."

Alvin stared at the bullet. Gypsies. He hated their breed. They were worse than the Blackfeet, even worse than Apaches. "You put a curse on my name?"

Harvey grinned at him. "I surely did."

Alvin shook his head. "That ain't right."

Harvey shrugged. "Come tomorrow, ain't gonna matter much to ya. Yer gonna be six feet under by the time the moon is up." He showed Alvin the bullet with his name on it again. "This bullet *will* kill you. The Gypsy woman guaranteed me that much." Harvey paused. "Word has it she ain't never had to refund nobody."

Alvin continued to shake his head. "This was supposed to be a fair draw," he said. "But you just changed the rules."

Harvey squinted at him. "I didn't change no rules. Tomorrow at noon, we draw." He pointed outside the saloon. "Right out there. We draw." He curled the bullet into his palm and closed his fingers around it. "We draw, and you die."

Alvin looked at Harvey's closed hand, but said nothing.

"You're a poker cheat. And poker cheats don't live long in Tombstone," Harvey said.

Alvin didn't argue against the accusation. He *was* a poker cheat. He was only angry and disappointed with himself that Harvey caught him. Harvey drew on him right in the saloon during the middle of a hand, but one of the saloon working girls screamed when she saw the Colt in Harvey's hand and that drew everyone's attention to Harvey. Ol' William, the saloon owner, told Harvey to stand down. He didn't want no killing in his establishment. It had never happened, not even once before, and Ol' William was going to make damned sure it never did. Harvey had no choice but to lower his Colt. But then Harvey challenged Alvin to a duel in front of dozens of witnesses. Alvin had to accept.

Alvin wondered if Harvey knew he had fucked his wife, too. Alvin was betting that he did. He knew Harvey would never accuse him of that publicly, too much shame and humiliation would accompany that, but there was a genuine anger simmering in Harvey that went beyond just catching a man cheating at poker.

And so tomorrow they were supposed to stand thirty paces apart in the dusty streets of Tombstone, and draw. Alvin knew it wasn't always the fastest draw who won the day; it was the one with the steadiest hand and quickest aim after the draw. He knew Harvey was fast, but the man had weak wrists and usually needed two hands to steady his shot. Alvin was pretty confident he could win the duel.

But the cursed bullet changed everything. There was no way he could beat a bullet with his name on it.

So Alvin followed Harvey that night, knifed him

repeatedly in the gut, took the cursed bullet from him, and left him dead in the dark and dusty streets of Tombstone.

Alvin checked on the bullet several times a day, constantly reassuring himself it was still in his possession.

And then a thought struck him. It was a bullet. It was made of brass and lead. He could melt it. He could change it into something that couldn't hurt him. He thought of the utensils he had just lost in the river. He rolled the bullet between his fingers. Probably not enough metal to make a full spoon out of, but he could make the cup of a spoon out of it and use some other metal to make the handle. Alvin contemplated that for a moment. He had just lost his bag of utensils. What if he lost them again? What if he turned the bullet into a spoon and lost it? What would happen then? Did it matter? What if someone else did find it? What could they do with it? They couldn't hurt him with a spoon. Sure, they could probably try to stab him with it, but he had yet to hear of a man dying of a spoon attack. He laughed inwardly at the silliness of such a thing.

Alvin continued to roll the bullet between his fingers, then stopped its movement and stared at the small projectile. He would go see Jake the blacksmith in the morning, get him to melt it down and make him a spoon. He smiled.

It was funny how much better his food tasted with

his new utensil. Alvin ate another spoonful of soup, slurping up the broth from his magnificent new spoon. Every bite had a delicious zest to it, as if he had sprinkled a dash of life onto each mouthful.

A bounty hunter tracked Alvin down a few weeks later for the cold-blooded murder of Harvey Posson, and hung a noose around his neck, stringing him up on a tree near Rock River. Alvin felt the rope tighten against his throat, felt the coarse fibers digging into his flesh. He clawed at the rope with his fingers, struggling to keep the air flowing through his body with desperate gulps.

The bounty hunter stood nearby with a bored looked on his face, watching him dangle, waiting for Alvin to die so he could collect his reward.

But Alvin didn't die. A tremendous windstorm developed, sending gusts so fierce whipping through the lands that they cracked the tree limb he was hanging from, sending him crashing to the ground.

The bounty hunter rushed over to him, but Alvin managed to kick him with a mighty kick, knocking the man violently backwards. The bounty hunter stumbled and tripped on a fallen branch. He fell hard to the ground, cracking his head on a large boulder. The bounty hunter died instantly, a massive pool of blood forming around the crack in his skull.

Alvin removed the noose around his neck and stared down at the dead bounty hunter. He couldn't believe it. He was still alive. He rubbed at his chafed neck. He had survived a hanging. He tossed the rope onto the man's corpse and the corded twine curled up on the bounty hunter's chest like a snake finding a cozy place to sleep.

Alvin thought about the cursed bullet, the deadly bullet he had transformed into a harmless spoon. Was that the *only* thing that could kill him? Wasn't that how those curses worked? He didn't know. He didn't know much about curses, but he had a strong feeling that's how this one worked. There was a cursed bullet with his name on it and now that was the only thing that could ever kill him. Except the bullet didn't even exist anymore. Alvin suddenly felt invincible. He threw his head back and laughed; the red welts on his neck no longer bothered him one bit.

Alvin usually hated the rain and the storms that came with it. Ever since he was a boy, he hated storms. They reminded him of his father, the vicious brute of a man who terrorized him from the day he was born. He remembered one storm very vividly; the heavens had cracked and the world had shook that night. Alvin had hidden under his bed, grabbing onto one of the bedposts and holding on for dear life. The bedpost was a log that his father had carved into one of the posts for his bed; its surface was still rough and coarse as no one had bothered to smooth its hacked edges. Thunder slapped the sky in the face with a resounding smack and the sky howled back with a whistling, screeching cry of wind. He feared the intense howling winds would reach into his room, grab him, and whisk him away if he didn't hold on tight enough.

A burst of lightning illuminated his father's face

staring straight at him; the old man was leaning down to peer under his bed. His big hand shot under the bed and ripped Alvin out from under the bed with one single yank. "What're you doing under there, boy?" his father asked. His breath was heated with the tangy bite of whiskey. His tone wasn't angry. He seemed more amused than agitated.

Alvin remembered he was too scared to answer the question. Another crack of thunder made him start in his father's grip. That seemed to aggravate his father, that little shuddering bit of movement. He remembered his father losing that amused look on his face. The expression on his face hardened. "You scared of the storm, boy?" his father asked. "Ain't no boy a mine gonna be scared by no storm." His father started to pull him towards the cabin door, but Alvin resisted, trying to plant his bare feet into the planks of the cabin floor. His father hadn't taken kindly to that resistance. He yanked him sharply towards the cabin door. "You need to face your fears, boy. Not hide like a chicken ninny."

His father whipped open the cabin door to reveal the ravaging effects of the storm. Outside, the night was filled with an eerie, ghostly glow from the full moon. Despite the storm, pockets of moonlight managed to smear the nearby gangly trees with a blueish tint. The sky was riddled with glowing raindrops that made Alvin think of a barrage of gunfire being shot towards the earth from some gang of gunfighters aiming down from above. Lightning ripped a ragged fork in the sky, tearing a jagged slash in the night's cloak. A booming cannon blast of thunder quickly followed, the sound echoing in Alvin's head.

His father moved behind him, blocking any hope of retreating back under his bed. "Get out there, boy," he said. "Get out there and shake your fist right back at God Almighty. Show Him you ain't afraid." His father pushed him in the back. "Go on."

"I don't want to," Alvin remembered saying. "I don't want to." That was a phrase his father could not tolerate. Ever. That set him off. He shoved Alvin roughly out of the door and into the thrashing rain. Alvin lost his footing in the wet earth and fell face first into the mud. The rain pounded his back like a hundred angry fists hammering at him. He pushed up away from the mud, spitting out the wet earth from his mouth. The wind howled around him, tugging at his clothes, pulling at his hair. Alvin thought that at any moment he would feel himself being lifted up off the ground as the wind grabbed him and threatened to whisk him away. But that didn't happen. He managed to get to his feet as the wind swirled around him. The cool rain continued to pound against his head, against his shoulders.

Lightning burst across the night sky, lacing it with yellow-white streaks that had the same shapes as the red streaks that often laced his father's eyes. Thunder boomed and rattled his teeth. The wind tugged and snatched at him.

But then a realization came over Alvin. He was still alive. The wind had not whisked him away. The lightning had not burned him. The thunder had not put holes in him. He was still alive. He raised his fist towards the dark sky. And he shook it. By God, he shook it with all the defiant fury he could muster.

Alvin turned to look back at his father, hoping to see a proud smile painted on his lips, hoping to see just a glint of acceptance in his father's eyes, but he saw none of that. He just saw the same angry grimace he always saw on his father's face. He moved back inside and his father cracked him across the cheek. "You bringin' mud into my house, boy?" he said with a snarl. "Ain't you got no respect for the hard work I do? Raisin' you without no woman to help me. Ain't you got none at all?"

As always, his father turned his minor triumph into scornful degradation and physical pain. The memory seemed to bring some of the pain back. His stomach rumbled and twisted. Alvin rubbed at his belly, trying to massage away the pain that flared up in his gut.

Alvin looked back out into the rain. Today he welcomed the storm with a grim smile. The rain would wash away his tracks. Not only wash them away, the torrential downpour and heavy winds would completely obliterate them. If there was a posse coming after him, they would probably give up. Alvin knew they would for a fact. As soon as a mission became difficult, someone in the posse would piss and moan and break off. This would start a chain reaction of defections, and soon another man would leave, then another. The posse would dissolve under its own lack of will. He had participated in enough posses in the past to know this to be true. Hell, sometimes he had been the one who pissed and moaned the loudest.

"You okay, mister?"

Alvin looked over at the woman. His head felt

foggy. A jolt of pain speared at his skull. He did his best to ignore it. He tried to focus on the woman. She was naked on the four post bed, looking at him over her shoulder, her ass up in the air waiting for him to put his cock into her from behind. She had long black hair that covered half her face. Her big breasts dangled down beneath her. Her ass was round and firm. Her dark skin marked her an Indian, or least as a half breed. He should've had a raging erection by now. Indian women always got him hard. A twinge of pain rumbled through his stomach. Alvin wondered if he had drunk too much whiskey, then remembered he hadn't touched a drop of the stuff for days.

"That thing work?" she asked, staring at his naked crotch. "It looks too scared to come out of its shell. I can barely even see it." She laughed.

Alvin didn't like the sound of her laugh. And he certainly didn't like the mocking tone of her words. He could tell she was no true Indian from the way she spoke. She was most assuredly a half-breed raised by whites. He felt anger as that realization came to him. He felt like she had deceived him, tricked him into thinking he was paying for real Indian pussy.

"I ain't seen a worm that limp and tiny since I helped my sister deliver her baby," she said and laughed.

Alvin didn't like the way she spoke at all. He didn't like any of the words coming out of her mouth. He didn't like them so much that he made sure she never uttered another word again in her life.

An Apache found Alvin four months later. Alvin

begged and pleaded for mercy, trying to buy the Indian off with what coins remained from the bag of coins he had taken from the bounty hunter's corpse, but the old Apache had no desire for coin. He only had desire for revenge. The whore Alvin had killed had been his brother's daughter. The Apache's niece. His blood. The Indian demanded blood for blood.

Alvin now sat on the ground, tied tightly to a large rock. The rope was wrapped around his chest three times, the knot tied on the other side of the rock behind him where he couldn't see it or reach it. His wrists were separately bound before him, his arms pinned behind the rope, his hands laying uselessly in his lap. He already pissed himself, unable to hold it in any longer. He forced the urge to defecate away, fighting it back as best he could, but he knew it was only a matter of time before he shit himself, too. His legs were also bound, another stretch of rope binding his ankles together.

The Apache didn't kill him immediately. He meant to torture him, to make him die slowly and painfully. It was called the Death of A Thousand Cuts. The Apache worked on him slowly, meticulously, making tiny incisions in his arms, his legs, his chest, his face. Each one was hardly painful by itself, but he knew the pain would build over time. He had come across a victim of this torture a few years back and it had not been a pretty sight. The body had been criss-crossed with a thousand cuts. But that's not what Alvin remembered most about that victim. What he remembered most was the terrified look that had been frozen on the victim's features. It was one of the most disturbing faces he had ever seen in his life. It was a face filled with the sure knowledge of its own imminent death; a face filled with dread and fear and the horrible anticipation of its own demise.

Alvin thought of Harvey and the bullet with his name on it and the Gypsy woman. Was the curse nothing but a lie? Had she really brought dark powers from the old world across the ocean? Had the Gypsy woman just told Harvey lies to get his gold? No. Alvin was positive she had spoken the truth to Harvey. There was something in Harvey's voice that made him continue to believe in the curse, a conviction that could not be denied. Alvin knew he would only die from the bullet that had his name on it. And that bullet didn't even exist anymore. He mentally laughed. It was just a spoon. A spoon he used to feed himself soup and porridge and many other delectable morsels. No, he would survive this. Somehow he would survive this Apache and the Death of a Thousand Cuts. He didn't know how, but he just knew he would.

But when the Apache found his leather pouch and pulled out the spoon, a tremendous feeling of dread threatened to overwhelm Alvin. The Apache looked at the spoon with little interest, but Alvin imagined a scenario that led to an ugly death. In his mind's eye he saw the Apache walk over to him and shove the end of the spoon straight into his eye, blinding him as he shoved the spoon deeper and deeper into his eye socket. Alvin quickly pushed that terrifying image away, but it was immediately replaced by another ghastly scenario. He saw the Indian walk over to him and start spoon-feeding him his own blood, and then he imagined the Apache shoving the spoon down his throat, gagging him and choking him to death with it. Alvin pushed that torturous image away, too.

The Apache tossed the spoon to the ground with disinterest and continued to rummage through his pouch, pulling out a few gold coins which he kept. The old Indian was interested in his coin after all, but only just to steal it.

Alvin never expected a mountain lion to be his savior, but that's just what happened.

The mountain lion came around while the Apache was making more cuts into his skin. Alvin lost track of how many cuts the Apache had nicked into his flesh at around thirty five. It was probably forty or more by this time. He felt a painful itch in the first cuts the Indian had made in his flesh. Red smears of blood now dotted his body on his arms, his chest, his legs. He couldn't see the ones on his face, but he could certainly feel their sting.

The Apache heard the lion, or somehow sensed its approach, long before Alvin did. The Indian had suddenly stopped just as he was about to carve another slice into Alvin's skin. The Apache's darkly weathered hand froze and his head cocked to the side, his long oily black hair shifting as his head tilted towards the nearby trees.

The Apache turned away from Alvin and looked into the woods, then quickly sprang away from him as the mountain lion padded into view. The beast stopped still and stared at the two men before it. The Apache moved into a crouch, his knife held at the ready before him. The tip of the blade was wet and red with Alvin's blood. The old Indian stayed very quiet and very still, intently watching the lion.

Alvin almost welcomed the lion's attack. At least he knew the mountain lion would probably kill him in a manner of minutes with its teeth and claws, thus sparing him from days of agony and a miserably slow torturous death.

The mountain lion moved closer, slowly, keeping its stare focused on the Apache. The animal was not going to just leave them alone, that much was clear. The lion intended to feed.

The Apache shifted left, moving away from the mountain lion, moving closer back towards Alvin. Was he trying to draw the lion to him? Part of Alvin wanted that to happen, part of him wanted the end to come quickly, but another part of him filled with quiet rage at the thought of what the Indian had been doing to him for the past half a day.

The mountain lion snarled, continuing to slowly creep closer, its tail softly swishing this way and that. And then the animal pounced, driving forward, leaping through the air at the Apache. The Apache raised his knife, meeting the lion's attack with a slashing strike of his own. The weight of the animal pushed the Apache back towards him, and both man and beast tumbled to the ground near Alvin. The ground exploded in a mad flurry of grass and dirt as the two combatants fought. Alvin saw flashes of claws and teeth and the glint of the blade. And then the mountain lion was on top of the Apache, lunging at the Indian with its sharp teeth. The Apache had his hand at the mountain lion's throat, fighting to keep the snapping teeth away from his own throat and face. The Indian's blade was no longer in his hand, the knife somehow knocked away in the scuffle with the mountain lion.

And then Alvin realized the Apache was right near his bound feet. He pulled his legs in, then kicked them out hard and fast, connecting solidly with the side of the Indian's head. The blow took the Apache by surprise and that's all the mountain lion needed. The animal raked a claw across the Apache's chest, then sank its sharply pointed teeth deep into the Apache's shoulder and neck. Blood sprayed everywhere and the Apache shrieked an awful shriek. Within seconds, the old Indian was dead. The mountain lion shook the Apache's body a few times, making sure his meal had no life left. Blood splattered across Alvin's legs and chest.

The mountain lion gripped the Apache's neck in its jaws and stared at Alvin with deadly serious eyes. Alvin stared right back. "He's all yours, big fella," he said to the lion.

The mountain lion adjusted its grip on the dead Indian. Alvin stared at the victorious wild animal, and damned if it didn't look like the animal nodded its head at him. The mountain lion abruptly turned away and moved back into the woods, its meal dangling from its jaws. The Apache's body dragged across the ground as the mountain lion disappeared into the trees with its prey.

It took Alvin another half a day to work himself free. He twisted and tugged at the ropes, contorting his body at every conceivable angle. He pulled his legs tightly under him and tried to stand, putting strain on the ropes around his chest. The rope rubbed against the coarse rock, his sharp movements cutting into the fibers, fraying the edges. Eventually, one part of the rope became so frayed he was able to snap it with a violent tug. After that, the rest of the rope loosened and Alvin was able to free himself away from the rock.

He gathered up his pouch and the Apache's fallen knife that he found in the grass a few feet away from the rock. He frantically searched for his spoon and eventually found it buried in the grass. Alvin smiled down at the lead utensil, breathing a heavy sigh of relief. His fingers twitched as he stared down at it, but he ignored their slight trembling. It was his good luck charm. He wiped the dirt from the spoon, finished cleaning it with his mouth, and then dropped it back into his pouch.

That's when Alvin saw the trees all staring at him. Somehow they all suddenly had faces carved into their trunks. Their eyes were dark and malevolent. Their limbs were like octopi arms, waving and weaving in the air. They reached out for him, the tips of their branches forming giant curled claws. He closed his eyes tightly, willing them to go away. When he opened his eyes, the trees were back to being just trees again.

I'm tired, Alvin thought. I'm just tired. It's all these damn cuts that fucking Apache put into me. I need to get them cleaned and bandaged before they all get infected and filled with that nasty thick yellow pus. He remembered seeing a drunk laying in the streets of Durango after the man had been on the unlucky end of a knife fight. The drunk had some deep cuts in his arms and his face that he never bothered to get properly treated. They got infected and started to get that horrid stink of pus about them.

I need to find a doctor, Alvin thought.

"I still keep getting these terrible stomach aches, too, Doc," Alvin said. He was sitting on the examination table in Doc McGill's office. Doc McGill had cleaned out his cuts and bandaged them up a few days ago, so today he had just come in for the doctor to give them a once-over to see how they were healing.

Doc McGill was a tall, thin man with deep black hair. He had a thick growth of beard that he kept well-trimmed and neat. "You think that Apache did something to you?"

Alvin shook his head. "No, I was gettin' them aches before that. Been gettin' them for a while now. Nothing seems to be helping. And I ain't got much piss left. It just dribbles out. Even after I drink a gallon o' water, it seems like I got no flow."

Doc McGill pursed his lips.

"And it don't stand up to attention no more, neither. I could be in a room full of naked Indian whores and it just dangles like a worm taking a nap."

Doc McGill listened.

"And sometimes…" Alvin's voice trailed off.

Doc McGill waited for him to continue.

"Sometimes I see things."

"Like what?"

"Things. Weird things," Alvin said.

"Lots of weird things in this world," Doc McGill said.

"No. I mean really weird."

Doc McGill looked at him with a slight cocking of his head.

"Like trees with faces and frogs that talk and horses with horns and spines on their backs."

Doc McGill studied him for a quiet moment.

"Okay, that *is* really weird. I'll grant you that." Doc McGill looked at Alvin closer, studying his eyes. "You drinking? You making your own hooch?"

Alvin shook his head. "No. I mean, just whiskey here and there. But I don't make my own. And I just drink it in the saloon. Little bit at a time. I don't even buy any jugs. Don't really like the stuff too much anymore."

Doc McGill pursed his lips. He reached his hand towards Alvin's mouth to look at his teeth. He saw a blue line along Alvin's gums, with a bluish-black edging to his teeth.

Alvin saw the serious look on the doc's face. "What? What is it, Doc?"

"You been poisoned."

"Poisoned? What kind of poison?"

Doc McGill shook his head. "I don't know exactly. But it looks like you've been poisoned. Not sure from what, but I've seen these symptoms before." The doctor looked at him. "You sure that Indian didn't poison you?"

"Yeah. I'm telling you, Doc, it started long before that damned Apache caught me and cut me up."

Doc McGill uncorked a bottle of medicine and looked around for a spoon.

Alvin produced his own spoon. His fingers trembled as he held the utensil out towards the doctor. "I got a clean spoon, Doc. Use this."

Doc McGill looked at Alvin's quivering fingers for a moment, but said nothing. He tipped the bottle and poured the treatment into the lead spoon. "Here, maybe this will help."

The elixir didn't help.

The old Gypsy woman shuffled up to the gravesite. The graveyard was empty but for the grave digger who stood at the side of the grave he had just dug moments earlier. He leaned on his shovel, patiently waiting for her. The old Gypsy woman reached the edge of the grave and stopped. A shawl was wrapped around her hunched shoulders, keeping some of the chill away. Her skin was nearly as wrinkled as the bark of the tree near the gravesite. She glanced down at the spoon in her hand and smiled. Not many people knew of the deadly effects lead could have on a person, but she did. She had guaranteed the man's death, had taken gold to seal the bargain, and her word was her bond.

The old Gypsy woman glanced down into the open grave at the corpse of Alvin Chaddock. A soft wind caressed her gray hair. It might not be a bullet now, and it might not have Alvin's name carved into it anymore, but she knew the lead had killed him all the same. She smiled. Bite the bullet took on a whole new meaning. She tossed the utensil down onto Alvin's chest, burying the spoon forged from his melted down lead bullet right along with him.

TERRORSTORY #34
ROAD RAGE

"Don't you think it's time for another one?"**
Trevor Kingsley grabbed at his can of Monster and
took a drink, then returned the blue can to the cup
holder that was situated between the front seats of
their car.

Outside the car, deep forest lined both sides of the
road, their tall trunks standing sentry over the narrow
two-lane highway that cut through Vickers Woods. It
was the road Trevor took back and forth to work
every day, and the only road that led into town from
their rural house.

Daisy Kingsley looked at her husband with
disbelief. "Another one?" She glanced back at the

73

sleeping baby snuggled in his car seat in the backseat of the car. Outside it was night and the sky was dark, but she could still see the outline of her baby boy in the moonlight. Ricky was sleeping peacefully, his tiny little hand clutching at his Spider-Man blankie. She looked back to Trevor. "Are you out of your mind? I feel like I just popped him out." Trevor's all-you-can-eat-buffet-and-still-stay-skinny lifestyle wasn't as kind to Daisy. She had put on a few pounds since they got married, plus the pregnancy hadn't helped her any. She promised Trevor she would lose a few pounds, but that was a promise going on almost seven months now. She was still cute, with her delicate nose and her soft rounded chin; there was just more cuteness to go around now. She went back to being a brunette a few weeks back, but there was still a hint of the fake blonde in parts of her hair.

Trevor took his right hand off the steering wheel and reached over to put his fingers on his wife's left thigh. Daisy's flesh was warm to the touch. Working at the local repair garage usually kept Trevor's fingers tattooed in a perpetual state of smeared dark stains, but he had put a little extra effort in cleaning them up today. He gave up trying to keep the dirt and grease and grime out from under his fingernails long ago, however, so his fingers were still tipped with a thin black line. Trevor was a few years shy of thirty. He was tall and lean; somehow he could still eat whatever he wanted and stay thin. His brown hair still held a hint of the curls that Daisy fell in love with years ago when they first met at Jo Jo's Western Saloon and Dance Hall. She made no effort to brush his hand away. Trevor looked away from the dark country road, moving his gaze to Daisy. "We always talked about having a big family."

"Yeah, but my pussy needs a break."

"Still?"

The doctor had to make a tiny cut in Daisy's perineum to make more room for Ricky to come out during delivery, so she was still nervous about even the thought of pushing out another baby. The cut in her vagina was healed, but the idea of getting her pussy sliced again still made her skittish. "Hey, big heads run on your side of the family, not mine."

"Oh, so that's my fault? Maybe I just need to keep fisting you to make more room for the next one." He squeezed her thigh.

Daisy squirmed in her seat. She reached over and put her hand on his crotch. "You twisted fuck. I knew that would get you hard."

"I'm gonna get that big black dildo out and shove it in you deep."

Daisy squirmed even more in her seat, feeling an excited flush flood through her. She glanced back out the front windshield. "Look out!" she shrieked and pointed to the beady eyes shining directly at them from the center of the road.

Trevor saw the small shape caught in the beams of the car's headlights. But instead of doing what a normal humane person might do, he kept straight on at the beady eyes, targeting the animal head-on.

"What are you doing? Turn the wheel!" Daisy shouted.

A sickening crunch could be heard as the car struck the animal. The car bounced up and down very slightly, as if going over a small speed bump.

"You fucking idiot!" Daisy screamed at Trevor. "You hit him on purpose." She punched her husband hard in the shoulder.

"He was on the wrong side of the road," Trevor said with an easy nonchalance. He took a casual drink of his blue Monster.

"You swerved right into him, you jerk." Daisy strained in the passenger seat, twisting her body to look out the back window of the car, but she couldn't see the smeared remains of the animal because the road behind them was too dark.

A gurgling sound in the backseat drew Daisy's gaze down. Little Ricky was awake now, squirming in his car seat. His eyes weren't open, but he was definitely fidgeting. His little fingers were wiggling and opening and closing. Daisy clenched her jaw. She could sense the baby was about to start crying and she had just gotten him to fall asleep. She knew she was in for a long night. She turned back around and glared at her husband. "You are such an ass."

Trevor shrugged. "Survival of the fittest."

"You woke Ricky up."

"*I* woke Ricky up? I'm not the one shrieking like a banshee."

Daisy's jaw clenched tighter. "Oh, so now I shriek? Now I'm a banshee?" She folded her arms under her large breasts. She hadn't been that big in the chest department before, but something about pregnancy really agreed with them because they had swelled up like watermelons. Trevor loved to play with them now more than ever. "We'll see how much I shriek for you tonight when you crawl into bed looking for some."

"Aww, c'mon baby, don't be sore," Trevor said, just a hint of pleading creeping into his voice. "You did scream loud." He reached out and put his hand back on her thigh. "I'll take care of Ricky tonight if he doesn't fall right back asleep. Just warm me up a bottle for him."

"You will?"

Trevor nodded. "Sure."

Daisy let his hand stay on her leg and he inched his fingers down closer to the inside of her thigh.

"You didn't have to run over that animal," she said. "What was it, anyway? A possum?" She opened her legs a bit wider, giving his fingers room to continue their roaming down the inside of her thigh.

"I don't know. Whatever it was, it was fucking stupid and it deserved to die." Trevor laughed.

The car sped off down the dark rural highway.

A pair of dark eyes glowed in the moonlight as the half-crescent orb slid out from behind a veil of wispy clouds in the night sky above to illuminate the road. The dark eyes watched the red taillights of the car recede into the distance.

Another pair of eyes joined the first, they too watching the car disappear into the gloom.

They both turned to gaze with a growing rage at the grotesquely flattened remains of one of their kits that was smeared across the road.

"What the hell?" Trevor muttered. He stared out the front window of the car at the mass of debris blocking the road. There were branches and twigs and piles of what looked like dirt and leaves splashed across the road. For a second, he thought about accelerating and just bursting through it all, but he wasn't sure what was behind all the dirt and leaves. There could be something hard hidden in there, like big rocks, or some chunk of metal that could cause some serious damage under his car. It wasn't worth the risk. Besides, he just went through the car wash yesterday and didn't really feel like smearing his Rio with dirt so soon after getting it cleaned.

He slowed the car to a stop, moving off to the side of the road to park the vehicle. Just a few yards beyond the car, the towering trees of Vickers Woods blocked the setting sun. Trevor clambered out of the vehicle and stared at the debris. Must have fallen off a truck, he thought. Dumb ass hick farmers. Trevor remembered the time two bushels of hay had blocked off Miller Road. That had been Granger and his stupid kid. Those assholes never secured their loads properly. It was probably them again.

Trevor neared the debris that was scattered all across the road, and paused. For a brief moment, he stared at the debris. It didn't look as randomly scattered across the road as it had the first time he saw it. It looked almost as if someone had purposely piled up the branches and twigs and debris to put up a blockade. Trevor scowled. Fucking punks. Fucking country bumpkins. He grabbed one of the large branches and dragged it off to the side of the road, tossing it into the patch of weeds that grew just off to the side of the asphalt roadway. He methodically cleared the road, angry at himself for chickening out and not just crashing through it. There were no rocks or metal parts hidden within the debris. It was all just sticks and mud and leaves.

Trevor returned to his car and resumed his way

down the road.

Tiny muddy smears now covered the rear bumper of his Rio. Smears that had not been present only a few moments ago. Smears that looked like they might have been caused by small, human-like paws searching for somewhere to grab onto.

⊰⊱

Trevor hit the garage door button on the wall and the large metal door slowly started to close, clanking and clunking as it lowered.

A dark shape stirred beneath the car near the rear bumper, but Trevor didn't see it as he moved into the house.

The light in the garage remained lit for a few minutes longer as another shape appeared near one of the rear wheel wells. And then another shape appeared, joining the first two. The three raccoons huddled together, communicating in grim silence. Each animal had a grayish coat of fur, their slightly rounded ears bordered by white fur. Each raccoon also had an area of deeply black fur around their eyes, giving them the infamous bandit's mask face that raccoons were so well known for. The mask enhanced their reputation for mischief, but these three angry raccoons were about to take mischief to a whole new level.

The largest of the three raccoons had deep set black eyes, and the band of black fur around his eyes was narrower than the band of fur that the other two raccoons had, giving the larger raccoon's face a tighter, sterner look. He also had whiskers far longer than the other two, the delicate tendrils stretching out a good inch longer on each side of his face. Whiskers rose up on his hind legs to get a better view of the garage.

The second raccoon had albino paws, instead of the usual black paws that most raccoons had. It gave her tiny paw fingers the look of being covered in white gloves. She was the smaller raccoon of the group. It was her kit who had been smeared across the road by the human's metal monster. Albino sat patiently on her haunches, staring at Whiskers.

The third raccoon was just a bit shorter than Whiskers. The third raccoon had several scars across his forehead, with one particularly ugly scar running across his nose; he also had only half of his right ear left. A tussle with a bear had led to those wounds. Scar had barely escaped with his life, and he still had a slight limp from that terrifying ordeal, but he had gotten away.

The garage light blinked out, but Whiskers had no problem quickly adapting his vision to the darkness. He saw where the human had headed and he led the other two raccoons towards the interior garage door.

A row of white metal shelves lined the wall just to the left of the door. The shelves were filled with metal buckets with lids on them, some claw-like things with wooden handles, some metal cylinders, and various other objects. Whiskers maneuvered his way to the shelves and hooked his hand-like paws onto the metal shelving, climbing up the shelves. He maneuvered cautiously up the shelves, careful to avoid knocking anything over. The metal buckets with lids had dried smears running down their sides, and they had very strong smells to them. He did his best to avoid going near them.

Whiskers stopped suddenly as he saw a coiled up object on one of the shelves. He snarled and hissed at the snake; he crouched low and tensed for battle. But the green snake didn't strike; the snake didn't even move. The large raccoon stared at the curled up green thing for a moment, assessed it wasn't a threat, and then continued climbing up the shelves until he was level with the doorknob. Whiskers had seen countless humans turn doorknobs in his life when he was out foraging for food in the human areas, and he knew exactly what the turning of the knob accomplished. He would need both paws to accomplish the task, but he knew he could do it. It took him only a matter of a few seconds to twist the knob and open the garage door that led to the interior of the human's house.

The large raccoon twittered softly down to his companions waiting near the door and they moved into the house.

The raccoons moved stealthily through the house, careful to keep quiet, padding silently along the carpeted floor. They heard sounds, the vibrations of human voices, up to their left, coming from the direction of a lit room in the distance. But first they came across an open doorway on their right, leading to a darkened room. A soft breathing noise came from the darkness. The sound was very low, very faint, but they still heard it. They paused at the doorway, listening for a moment, and then moved into the room.

Whiskers saw a crate with wide slats of wood positioned against the far wall; the crate was raised up several feet off the floor on four thin posts. The crate reminded the raccoon of the crates filled with oranges in the human food markets they raided, except this crate was much bigger, much longer. Whiskers licked his lips. He loved oranges. The crate, which unbeknownst to Whiskers was a human crib, was where the soft breathing sound was coming from, so the raccoons moved closer.

Some objects floated in the air above the crib. Again unbeknownst to Whiskers, it was a mobile that dangled above the crib, comprised of tiny rocket ships, the spaceships now still and motionless. A cloth bumper decorated with little bunnies lined the crib, blocking the raccoon's view of what lay inside the crib.

Whiskers climbed up onto a nearby dresser, his claws clacking very faintly on the wood as he climbed. He sat down on his haunches and stared down into the crib. His eyes gleamed.

A human kit lay in the crib, a tiny hat atop its head. The baby was asleep, a chunk of rubber attached to a plastic holder resting next to its mouth.

Scar joined Whiskers atop the dresser. Both animals stared down at the sleeping baby. Their eyes gleamed.

Albino climbed up the side of the crib, the wood creaking slightly as she maneuvered her way to the rim of the crib, her white paws adroitly clutching at the wood slats of the crib. She couldn't maintain a stable position on the thin edge of the crib, so she crawled down into the crib. Albino sat down on the mattress next to the human baby, watching it breathe.

All three raccoons had seen human babies before. They had seen them riding around in wheeled boxes in the human areas. They had seen them being held in sacks tight against human chests as the humans walked the forest trails. They had seen them laying in baskets on the ground, or laying in baskets on top of picnic tables in the clearings. They had seen human babies many places. And the raccoons knew they were weak and helpless. They would start with this one. It was only fitting after what the humans had done to one of their kits.

Albino stared at the human baby. Her eyes gleamed.

The raccoons exited the baby human's room, the fur around their mouths streaked with a shining red wetness. Albino's abnormally white paws were now smeared with a thin layer of wet redness. The flesh of the human kit had been so tender, and so juicy. The taste of it had been delicious beyond all they had ever tasted before. The pink human meat was something they had never known before. It was far better than the taste of bugs, or crawfish, or anything else they had ever eaten before. The pink human meat was good meat. The taste of the pink human meat was something they needed to share with all the other raccoons in their gaze.

But first they had more work to do. The raccoons headed towards the human voices.

"Go check on Ricky, will you?" Daisy said. "He's being awfully quiet." She reached for another piece of the jigsaw puzzle, holding it above the half-completed puzzle, turning the piece this way and that to see if it would fit where she thought it would fit. It didn't.

"He's being quiet because he's asleep," Trevor said. "Leave him be." Trevor was helping with the puzzle, sitting on the side of the folding table next to his wife. A can of beer rested on a plastic cork-filled coaster near him. He took a drink from the beer and set it back down, smacking his lips.

The small television in the living room just beyond the kitchen was off, its screen dark. They just canceled their cable TV a few weeks ago because they felt it wasn't really worth the high monthly fee. They kept their internet access, but not the cable TV. Netflix was all they really needed anyway. They liked binge-watching an entire season at once. It was more fun that way. And no commercials. It was worth it just for that. They could knock out a sitcom episode in twenty two minutes or so instead of thirty. "How freakin' cool was that?" Trevor had said the first time they watched an entire episode of Friends without it getting interrupted by a car commercial or by some new prescription drug commercial with warnings longer than the damn commercial itself. Canceling cable was one of the best things they ever did. They found themselves doing more activities together, even if it was just simple things like going for a drive or working on a jigsaw puzzle.

Trevor's face lit up as he grabbed a loose puzzle piece and promptly added it to the puzzle. They were building a puzzle of a tropical beach paradise, complete with a sailboat in the distance on the ocean. He had found part of the sailboat and put it in its correct place near the top edge of the puzzle. Earlier, the exotic picture on the puzzle box had led them to talk wistfully about how great it would be to spend a few weeks on a boat like the one in the puzzle, sailing through the tropics with the wind at their backs. Then, being the pessimist she often was, Daisy talked about the pirates roaming the oceans and asked Trevor what would happen if they got captured by those cutthroats. That had led to a pirate prisoner fantasy and Trevor the mighty Somali pirate captain fucked the shit out of Daisy the helpless American tourist prisoner.

"Geez, give me a chance, will you?" Daisy muttered. "What are you, some kind of puzzle whisperer?"

Trevor smiled lazily at Daisy. He had a good buzz going from his third beer. She still had a bit of a red mark around her throat where he had grabbed her while he was pounding his pirate captain prick into her. He thought he had been squeezing her too tight, but Daisy said no. She liked it. It really got her off.

Daisy grabbed another piece of the puzzle and moved it about over the half-completed picture, looking for its place in the puzzle, but this piece didn't fit anywhere either, so she gave it a quick toss back onto the table. The piece bounced off the table and fell to the floor. Daisy bent down to pick it up, but froze as she saw a pair of gleaming eyes staring up at her from down the darkened hallway a few feet away.

"Trevor!" Daisy screamed. She bolted out of her chair, knocking the folding chair over as she scrambled away from the table. Her arm hit Trevor's beer, spilling it across the table, sending the pale amber liquid flowing across half the puzzle, the white wave of foam from the spilled beer rolling over the image of the sailboat in the puzzle.

Trevor drew back from the table and the spilled beer, throwing his hands up into the air. "Shit, Daisy, what the hell?"

"Trevor!" she screamed again, pointing down the hallway with a shaking finger.

Trevor turned to see three raccoons standing just inside the room. Each one of the animals had a muzzle streaked with red. Behind the raccoons, he could see dark paw prints on the carpeting. For a moment, the paw prints looked black in the soft light, but then Trevor realized they were a dark red. A blood red. He sobered up very quickly.

The largest of the raccoons hissed and charged forward, leaping for Daisy. She screamed and threw her hands protectively up in front of her face as Whiskers attacked her.

Trevor scrambled towards the kitchen, going for the knife block on the kitchen counter. He didn't make it. Scar and Albino pounced on Trevor's back, clawing and tearing at him, ripping his shirt to shreds in a matter of seconds, tearing deep gouges into his flesh. Trevor howled in pain, grabbing at the raccoons that were slashing and biting him with a fierce savagery. Blood spurted out of Trevor as he twisted and turned, the red fluid geysering out of his body hitting the kitchen cabinets, splashing across the counter, splattering against the coffee maker. Trevor managed to grab Scar by the scruff of his neck and yanked the raccoon away from his body. Trevor hurled Scar away from him and the raccoon slammed hard against the refrigerator, falling dazed to the cracked linoleum floor. Scar snarled at Trevor, showing Trevor his own blood on his teeth.

Daisy pulled at the raccoon that was clutching at her upper chest. "Get it off me!" Whiskers had sunk his claws deep into one of her breasts, anchoring himself to her chest. The raccoon's teeth were embedded deep into her shoulder and blood oozed out from around the area where Whisker's mouth was clamped tight to her flesh. The raccoon sunk its sharp clawed feet into her gut, easily driving them into her like nails through butter. Daisy shrieked like a banshee as her blood spurted in all directions. "Get it off me! Get it the fuck off me!"

Trevor finally managed to reach the knife block and pulled out a knife. The blade was long and thick; its silver surface glistened for a brief moment as he drew the sharp knife fully out from the wooden block. He attacked immediately, swinging the knife wildly behind him, but at such an awkward angle he couldn't reach the raccoon clinging to his back. Daisy's shriek drew his gaze and Trevor staggered over to his wife, swinging the knife at the raccoon clutching her chest.

But Daisy turned her body, still desperately trying to dislodge the raccoon from her chest, and the knife slashed across her arm. "You stupid fuck!" Daisy cried. She grabbed at her slashed arm, the blood pouring through her fingers; tears streamed down her cheeks. She slipped on all the blood coating the linoleum tiles and went crashing hard to the floor. "Trevor! Help me!" she screamed.

"Daisy!" Trevor screamed. He continued to swing the knife wildly, trying to dislodge Albino from his back.

Whiskers took advantage of Daisy's fall and lunged for her exposed neck, sinking his teeth deep into her throat. Daisy stopped shrieking like a banshee. Her cry of pain turned into a wet gurgle. And then she was silent. Her body spasmed on the tiles as more blood poured out of her.

"You mother fucker!" Trevor twisted and contorted his body, slashing futilely at the air, unable to strike the white-pawed raccoon embedded into his back. Ragged pain seared through Trevor as the feral beast continued to savage his soft flesh.

Scar recovered from his daze and hissed at Trevor from his position on the floor near the refrigerator. His muzzle was coated in a thick red smear, his fur soaked with Trevor's blood. The raccoon sprang upward, going for Trevor's crotch, biting hard and deep, easily puncturing the fabric of Trevor's shorts. Scar's sharp teeth punctured Trevor's scrotum, piercing one of his balls. Trevor howled and dropped the knife, bending over to clutch at his groin. Blood seeped through his shorts, staining his fingers red. Trevor's vision dimmed and he dropped to his knees, howling in agony.

Albino moved up Trevor's body, going for the back of the human's exposed neck.

The pink human meat was good. Not as good as the tender human kit meat, but the chewy meaty flesh was still satisfying.

Nancy Yorr looked into the rearview mirror and frowned as her son wet his index finger with his mouth and stuck it into his friend's ear to give him a wet willy. The friend squirmed and smacked her son on the side of his head. Then her son turned and flicked the boy sitting on the other side of him in the head. The boys shoved and poked and punched each other. "Stuart, knock it off."

"Aww, look, Mommy. Raccoons. They're so cute." Amanda Yorr pointed out the right side window of the car to the animals sitting calmly near the side of the road. Amanda was five years old, fresh out of a fun day in kindergarten. Cute as a daisy, and smart, too. Such a calming counter to the rambunctious boys. Amanda was sitting by herself in the middle seat of their passenger van, the boys all behind her in the far back row seat.

Nancy raised her foot off the accelerator, slowing the car down, cautious of the animals so near the side of the road.

The boys in the back seat took notice, all three of them fighting to get a glimpse of the raccoons outside. "Hey, there's some over on this side, too," Stuart said, looking out the side window to his left.

Nancy turned her head left to look out the driver's side window. Sure enough, there were half a dozen more raccoons sitting near the side of the road. They were all very still, very eerily still, just watching the road from behind their little black masks. Nancy put her foot back down on the accelerator, suddenly very anxious to get away from these creepy animals.

Amanda continued to watch the raccoons out the passenger side window. There were seven of them. They all sat calmly on the side of the road, watching the rural highway as if they were spectators watching a race. It looked like a mommy raccoon, a daddy raccoon, and five baby raccoons. One of them, maybe the mommy raccoon, looked up at Amanda as the car passed. Amanda smiled and waved at the animals.

Another one of the raccoons, the daddy raccoon probably, stared back at Amanda. He had a thick black mask of fur across his eyes and a large black nose. His eyes looked just as black as his nose. And she noticed he had very long whiskers, whiskers much longer than any of the other raccoons. The daddy raccoon turned his head to trail the motion of the car. He gave a slow nod of his head and the other raccoons scattered, disappearing back into the brush near the road. The daddy raccoon continued to stare at Amanda.

Amanda stared back, turning her head to keep the daddy raccoon in view as the car accelerated away from him. There was something wild and scary in the raccoon's stare. He didn't look like the friendly little animal she had seen in some of her cartoons. Amanda's smile faded and she slowly lowered her waving hand.

Suddenly, Nancy slammed on the brakes, thrusting her right arm out to protectively shield the baby sleeping in the car seat belted in right next to her on the front seat. The quick deceleration thrust Amanda harshly against her seat belt and she exhaled a hard grunt. "Oww, Mom!" The boys hit the back of the middle seat, since none of them were wearing their seat belts like they were supposed to be, and fell into a heap, howling and laughing and giggling.

Nancy quickly looked down at Penelope, making sure she was okay. The baby just cooed at her.

"What the heck, Mom?" Stuart said as he righted himself in the back seat.

Nancy didn't answer her son. She stared transfixed

out the front windshield as an eerie quiet settled around the car.

A huge scattered pile of branches, twigs, leaves, and mud debris blocked the road.

His latest brood of kits were almost fully grown now. Soon, Whiskers knew they would leave the family and find their own territories to rule. Maybe they could even start roaming the human areas directly. There were so many more of the tasty humans in the human areas. So many more. And the pink human meat was good. Especially the tender meat of the little humans. It was so very good.

Whiskers looked over to Albino. It was time to make more kits and teach them to enjoy the taste of the pink human meat.

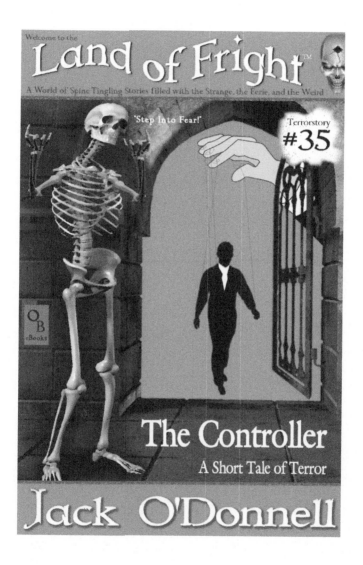

TERRORSTORY #35
THE CONTROLLER

"How could the guy be dead for weeks and still rob a bank yesterday?" Hagan Broome puffed on his cherry e-cig and looked at the coroner. Hagan was a gruff man in his fifties, grizzled, his hair kept short and neat. Lines of wrinkles creased his forehead. He had frowned so much in his life that his lips were perpetually curved down at the corners.

"That's your job to figure out," the coroner said. The coroner reminded Hagan of Vincent Price; the guy was tall with an old school British elegance about his movements. "I only know the guy's been dead for weeks." The coroner glanced at the electronic cigarette and frowned at Broome. "Do you really need to do that here?"

Hagan shrugged. "It's just vapor." He looked at the corpse lying on the metal table. "You realize that's not possible."

"I'm trying not to think about it."

"Maybe you're wrong," Hagan said. "Maybe he had some weird aging disease, or something? I've seen pictures of ten year olds who look like they are fifty."

The coroner stiffened. "I am not wrong. He's been dead for two weeks. Every test I ran and re-ran verifies that fact."

"Okay, okay. No need to get testy with me." Hagan nudged the coroner with his elbow. "Testy. Get it?"

The coroner ignored him. He reached down to grab the edges of the white sheet that lay on the corpse's upper chest. "Are we done here?"

Hagan nodded. "Yeah, yeah."

The coroner pulled the sheet up to cover the corpse's head.

"Oh, shit, he moved," Hagan said.

The coroner leaped back away from the table, spilling a tray of instruments. The implements hit the tiled floor with a loud clatter.

"Just kidding, doc."

The coroner looked at Hagan with wide eyes. A scowl darkened his face. "Are you crazy?"

Hagan nodded. "That's what they tell me." He puffed on his e-cig, the tip glowing an electronic bright red. "Been on this job too long." He shook his head. "Seen too much shit."

"And don't tell me," the coroner said. "Only a week until you can retire, right?"

Hagan frowned at him. "No, fuck that. You've

seen too many cop movies. I could've retired five years ago, but I ain't got nothing better to do, so I'm still pluggin' away at it."

Give this one to Broome. It's right up his alley. Hagan could just hear the Sergeant yelling out to Marie when the case came across his desk. He always got the weird ones. And this one was really up there in the stratosphere of weirdness. Zombies who rob banks.

Hagan stared at the case notes on his computer screen. He thought zombies only cared about eating brains. Since when did they need money? He puffed on his e-cig. There's no way the guy could have been dead for weeks, he thought again for the hundredth time. The coroner had to be wrong.

But Hagan knew he wasn't. The lab had three separate experts examine the body and they had all come to the same conclusion. The guy had been dead for weeks. Hagan rubbed at his temples. And yet a dozen witnesses had seen him rob a bank two days ago. And it wasn't a case of twins or triplets or anything like that. This *was* the guy who robbed the bank. He had four bullet holes in his chest as proof. Ballistics matched most of the slugs to the gun of the bank guard who shot him, and one slug to the gun of the off-duty cop who happened to be in the bank at the same time who also put a bullet into the guy.

Hagan exhaled a mouthful of vapor and looked at the name on the screen. Becky Reingold. The zombie bank robber's sister. Time to pay her a visit.

"I hope you don't find offense, ma'am, but did a skunk die in here?" Hagan asked.

Becky Reingold's face was plastered with make-up. She reminded Hagan of his second grade teacher, Miss Nelson. Her make-up had looked so thick it was like Miss Nelson had been wearing a cream-colored mask. He envisioned Miss Nelson just peeling it off at night when she got home from the elementary school and laying it down on her night stand so she could just grab it in the morning and slide it back onto her face. Becky had a similar thick coat of cosmetics smeared over her face, except Becky's didn't have a cream color to it; hers looked a bit off, as if the colors were mixed to simulate a flesh tone except the color combinations were wrong. The make-up had hints of blue, white, brown, all smeared together. She looked part alien, part Hispanic, and part something he had never seen before.

"No," she said. Her lips seemed to have difficulty forming the word. Her voice was low and guttural. Usually that was a turn-on for him, but not this time.

The off-white blouse she was wearing was severely wrinkled and stained yellow under her pits. Hagan looked at the odd shaped yellow stains and saw a frog, a golf club, and a stripper amongst all the shapes. Knock it off, Broome, he warned himself. You're gonna drive yourself nuts. Ha, too late. He looked away from the stains, up to the woman's caked-on-cosmetics face. "Have you seen your brother lately, Miss Reingold?"

"No."

Hagan glanced down at the table and saw a funeral card sitting near a pile of unopened mail. The card rested next to a teacup, the edge of the card stained by what was most likely spilled tea. He reached down and picked up the funeral card. "In Loving Memory of Bart Reingold," he read aloud. He held up the card to her. "This is your brother, yes? You went to his funeral, yes?"

"Yes."

"So you saw him there?"

"Yes."

"You saw him put into the ground?"

"Yes."

"Is that all I'm going to get from you, Miss Reingold? Yes or no answers?"

"Yes."

He smiled wanly. "What would you say if your brother was caught robbing a bank two days ago? What would you say to that?" He waved the funeral card in front of her. "Now how can that be if he was buried 15 days ago? I'm thinking maybe he wasn't really dead. Maybe he got buried alive and clawed his way out."

Becky said nothing.

"Or maybe you and him had some scam going down and you dug him back up. Maybe he faked being dead to try and get his name taken out of the system. He's got a laundry list of dirty deeds on file that needs a serious cleaning. Like a brillo pad kind of scrubbing, if you know what I mean."

The woman remained silent.

"What do you think?" Hagan asked, trying to simply prompt the woman into saying more.

Becky said nothing.

"Hmm. Well, I'm thinking maybe I need to exhume his grave and see if he's still in his coffin. What do you think?"

"Diggin' up the dead ain't right."

"Ahhh." Hagan smiled and pointed the funeral card at Becky. "Now we're getting somewhere." He set the funeral card back down on the table.

"You need to leave, mister."

Hagan frowned. "We were just starting to have a nice conversation." The sour smell of the place hit him again and he scrunched up his nose. There was something else *off* with this woman, but he couldn't quite put his finger on it.

"You're asking too many questions. They're not gonna like you asking so many questions."

"*They're* not gonna like? Who's *they?*"

"Them," Becky said. "And the controller."

"The mysterious *them*, eh?" Hagan pursed his lips. "And who exactly is this *controller?*"

"You'll find out."

Hagan frowned deeply at the woman. "Are you threatening me, Miss Reingold? I don't take kindly to threats. No, I don't, ma'am. No I do not." He looked at her with a sharp squint to his eyes. "I think a little trip down to the station will do us both some good. Clear the air, so to speak."

"You charging me with something?"

"Yeah, with pissing me off. Let's go." Hagan rose out of his chair.

The teacup in the saucer rattled. Hagan stared down at the cup on the table. No one had touched it. Maybe he had bumped the table when he had stood up. No, it rattled after I stood up, he thought. And I did not bump the table when I got up.

Then the teacup rose up off the saucer and floated in mid-air a few feet above the table.

Hagan just stared at it. I *have* seen too much shit.

That thought came slamming into the forefront of his thoughts.

The teacup started to spin, slowly at first, but it quickly picked up speed and started turning faster and faster. Within seconds, it was twirling in mid-air like a top on crack.

Seriously, Hagan thought. I have seen way too much shit.

Becky slowly raised her hand and hit the spinning cup with a quick flick of her finger.

The cup rocketed straight towards Hagan with the velocity of a bullet blasting out of a gun barrel. He didn't have time to physically react. But in that microsecond he suddenly realized what was odd about the woman; she never blinked. The cup smashed hard against his forehead. Hagan heard the thunderous crunch just a split second before everything went black.

Hagan saw his own arm raise and lower, but he wasn't doing it. His vision had slowly returned and he came back to consciousness to find himself looking at his own arm in front of his body. He wasn't controlling the movement of his own limb, though. Somebody else was. He could feel their presence in his head. He wasn't sure how or why, or what the hell was going on, but he could definitely feel a presence in his mind like someone was standing behind him just out of his field of view. He was no longer in Becky Reingold's apartment; he had no idea where he was now.

"I think he's still in there," Hagan heard a voice

say.

"No, man, he's dead," the voice of a second man said, countering the first man's voice.

"You sure?"

"Yeah, I'm sure. How else do you think we can control him?"

"I don't know. Look at his eyes," the second man said. "I think he's still in there. We never had one so fresh before. I mean we got to him right away at Becky's. All the others we had to dig out of the ground."

"He's dead, man."

"Derek, I know he's dead. I strangled him with my own hands. I know he's dead. But I think he's still in there. Maybe you got in there too soon. Maybe he wasn't dead long enough. Maybe you brought him back. For real."

Hagan heard footsteps and felt the presence of another person in the room, but he couldn't see anyone. He couldn't move his head. He couldn't even move his eyes. They were frozen in place. He desperately, urgently wanted to just shift his eyes to the left, but he couldn't. He couldn't move. He couldn't speak. He couldn't scream. He was trapped inside his own body. All of his senses were functioning. He could see. He could hear. He could smell. But he couldn't move. He couldn't react to any of it. What the fuck was going on? He wanted to scream. He wanted to shout. He wanted to take a swing at the two fuckers sitting in front of him ogling him like two drunk slobs checking out a pole dancer at a strip joint.

Then one of the things one of the guys had said registered in his mind. Something about strangling, the guy had said. I strangled him with my own hands, the guy said. And he was looking right at me, Hagan thought. Right at me. Was he talking about me? Did he strangle me? No, I'm still alive, Hagan thought. Are you? Are you still alive? The questioning voice repeated the same question over and over in his head.

One of the men in front of Hagan raised his hand. Derek, the other guy called him. Derek was his name. He was an average looking guy with brown hair and a plain face. You'd see him on the street and forget what he looked like minutes later. Except Hagan would remember him. Derek had a slight bump in his nose, very slight, but Hagan saw it. Probably had been broken in the past. Derek raised his hand and Hagan felt his own hand do the same thing, mirroring the movement of Derek's hand precisely. Derek raised his other hand in front of his face and wiggled his fingers.

Hagan saw his own hand do the same thing. His own fingers wiggled in front of his face.

"Man, that's smooth. Look how fluid that is," Derek said, looking at his moving fingers, then at Hagan's. "I think we're on to something here. He don't even look like a stiff."

"Ooh, he looks fresh," a woman's voice said.

"Candice, come check it out."

The woman Derek had called Candice stepped into Hagan's view and rubbed her hands across Hagan's face. "He don't stink none at all." She moved closer and sniffed at him. "Kinda smells like cherries," she said, the words cooing out of her mouth with a soft purr. Candice looked closer at him, staring into Hagan's eyes. "Damn," she said. "I think he's still in there." She was a blonde gone bad. Her face and her figure had obviously been knocked around a few times by what life had thrown at her. She might have been very attractive once, but she wasn't any more. Too much time had hit her. Too many weight loss programs that didn't work. Too much stress had slapped her around. Hagan could almost see the slender woman beneath the extra weight, but he knew she would never see that woman in the mirror again.

Hagan saw a hand slap Derek on the shoulder, but he couldn't see who the hand belonged to. "I told you. I told you I thought he was still in there." It was the voice of the second man.

Candice circled Hagan, moving in and out of his view as she went around him. She stared intently at him, obviously studying him.

"I was right, wasn't I, Candy?"

"You was right, Izaak. He's still in there. He's mighty pissed, too. I can see that in his eyes." She pointed straight at Hagan's eyes. "See that. He can't do nothing about it, but he's in there." Candice continued to circle Hagan. "So what are we gonna do with him?"

"The usual," Derek said.

Candice pursed her lips, continuing to circle Hagan. "Seems like a waste, don't it?"

"What do you mean?" the man they called Izaak asked. Izaak moved more fully into Hagan's line of sight. He was a stocky guy with tight black curls on his head. He had a five o'clock shadow on his face and it looked like he was starting to grow a mustache because the line of hair under his nose was a bit thicker than the rest of the hair on his face.

"I mean with him looking so fresh and all. Maybe we ought to figure out something else," Candice said.

"Something bigger."

They waited for Candice to continue. She didn't say anything.

"Like what?" Izaak finally asked.

Candice shook her head. "I don't know. Just something." She stared at Hagan's face, his lips. "Can you make him talk?"

"Are you serious?" Derek asked.

Candice nodded. "Try it. Come on, just try."

"I ain't no master ventriloquist," Derek said, shaking his head.

"You can do it with Becky," Candice countered.

"That's only because I knew how her voice was supposed to sound and I practiced on her for weeks. I don't know this guy."

"Come on, just try. You can make his hands move. You can make his fingers move. See if you can make his mouth move and his vocal cords."

Derek grinned. "I'll tell you what I can make move."

Candice waited.

"You're looking too high," Derek told her.

Hagan felt his head move and he stared down at his crotch to see his cock bulging against his pants.

"Look, I think he likes you," Izaak said. "He's got a stiffie. Get it? A stiffie." Izaak hooted.

At any other time, Hagan would have enjoyed Izaak's stupid joke, but right now he just wanted to rip his wise-ass head off his body and drop kick it through the window.

"Knock it off," Candice said. "Have some respect for the dead."

Hagan watched his bulge recede. His head raised back up and he looked at the two men and the woman before him.

"What do you want him to say?" Derek asked.

"I don't know," Candice said. "Just make him say something."

Hagan felt his lips move, but no sound came out. Then, an incoherent guttural noise came out of Hagan's mouth.

"Hey!" Derek said. "I can feel 'em. I can feel his vocal cords! I think I got this."

Hagan's lips moved, but the sounds coming out were still garbled and unintelligible.

"Uhh, he sure sounds like you," Izaak said.

"Shut up, I'm tryin'."

Hagan watched Derek close his eyes for a moment as the man obviously forced himself to concentrate on the task at hand. Hagan felt his own lips move again and this time a few discernible words came out. "This is a stick up," he heard himself say.

Candice clapped her hands gleefully. "Ha, nice!" She looked at Derek, then back to Hagan. "Keep going. Make him say more stuff."

"Candice," Hagan's lips said. "Suck my dick."

Candice slapped Hagan in the face. And he felt it. Hagan felt the stinging slap, but he couldn't do anything about it. Inside his mind, he screamed. *Motherfuckers!* Inside his mind, he stomped his feet and waved his arms and shouted and cursed. The three people gathered around him saw none of this, heard none of this. This made him want to scream and stomp his feet even more. And he did so, but only inside his head. *I'll kill all of you! Motherfuckers!*

"Does he got a wallet?" Candice asked.

Izaak pursed his lips. "Dunno. Let me see." Izaak stepped forward towards Hagan, reaching for his back pocket.

Candice grabbed Izaak's arm and pulled him back. She made a tossing motion with her head at Hagan. "No, make him dig it out."

Hagan saw Izaak look over at Derek. Derek nodded his head. He looked at Hagan, clearly concentrating heavily. He made Hagan move his hand to his crotch and start rubbing it. "Suck my dick," Hagan's lips said again.

"It's like you can walk and chew gum at the same time," Candice said, with obvious distaste. "Real impressive, Derek."

Derek frowned. "I'm just messing with you, Candy."

"Yeah? Well, mess with him. Get that wallet out."

"What you want his wallet for?" Izaak asked.

"I want to see what's in there."

"We know he's a cop or a detective or something like that already," Izaak said. "It's a good thing we was with Becky when he first showed up. He didn't see us and we got the drop on him."

"We?" Derek asked.

"Okay. Derek got the drop on him."

"I know he's some kind of cop," Candice said, trying to hold back her exasperation. "I want to see if he's got some blank checks, or deposit slips, something with his bank info on it. My dad always used to keep one or two blank checks in his wallet in case he needed one."

"What you want with blank checks?" Izaak asked. "I mean, they're blank, right? That don't do us no good."

Candice stared at Izaak. "You really can't be that dumb." She studied Izaak a bit more intently. "No, maybe you really are."

"I got it!" Derek shouted and Candice and Izaak turned towards him.

Hagan felt his fingers clutching the leather of his wallet, felt a tugging sensation around his buttocks near his back pocket as Derek struggled to get the wallet out. In a matter of moments, Hagan saw his own hand rise in front of him, his fingers holding his wallet out to Candice.

"Ha!" Derek shouted with triumphant glee.

Candice took the wallet and rifled through it. She pulled out a blank check and whooped, waving the thin piece of paper in the air like she was waving the American flag on the fourth of July. "We're in business, boys."

Izaak squinted at her.

"Don't you get it?" Candice asked.

Izaak didn't answer.

"We're gonna hit his own bank," she said.

"We're gonna use him to rob his own bank?" Izaak asked.

"No, not rob. He's gonna walk right in, cash a big fat check, walk out and hand us the money. Nobody's robbing anybody." She smiled at Izaak. "Get it?"

"Nice, Candy," Derek said, his head nodding slowly up and down. "Nice."

Candice raised the blank check up to her nose and gave it a sniff. "Smells like a score."

Derek grinned.

"Then can we splat him after the score?" Izaak asked.

Derek frowned. "Splat?"

"Yeah, like a watermelon."

"What the fuck are you talking about?"

"You know, like dropping a watermelon off a big building. It hits the ground with a big ol' splat. I love that shit." Izaak grinned.

"You wanna splat this poor guy?" Derek asked.

"Yeah." Izaak looked at Hagan, studying his face like he was studying a fine painting. "What do you think about that, detective? Want us to splat you?" Izaak turned to Derek. "He said yes."

Derek frowned. "Shut up. He didn't say that."

"He don't have to. I can see it in his eyes," Izaak said. "He wants us to splat him."

"Are you two morons finished yet?"

Both men turned to look at Candice.

"We are not going to splat him. Not until we make a fuck load of money off him." She smiled pleasantly at the two men. "Then you can splat him."

"Hey, Mr. Broome," Chloe Sullivan said from behind the bank teller counter. "How are you?" Chloe was in her mid-fifties. Divorced. Alone. Still had her looks, but didn't go out much. She had tried Our Time, but didn't like any of the men that she had dated, so she gave up on it. The local bars were just dingy and dark and full of dumb shits, so she gave up on that, too. She had a thing for Mr. Broome, though. He was always friendly when he came in to the bank, always took a few minutes to talk to her. She had been laying down lots of hints, talking about her divorce, how she had a lot of free time on her hands. She was hoping he'd get the hint that she was available. Hell, he was supposed to be a detective. You would have thought he would have gotten the hint by now to ask her out to dinner. She'd give him some on the first date, she was certain of that. It had been way too long since the last time she got laid to play games. She already knew she liked him and found him quite attractive in that gruff movie-detective fantasy sort of way.

"Fine," Hagan said.

Chloe paused and looked up at him. His voice sounded a bit strange, a bit off. A little hoarse, maybe. Maybe he was coming down with something. She didn't care. She'd still kiss him. "What can I do for you today?" she asked.

He slid a check across to her. "Cash this," he said.

She grabbed the check and looked at the amount. Nine thousand dollars. It was a pretty large amount, much larger than anything he had ever cashed before. "Going on vacation?" she asked.

Mr. Broome said nothing. He just stood there, staring at her with a weird stare. His eyes looked both blank and alive all at the same time. It was one of the oddest, most unsettling stares she had ever seen. There was clearly something wrong with him.

"Are you okay, Hagan?" Chloe asked. She felt a touch uncomfortable using his first name, but it felt right to use it in this instance. He really did not look well.

"Cash this," he repeated.

Chloe frowned at his abruptness. That was a bit brisk. He continued to stare straight ahead. She finished up the transaction, pushing the stack of bills to him. He grabbed at the money, but it took a few tries before he was able to grab hold of all the bills. Chloe frowned again. The poor man was clearly not well. She thought of calling someone else over, but she didn't. She didn't want to make a fuss for herself, or for Mr. Broome.

She watched him walk out the door with an odd gait. It was almost like he was drunk, but she hadn't smelled a whit of liquor on his breath, so she didn't think that was it. Maybe he was stoned. She didn't know what marijuana smelled like, so she couldn't be sure.

Chloe looked up at her computer screen at the account of Hagan Broome. She looked closer at his address.

Candice fanned the wad of cash under her nose, sniffing obscenely at the bills. She laughed with a truly joyous laugh. "That was the easiest haul ever!" They were back at the apartment, all three of them giddy with delight at the ease of their latest heist.

"And we wasn't even really stealin'," Izaak said.

Candice whacked Izaak on the side of the head with the stack of money. "Of course we are stealing." She patted Hagan on the cheek. "We're stealing from this dead fool." She waved the money under Hagan's nostrils, the bills making a flapping sound like a baseball card slapping against the spokes of a fast-moving bike wheel. "We're stealing right from under his nose." She laughed again, this time even more shrilly.

Derek looked at Hagan. "So what do we do with him now?"

"We keep draining his account," Candice said. "We keep draining it until it's dry."

"We should at least leave him a dollar," Izaak

muttered.

Derek and Candice turned to look at him.

"Don't want to leave no man completely destitute," Izaak said.

"You feel the burning need to leave a dead man, a corpse mind you, one dollar in his bank account?" Derek asked.

Izaak shrugged.

Derek squinted at Izaak. "What on earth is a dead man going to do with a dollar?"

Candice frowned at Izaak. "Aren't you the one who wants to splat this dead fool?"

Izaak shrugged. "Yeah. But it just don't seem right to me leaving him with absolutely nothin'. It'd be like he never existed at all. I wouldn't want that happenin' to me."

Derek look to Candice. "I told you he was getting soft." Derek tapped at his own head. "I told you."

⚜

Chloe sat at her teller station in the bank, looking at her computer screen. Mr. Broome had been coming in every few days and withdrawing funds. He barely said more than a few words to her, and he still had that weird distant stare in his eyes. She looked at the number on the screen. It was the balance left in Mr. Broome's account. For some reason it flashed at her. It had never done that before. Probably just some glitch in the matrix, she thought, and fought back a giggle at her own cleverness. The $1.00 continued to flash at her. This just felt all wrong to her. Why leave one dollar? He was going to get charged for letting the balance go under a hundred,

112

anyway. She had told him that, but he didn't even respond.

There was clearly something wrong with the man. Chloe knew it. Maybe Mr. Broome has a terminal illness, she thought, and immediately felt very saddened by the possibility. He was such a nice man.

Chloe looked at his account information, her gaze again shifting over to his home address. There was a gas station a block away from that address, a pizza place, and a dry cleaners. She could use any of those as an excuse to be in his neighborhood. I'll just drive past his house first, she thought.

Mr. Broome's house was dark and quiet. The lawn clearly hadn't been mowed for weeks and was starting to look overgrown and sloppy. Mr. Broome didn't strike her as the kind of man who would let his nice lawn get overgrown and sloppy. Chloe drove by slowly, then decided to circle the block and drive by on the other side of the street, closer to his house.

When she came around the corner, she saw a car parked in his driveway. A man stepped out of the car and glanced around the area, clearly looking around to see if anyone was watching him. Chloe knew that look. It was the same look she knew she used to have when she shoplifted years ago. A surreptitious glance that wasn't really very sneaky at all; in fact it was grossly obvious. The man looked around a few seconds more, then headed for the front door.

Either the door was unlocked or the man had a key because the door quickly opened. The man made another cursory glance around the neighborhood and then went inside, closing the door behind him.

Chloe waited until the man came back out. He was only in the house for about ten minutes. She saw him come back out with some documents in his hand, some kind of papers. She couldn't tell what they were from this distance. The man was also clutching a plastic bag, with what looked like clothing stuffed inside; she saw the legs of some pants and a shirt-sleeve sticking out of the top of the bag. This is suspicious as hell, she thought. She had to find out what this man was up to. Maybe he was just a family member coming to check on Mr. Broome. But something told her he wasn't. He wasn't a family member. Family members don't have that kind of look on their faces visiting a sick relative. She was going to follow him. Chloe watched the man through the passenger window of her car as he moved back to his vehicle.

She felt a tingling excitement coursing through her and quite a bit of fear. What the hell was she doing? Playing Miss Marple? Being a junior Sherlock Holmes? Chloe Holmes. His smarter older sister. Chloe smiled softly. Yeah, Chloe Holmes. Then a rational voice inside her countered her silly daydream. *What you are doing is ridiculous. And probably dangerously stupid.* Maybe so, but she felt like she owed it to Mr. Broome. He was a nice man and something bad has happened to him; she just knew it.

A sudden knock on her window made Chloe scream.

"What the hell we gonna do with her?" Izaak

asked.

"Who the hell is she?" Derek frowned at Chloe.

Candice pulled a driver's license out of Chloe's purse and looked at it. "Says she's Chloe Sullivan." Candice continued to rifle through her purse. She pulled out an ID. She waved it at Chloe. "Hot damn. You work at the bank?"

Chloe said nothing.

Derek leaned in menacingly towards Chloe. "She asked you a question."

"Yes," Chloe said, her voice cracking nervously.

"You following me?" Derek asked.

"I was going to," Chloe said.

Derek reared back from her. "Fuck. Why? How do you know me?"

"I went to Mister Broome's house because he was acting strange." Chloe paused. "He looked sick." She paused again. "I wanted to see if he was all right."

Candice looked at Chloe. "You always check on customers who look sick?"

Chloe shook her head.

Candice looked at Hagan, then back to Chloe. She stared at Chloe for a long moment, studying her face. "You got a thing for him?"

Chloe said nothing.

"Fuck, she does." Candice looked at Derek and Izaak. "Fucking bitch has got a thing for our guy."

Derek looked at Chloe, then at Hagan, then back to Chloe. "Seriously? You got a thing for this old fuck?"

"She ain't no spring chicken herself," Izaak said.

"Fuck you," Chloe said to Izaak.

"Whoa! Hey, she's got some spunk!" Izaak laughed.

Candice continued to rummage through Chloe's purse. She pulled out a black rectangular object and waved it in the air. "Hoo whee, lookie here, boys. Our new lady friend's got some serious self-defense weaponry."

"What is that?" Izaak asked.

Derek frowned at Izaak. "Damn, ain't you ever seen a taser before?"

"Not in real life."

Suddenly, Chloe sprang forward and grabbed the taser. She flipped it on and swung it around towards Izaak, targeting his chest. Izaak reacted quickly, deflecting her strike by blocking her arm with his forearm and pushing her sharply away. The taser swung toward Hagan and hit him square in the chest, right over his heart. The taser buzzed and crackled.

<hr/>

Hagan moved his eyes. He moved his eyes. I can move my eyes! He moved his fingers. I can move my fingers! He moved his arm, raising it up. He felt something squirming about in his brain, but he pushed it away. He looked out at the four people in the room, at Chloe from the bank who had tried to help him, then at the three son of a bitches who did this to him. And he was sorely fucking pissed.

"He's alive! He's alive!" Izaak shouted.

"You doing that, Derek?" Candice asked, her voice clearly unsettled.

"No, I'm not doing that," Derek said, shaking his head. He stared at Hagan with widening eyes. "*He's* doing that."

"Take him back," Candice said. "Get him back

under your control."

"I'm trying." Sweat broke out on Derek's forehead. "He isn't letting me."

Hagan struck, swinging with a mad fury. He hit Izaak in the face hard, his punch landing squarely on his jaw. The force of the blow sent him reeling and he spilled over the table, knocking cups and plates and food everywhere as he went tumbling to the ground. Hagan leaped on him and grabbed his head, pounding it against the tile floor with vicious fury until he heard Izaak's skull crack with a loud splat and he felt his brains in his fingers.

Something landed hard and heavy on Hagan's back. It was Candice, grabbing him, tussling with him, trying to pin his arms down. Hagan whipped his body around and Candice flew off of him. She crashed into the wall, putting a big hole in the drywall with her shoulder.

A gunshot rang out and Hagan looked down to see a hole in his shirt and his chest. He felt the searing pain of the bullet, but there was no blood. Then another gunshot rang out and another hole appeared in his shirt and his chest. Hagan looked up to see Derek gripping a gun with two hands, pointing the weapon at him.

Chloe went at Derek with the taser, lunging towards him.

Derek spun towards her and fired.

Blood blew out from Chloe's back as the bullets exited her body and she fell to the floor in a heap. The taser clattered to the floor. More blood oozed out of the holes in Chloe's chest and her back.

"No!" Hagan cried out, his voice raspy and rough.

Derek spun back to Hagan and aimed for his head.

Derek pulled the trigger. Click. The gun was out of ammo. Derek hurled the gun, hitting Hagan in the neck. The gun stung as its hard metal edges hit Hagan, but it otherwise bounced harmlessly off his dead flesh.

And then Hagan couldn't move anymore. The effect of the taser charge wore off. He was frozen again, unable to move his limbs, unable to move his eyes. All he could see was part of the dead woman on the floor, just at the bottom corner of his vision. The woman who had come to save him. The woman he had never asked out on a date although he knew he should have. He had just been too nervous to do it. And now she was dead.

Hagan felt the slimy presence of Derek working its way back into his head.

Hagan was seated at the kitchen table, naked. Chloe was seated across from him, also naked. They both stared at each other. Hagan knew she was in there, trapped in her naked body, staring back at him. They hadn't even bothered to clean the blood off her chest.

"Look, the two love birds are having tea," Candice said and laughed. She looked at Hagan from over Chloe's shoulder. She cupped Chloe's bare breast and wagged it grotesquely in Hagan's direction.

Hagan watched Chloe's lips move. "I love you, Hagan," her mouth said. Hagan felt his own lips move. "I love you, you fucking dumb bitch."

The room filled with raucous laughter. Derek had made them do all sorts of obscene things to each other; it was their own petty way of getting revenge for Izaak's death and for the pain and chaos they had caused. Derek and Candice never seemed to tire of it. And Derek was getting better and better at controlling both of them every day. He could only control one of them at a time, but he was getting better at making them speak longer sentences and more complex words. And every once in a while, he brought in Becky to play sordid sex games with them. Becky's body was really begin to decompose badly and one of her nipples had fallen off right into Chloe's mouth; that made Derek and Candice cackle insanely for about an hour straight.

Hagan could only hope his flesh would start to rot and fall off his bones, but something in Derek's power was preventing that. His flesh wasn't vibrant and healthy, but it wasn't rotting away either. And neither was Chloe's. They both looked pale and a bit sickly, but neither one of them was decaying beyond that. He had a sudden craving for a smoke, like some weird phantom pull that he couldn't shake even in death, but he couldn't do anything about it.

Hagan wondered where Derek had learned the skill to control the dead, but he knew he would never find out. It would just be one of those great mysteries, and that really gnawed at him. Here he was, a detective with the greatest mystery in his life to solve but with no means to solve it.

Hagan continued to stare straight at Chloe. He thought he saw a shimmer of life still in Chloe's eyes, too, but he wasn't sure. Neither one of them could move their eyes on their own, or even blink. They had no way of communicating with each other even though they were only a few feet away from each other and staring straight at each other.

He caught flashes of metal as Derek and Candice moved in and out of his field of vision. Hagan was pretty sure the flashes of black metal were guns. Some kind of automatic weapons. He wasn't sure if they were sending them out an a big heist, or if they were just going to send them on some mad shooting spree; Derek and Candice had discussed both, but hadn't made up their minds yet.

Either way, they were finally going to send Chloe and him out together on their first date. A date from Hell.

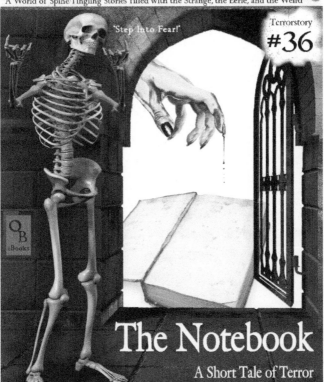

Welcome to the

Land of Fright™

A World of Spine-Tingling Stories filled with the Strange, the Eerie, and the Weird

"Step Into Fear!"

Terrorstory
#36

The Notebook

A Short Tale of Terror

Jack O'Donnell

TERRORSTORY #36
THE NOTEBOOK

The words wouldn't come.

Marla Walker sat glumly before her desk. The blank computer screen radiated its whiteness back at her. She stared into the milky glow. There were words buried in there somewhere, words hidden in that vast whiteness, and all she had to do was move her fingers across the keyboard and reveal them with tiny taps of her fingers. The thin black line of the cursor flashed, taunting her like a digital tongue being stuck out of the computer's mouth. In and out. In and out.

She frowned and gave the cursor the finger, pushing herself away from her desk. Marla was in her late forties, a single parent doing her best to raise two hungry boys and keep food on the table. Who the fuck am I kidding? I'm no writer. She looked up at the clock on the kitchen wall. Two hours before she had to go to her shift at ShopMart. *I'm a cashier. I'm a minimum wage monkey, that's what I am, and that's all I'll ever be.* She swiped a lock of her brown hair away from her face.

Her right contact lens bugged the crap out of her and she blinked her right eye repeatedly, trying to force the contact back into place. It's always something, she mentally moaned. *Always something stopping me from writing.* She rubbed her right eyelid, maneuvering the contact back to a more comfortable position.

"Mom, what's for lunch?" Curtis asked as he stumbled up from his basement room. Her son padded across the fake hardwood floor of their living room in his bare feet, wearing nothing but shorts. "It better not be hamburgers again. You know I'm cutting. I can't eat all that red meat. I need turkey or fish."

Marla glanced over at Curtis. Her oldest son was nearly twenty, incredibly fit, incredibly buff. He didn't have much time for a job or for his community college homework, but he found a lot of time for the local fitness center. She knew she should exercise, too, but she never seemed to have the energy for it. Every time she saw her son's muscular body, it just made her feel more tired. "I'm making spaghetti," she told him.

"God damn it. Again?"

"Relax. I'm using low fat ground turkey and whole wheat pasta."

Curtis said nothing. He moved to the refrigerator

and defrosted it while he stared inside it. "Who the hell ate my blueberries? Did Rudy eat my blueberries? I'm gonna kill that little fucker."

"Watch your mouth. You know I don't like you cursing in the house."

"Shut the fuck up, Mom," Curtis said, his head still buried in the refrigerator.

Marla scowled. "No, *you* shut the fuck up," she snapped back.

Curtis pulled his head out of the refrigerator and looked at her with a stupid grin on his face. "I was just kidding, Mom."

"Yeah? Well, it's not funny. Stop being such an ass."

"Jeez, you can't take a fucking joke."

Marla felt her blood start to boil, but she forced herself to be calm. Curtis was just trying to rile her up. *Just stay calm.* She turned back to the computer and stabbed at the monitor power button, turning the display off. She would get no writing done today. She mentally scoffed. Not that she would have gotten any writing done anyway.

***

Marla purchased a stack of hand-sewn parchment notebooks from the local Saver Plus store. Saver Plus was a local chain of stores, each one of the stores full of used items like clothing, plates, toys, kitchen gadgets, books, shoes, coats, even furniture. Wandering through Saver Plus was like wandering through a massive garage sale under one big roof. It was more like a mini flea market all unto itself. Marla liked it. She liked meandering through the aisles, looking at the assorted discards of other people's lives. Someone's trash is someone else's treasure. She almost always found a good deal on something she needed. The low prices at Saver Plus helped her limited funds go much further than always buying new.

She had been shopping for some new jeans for herself and for her youngest boy Rudy, but hadn't really found anything she liked so she wandered around the store. She strolled amongst the rows of discarded plates and mugs and kitchen utensils, eventually finding herself amongst the books and videos. She skimmed through the DVDs but saw nothing of interest, just a bunch of old exercise DVDs from people she had never heard of, some old action movies, some ancient TV shows. She snorted at the box of VHS tapes on the floor and moved on. She cocked her head sideways to read the book titles printed on the spines of the books that lined several rows of wooden shelves next to the DVDs. A lot of romance, a ton of mysteries, and a smattering of non-fiction. Nothing really leaped out at her; nothing worth buying even for a few bucks.

Marla paused as she came across some journals and pens and notebooks on a nearby table. One of the notebooks immediately caught her eye. It was a hand-sewn notebook bound in leather, sitting on a stack of similar notebooks. It was about 4 inches by 5 inches, about half the size of the regular notebooks Rudy used for school. The stitches were large and pronounced, criss-crossing down the spine. The notebook was a good inch or so thick. Marla picked it up. It had a decent heft to it and the worn leather felt smooth in her hand. She flipped it open to see the inside was comprised of a parchment-type paper, almost linen-like. The color of the parchment was a faint brown with a hint of a very faint pinkish white pattern swirling across the page. For just a brief second, she thought of human flesh, but then just dismissed that thought as being absurd. She flipped through a few pages. The pages were a bit stiff, nearly crisp, but at least they were all blank and not scribbled on. The notebook was as good as new. She looked at the price sticker on the back. A dollar. *I'd buy that for a dollar.*

Maybe this will help, Marla thought. She hadn't written in a notebook since taking notes in high school. *Crap, that was a long time ago.* She wondered if Peter Osterly was still living in town. She hadn't seen him for over twenty years, but she still thought about him every once in a while. *He probably would've made a better husband than the drunk who ran out on me.* She might get out the old vibrator tonight and give Peter a good fucking. She wondered if any other women named their vibrator after their old high school boyfriends. Of course not, she scoffed at herself. *They're not as pathetic as you are.*

Marla ran her fingers over the warm leather of the notebook. Maybe trying some good old fashioned long-hand writing might help me conquer this goddamn writer's block, she thought. At this point, I'm willing to try anything. She grabbed the rest of the notebooks and bought the whole stack, nine notebooks in all for nine bucks; she felt a little indulgent spending nine bucks on herself, but she did it anyway.

The notebooks did eventually help her. But not in the way Marla had expected them to help her.

The words were still not coming. Marla threw the pencil down in disgust. The parchment notebook lay open in her lap, the first page still blank. Nothing was working. She looked over at the blank computer screen to her left on her desk; its stark whiteness taunted her with the emptiness of failure. The words weren't coming no matter what she tried.

She truly thought getting away from the computer and her laptop and doing some old-fashioned scribbling by hand in a notebook would help, but it didn't. None of it had helped.

Marla whipped the notebook shut with an angry swipe and immediately gave out a small yelp. She looked at her finger to see a paper cut starting to ooze a thin line of red. *Damn it. Even the writing gods are mocking me. I'm trying to feed my muse, and all it did was bite me back.*

She threw the notebook back down on her desk in disgust. She lay down on the couch that was situated in the den near her desk, and put her hand over her forehead, pressing the backs of her fingers against her head. *I'm never going to be a writer. Why am I torturing myself?*

"Mom, what the fuck's for dinner?" Curtis asked as he walked past the den on his way to the kitchen.

Marla felt a wetness pooling in the corner of her eyes and didn't even bother to stop the tears from sliding down her face.

Marla sat back down at her desk. Curtis was off working out at the gym and Rudy was at a friend's house, so she knew she had at least an hour of peace and quiet. She was going to give the notebook the old college try and have a go at it again. Every miserable night working her shift at ShopMart fueled her determination to at least get one book written. What other choice did she have? Sure, it was a long shot to make money writing a book, but she couldn't think of any other alternatives. She couldn't think of any other way out of her present situation. Hell, it didn't even have to be a full length novel. She'd settle for a novella, or even a short story. Something. Anything.

Marla opened the notebook and stared. She had a hard time believing what she saw in the leather-bound journal. There were words on the page. Words she didn't remember writing. Words she *knew* she had not written. Because they were written in blood.

She slapped the notebook shut and immediately pushed it off her lap, standing up quickly to get away from it. What the hell? She stared down at the notebook sitting on the carpet, feeling her heart pounding in her chest. The notebook lay motionless on the floor. She half-expected it to growl at her like it was some possessed creature, but it wasn't making any noise. It wasn't moving. It wasn't slithering across the floor. It just sat there.

Waiting for her to pick it back up.

Marla let the notebook sit on the floor for a full day. Neither one of her boys noticed it, or if they did they didn't say anything about the notebook just sitting on the floor in the middle of the den. Neither one bothered to pick it up, either.

She stared down at the notebook. It hadn't moved. It still lay exactly where it had fallen. It still made no noise.

She finally got the nerve to move closer to it. She stood right over it, staring down at it. And then she picked it back up, crouching quickly to snatch it and then rise back up to her feet. It felt like a normal notebook in her hand. She turned it over in her hands. It still looked the same.

Marla slowly peeled back the cover and looked at the first page. The words were still there. Still written in blood. She quickly closed the cover, but this time she still held on to the notebook. She forced herself to be calm, taking a slow, even breath.

She moved over to the couch near her desk and sat down, placing the small notebook squarely in her lap. She took another slow breath and opened the cover. And started to read the words on the page. They were good. They were damn good. She found herself immediately absorbed in the story and the characters. She reached the last sentence at the bottom of the page, eagerly anticipating more of the story. She turned the page only to stare with disappointed eyes at a sheet of blank parchment. She wanted to read more, but the words had ended. She flipped back to the first page filled with the dark words, then flipped forward to the next page. The second page was still blank.

Marla sterilized the needle on her stove, holding

the small piece of metal in her hands, watching the tip turn blue hot in the flame, then blacken. The absurdity of what she was doing struck her. *No, it's not just absurd. This is insane.* But despite that inner ridicule, she continued on with what she was doing. She had to know.

She moved the tip of the needle closer to her opposite hand and pricked her finger. A tiny round ball of redness appeared on her flesh and she let a drop of her blood fall onto the empty notebook page. The blood hit the parchment and soaked into the thick paper. She watched the blood stain spread. No words appeared. She frowned, disappointed in the outcome. Again, the madness of what she was doing struck her. Here she was pricking her finger and dripping blood onto a blank page so a magical notebook would write more words for her! That was sheer madness.

Scared of her own actions, and suddenly terrified of the level of her desperation, Marla closed the notebook quickly and set it down on her desk.

It took a few days, but the lure of the notebook could not be denied. Marla waited for a time when the boys weren't at home, afraid of what she might do when she looked into the notebook, afraid of her own reaction to what she might see. Part of her was afraid she might burst into tears and embarrass herself in front of her boys. She tried her best to always be strong for them, but lately she had felt bone-tired and feared her weariness might lead her into doing or saying something stupid, or even hurtful.

Just look, the voice inside her goaded. *Just pick up the damn thing and look.* She picked up the notebook and opened it to find the second page filled with words. She felt her heart start beating faster. *This is crazy!* But incredibly exciting at the same time. She read the words and her excitement fizzled. They were the same words she had read the day before. She flipped back to the first page and read the words again. Yes, they were identical. The exact same sentences filled both pages. The disappointment was crushing. The story hadn't advanced. No new characters were introduced, no new twists in the plot. It was just the same exact words scrawled in blood across the page.

Because it was your blood again, a voice whispered. *These words came from your blood. Maybe you need different blood? Maybe you need someone else's blood?* The questioning thought disturbed her. *That's just sick.* She didn't want to touch someone else's blood.

Marla's fingers trembled as she shut the notebook.

Marla couldn't help herself. She stared at the cut on the boy's knee. Troy, a friend of her son Rudy, had scraped himself on the street playing touch football with Rudy and his buddies. She felt like she was in a daze. Sunlight sparkled in through the kitchen window, giving the entire room a warm golden glow. A beam of sunlight shone right on the boy's wound, as if putting a miniature spotlight directly on Troy's bleeding cut.

"Mom, c'mon," Rudy said, looking away from her towards the open front door and the street beyond, then back to her. "The guys are waiting for us."

Marla looked slowly away from the blood on Troy's knee and up to her son's face. The sun made the tiny patches of freckles on Rudy's face sparkle. He was a good looking kid, Marla thought. *Took after his father.* Such sweet eyes, she thought. *He always had the sweetest eyes. And those cute little freckles. Like little tiny circles of blood on his face.* Horrified by that thought, Marla looked away from her son. The magnetic pull of Troy's fresh blood easily pulled her gaze back to the glistening wet redness on the boy's knee. The blood also sparkled in the sunlight, shimmering with a soft aura. The fresh blood.

"Mom, Jeez, come on. It's a scratch." Rudy's voice was clearly full of exasperation. "It's fine, just put a band-aid on it."

"Okay, okay," Marla said, forcing the fog away from her brain. She dabbed at the cut on Troy's knee with a clean cloth, wiping away the excess blood, and disinfected his scrape with a squirt of disinfectant spray. She secured a bandage over the scrape.

"Thanks, Mrs. Walker," Troy said.

Marla sent Rudy and his friend Troy back out to play with a smile and a nod. Marla stared at the bloody cloth on the table. *No. Thank you, Troy.* She stared hard.

⬥⬥⬥

Marla gazed with a sick thrill at the words on the page. The words on the parchment were new! She read the new sentences, getting even more engrossed in the story, really wanting to know what would happen next. She reached the end of the writing, just as a character was getting into a deep fix, and reflexively turned the page.

The page staring at her was blank.

I need more blood. The thought was horrifying, but she could not deny it. She needed more blood to continue the story.

⚜

"Would you like to apply for a ShopMart card today?" The question came out mechanical, robotic. It was a question Marla had to ask every customer as they came through her checkout lane.

The man in line shook his head. "No, thanks. Trying to get out of debt, not deeper in."

Marla smiled politely and nodded. She grabbed the garden spade the man put on the conveyor belt and swiped it across the scanner. The man reached into his shopping basket for the packets of vegetable seeds that were on the bottom of the basket. That's when she noticed the blood-stained bandage on the man's elbow. Marla found herself transfixed by the sight of it. By the possibilities of it.

The man must have felt the intensity of her stare because he looked up at her.

"You ought to change that," Marla said.

The man squinted at her. "What?"

She pointed to his bandaged elbow. "Your bandage."

The man glanced at his elbow, at the red smear threatening to soak through, then back up to her. "Yeah, I will." He looked curiously at her, clearly not quite knowing what else to say to her. "Thanks," he finally said.

"I've got some fresh ones in my first aid kit."

Marla reached under the register and pulled out a tiny white box with a thick red plus symbol painted on it. She fumbled at the plastic clip holding the kit closed, then managed to open it.

"That's okay," the man said. "Don't bother."

"No trouble," she said. She held out a bandage to him.

He looked curiously at her, but took the offered bandage. "Thanks."

Marla looked at him expectantly. He pocketed the bandage in his shirt pocket. She stared at him.

"Umm, can you finish checking me out?" he asked.

"What? Oh, yeah, sorry." Marla fumbled at the rest of the items he had placed on the belt, finishing up his order. He paid with cash and she gave him his change, forcing herself not to stare at the blood-soaked bandage on his elbow. He grabbed his bag and moved quickly away.

Marla had a mad thought to follow him, to wait for him to change his bandage and then just grab it out of the garbage when he threw it away.

"Excuse me?"

Marla turned to see a woman staring at her with a sour expression.

"Can you do your flirting some other time?" The woman pointed to the items she had placed on the conveyer belt.

"I wasn't flirting. I was—" *Just staring at the blood I need.* Marla closed her mouth. She looked away from the woman and forced her attention back to her job. She grabbed one of the cans of cat food the woman had placed on the conveyer belt and swiped it across the scanner.

Marla watched the children play in the park. Someone was bound to scrape a knee or cut a finger sooner or later. She heard a little girl cry and looked over to see the girl grab her knee. The little girl pointed to the balance beam she must have just fallen off of as she continued to wail. The girl's mother comforted her, herding her away from the wooden beam.

Marla stood up and slowly moved toward the beam, trying to be as casual as she could, fingering the cloth she had brought with her in the pocket of her jeans. She reached the beam and stared down at the strip of wood. It was only about a foot off the ground, but the beam had firm edges that could still cause some damage if someone slipped and cracked their knee on it. Marla frowned. She didn't see any wetness on the edges. No red smears. The girl had just banged her knee, not cut it.

She felt a horrible guilt well up inside her. Had she really wanted that girl to cut herself? Had she really wanted some little child to feel pain just so she could collect some of her blood? Marla felt a sickening churn in her stomach. I can't do this, she thought. *This is too much. This is disgusting.*

The sound of metal crunching against metal suddenly filled the air. Someone shouted. Someone screamed. More people shouted.

Marla looked over to the street near the park entrance. Two cars had just collided. They must have hit hard because there was glass and debris all over the street. A woman stumbled out of one of the vehicles, clutching at her head. Blood dripped down her face, her head wound bleeding profusely.

Marla looked down at the cloth she held in her hand. She hurried over to the crash site. The woman who had struck her head was still walking around in a daze. The driver in the other car still had not exited the vehicle. Marla couldn't see much of the interior because the wounded woman's vehicle was blocking her view. She moved up to the bleeding woman. "Are you okay?" Marla asked.

The woman looked up at Marla, her hand still to her head, blood still streaming down her face. The woman didn't say anything; she was clearly in shock.

Marla put a hand on the woman's shoulder, gently guiding her off the street and sitting her down on one of the park benches.

"Did anyone call the cops?" someone shouted.

Marla thought about pulling out her phone. But she didn't. She gently pulled the woman's fingers away from her bleeding head and pressed the white cloth against the gash in the woman's head. The cloth immediately drank up the blood and Marla felt a thrill as the red stain spread across the cloth.

"Erin? Erin, are you okay?"

Marla looked up to see a man stumbling towards them. He was clutching at his arm, his face racked with pain, but Marla didn't detect any blood on him, so she turned her attention back to the wounded woman. The cloth grew heavier and wetter with blood. Marla wondered how much she actually needed. Just a drop would probably work as well as a pint. She pulled the cloth away and the woman continued to bleed. Marla stared at the bloody cloth in her hand.

"What the hell are you doing?"

Marla looked up to see the wounded man staring down at her.

"Put that back on her head. She's still bleeding." The man pointed to the wounded woman. "Put that back on her head."

"Sorry, it's mine," Marla said.

The man scowled at her. He reached for the cloth, but Marla pulled it away, causing him to stumble. The man winced and grabbed at his wounded arm.

"What the hell?" He again pointed urgently at the bleeding woman. "My wife is bleeding. Put that back. We need to stop the bleeding."

Marla stood up, stepping away from them.

"What the hell is wrong with you? Give me that." The man snatched at the bloody cloth, but again Marla jerked it away from his grasping fingers. "What the fuck is wrong with you?" the man shouted. "She's hurt!"

Marla turned and ran.

"Come back here!"

Marla quickened her pace, clutching the bloody cloth tightly in her hands. She felt like laughing hysterically as a giddy high exploded through her.

<hr />

Marla opened the notebook and turned the page. A happy smile lit up her face. There were more words on the page. New words. New sentences. New paragraphs. The story continued. And it was good. It was so good. The best thing she had ever written.

But you didn't write it, a tiny voice countered. *You didn't write it.*

She mentally shook her head. *I don't care. It's my notebook. It's my story. It's mine.*

"Mom, what's this?"

Marla glanced up to see Rudy holding the corner of the bloody cloth.

"Are you hurt?" Rudy asked.

She closed the notebook and quickly moved over to Rudy, taking the cloth out of his hands. She hurried to the garbage bin and tossed it inside. "Go wash your hands," she told her son.

"Are you hurt?" Rudy asked again.

She shook her head. "No. Now go wash your hands."

"Whose blood is that? Did you finally stab Curtis?" Rudy's voice held a hint of sarcasm, but not much.

"I said go wash your hands." She pushed at him. "Now go!"

<hr />

Did you finally stab Curtis? Rudy's question echoed in her mind, repeating itself over and over again. Marla stared down at the open kitchen drawer. The object of her gaze was sitting off to the side of the plastic utensil holder, right next to the compartment holding the dull butter knives. It was a large steak knife. Very large and very sharp.

What the hell are you doing? Are you out of your fucking mind? Are you really considering such a thing?

Marla shuddered at her own dark thoughts and pushed the drawer closed. There had to be an easier way to get blood. Maybe she could attend more sporting events, football games or something. Or soccer. No, MMA. She should go to those ultimate fighting shows that Curtis loved so much. Those men, and women, pounded on each other pretty hard with some savage punches and kicks. There always seemed to be blood involved in those fights.

The TV droned on in the living room, the sound catching her attention. Marla moved in front of the television and stood before it, watching the show that was playing out on the screen. Of course, she thought. She felt like smacking herself in the forehead. She didn't know what show it was, but it didn't matter. All those medical shows were pretty much the same, each episode just highlighting a different disease or emergency of the week. She smiled. Emergency.

⋘⋘◦◦◦⋙⋙

Marla had no illusions about becoming a nurse or a CNA, but that didn't mean she still couldn't get a different type of job. She stared at the job category listing. *Janitorial services for health care facilities.* Somebody had to clean up those places.

Proper sanitation in the emergency room is essential to preventing the spread of infectious diseases. The largest emergency rooms see thousands of patients each week, and the ER must be kept constantly clean and free from germs. She read that part of the description again. *Thousands of patients each week.* She thought about that for a long moment, then continued reading. *Sanitation specialists must ensure that biohazardous material is disposed of properly and patient rooms are thoroughly cleaned after each use.*

Marla scrolled down the page and read one of the job listings again.

Numerous healthcare settings require frequent and intensive cleaning. These include, but are not limited to, waiting rooms, hallways, bathrooms, the hospital cafeterias, gift centers, doctor's offices, nurse stations, emergency rooms and operating rooms. HCSW (Health Care Sanitation Workers) employees work with medical professionals to determine the best products to use in these capacities, focusing on the dual functions of cleanliness and infection control. All HCSW employees assigned to medical facilities receive training in blood borne pathogen handling…

She stopped scrolling down after that and kept reading the same line over and over again. Blood borne pathogen… blood borne… blood.

Marla finished filling out the online job application and hit submit.

Gunshot wounds. Stabbing victims. Car accident casualties. Head trauma. Blood transfusions. Soiled hospital gowns. Stained disposable gloves. Marla felt giddy.

Quitting her job as a cashier and working for HCSW as a glorified cleaning lady in the emergency room was the best decision she had ever made. Every time the doors burst open and they wheeled in a gurney, Marla got a thrill. One man being wheeled in on a gurney spit up blood right towards her as she was standing in the facility hallway, and she nearly climaxed when the red liquid splashed on her shoes. The dark stain held the secret of more hidden words. Another page would be filled with glorious sentences.

It was the ideal job for what she needed to do. No one bothered her. No one cared what she did with all the blood-stained dirty clothes, the blood-smeared hospital garb, the blood-soaked mops. No one questioned her. They all just wanted the place to be kept clean and sanitized, and she was happy to oblige.

Marla realized quickly that the late shift was the ideal shift for her. Most of the other HCSW employees had no desire to work the dark hours, so she had little internal competition for time slots. She took the late shift because so much crazy violence happened after the sun went down. That's when all the real action happened. She loved it when the gangs started shooting at each other. That usually meant a good two or three victims a night. One particularly ugly turf war had brought in five shooting victims and two stabbing victims. That was a good night! She had to cut up a cleaning cloth into small segments to keep the blood from each wounded patient separate. She went home with a full pocket of stained cloths that night.

So many different fatalities. So much blood. Marla didn't know if she would ever stop smiling. The words were coming in a flood. The notebook was three quarters full and the story was so good. So damn good!

Marla scurried forward, pushing her mop and bucket towards room B. A multi-car accident had just brought in four victims. The night was early, but was already a frenzy of activity.

The emergency door wheezed open and two paramedics wheeled in a gurney. She couldn't see who was on the gurney because the victim was curled up, facing away from her. She heard a splutter and saw a glob of blood hit the floor. She waited for the paramedics to push the gurney past, then moved for the blood splatter, soaking it up with one of the cloths she kept ready at hand for such opportunities. She wiped at the blood, absorbing a good portion of it, then shoved the bloody cloth into a plastic disposal bag, sealing it shut with a quick pull of the sealing zipper.

"Mom?"

Marla looked up to see a disheveled Curtis staring down at her. She rose up to her feet. "What are you doing here?"

"Where's Rudy? Where did they take him?"

Marla frowned at him. She felt her heart quicken and a tightness squeezed at her chest. "What are you talking about?"

"They just brought him in here. Where did they take him?"

She thought of the body on the gurney that had just passed. Oh my God. That was Rudy on that gurney. Marla stared with a sickening feeling at the plastic disposal bag in her hand. The bag containing her son's blood.

"I didn't mean to hit him so hard," Curtis said. "But he took my sandwich. I told him not to touch my stuff. I told him to keep his fucking grubby hands off my food. He did it just to piss me off."

Marla felt paralyzed. She suddenly felt very weak. A dizziness washed over her and she felt her vision dim. She stared at the blood-stained cloth. Then she turned and raced after the gurney.

⚜

Marla stared at the notebook. It sat on her desk, untouched for a week now. There was a slight bulge in the notebook, a bulge where the strip of bloody cloth lay on the last page. She hadn't touched it since Rudy's funeral.

The house was so quiet with Curtis in jail awaiting trial for involuntary manslaughter. She felt like she was encased in a giant mausoleum. She didn't want any visitors. She didn't want any friends to come over, not that she really had many friends in the first place. She just wanted to be left alone.

With her notebook.

Marla reached down and opened the notebook, her face flat and expressionless. She gently removed the bloody piece of cloth, revealing the red words written on the parchment that lay hidden beneath the stained shred of fabric. She read the words. Tears started to stream down her cheeks as she read. She reached the end of the tale and closed her eyes, squeezing more tears out. It was such a good story. Marla gently closed the notebook and held it in her lap, feeling the hot tears sliding down her cheek. Such a good story…such a perfect ending…

One of her tears hit the cover of the notebook, the liquid soaking into the leathery cover. Marla stared with rapt fascination as a shape began to appear on the cover, the wetness of her tears revealing a hidden image. It was as if the image had been drawn in some ancient invisible ink, buried deep in the hidden layers of the leather cover, and her tears had made the artwork rise up to the surface. It was a woman's face. A face Marla recognized. It was a face she had seen before in her studies of Greek mythology. It was the face of a Muse. The face of one Muse in particular. The face of Melpomene, the Muse who presided over tragedy.

She looked over at the other notebooks that had been part of the stack she had bought at the Saver Plus store. There were eight more notebooks in the pile on the far edge of her desk. Could it be, she wondered. There were nine Muses in Greek mythology. Nine notebooks. Nine muses. Was there a Muse trapped within each one? More importantly, were they hungry?

Marla reached for another notebook.

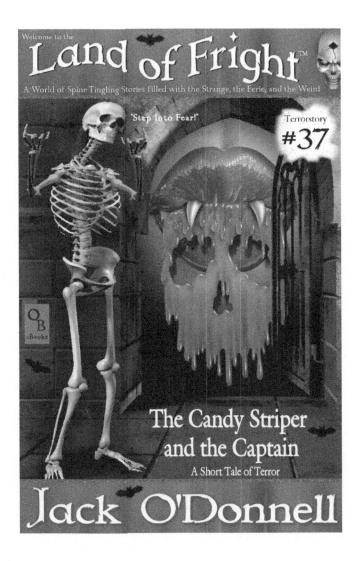

TERRORSTORY #37
THE CANDY STRIPER AND
THE CAPTAIN

I **can't wait to get back to the States. Or do I feel** this way because *she* wants me to feel it? Do I yearn to get back home to Hobart because she is guiding me there? Because she wants me to help her extend the range of her influence? Ever since... ever since the war I'm not sure any of my actions are truly my own. I know she has a power over me, but how far does it extend? How far can she reach me?

The thing that unsettles me the most is that I'm uncertain of the true reason why I'm so eager to get back home. I want to get back to Indiana just to see my wife and daughter. I mean, right? Seems pretty obvious. Who wouldn't want to see their family after that brutal war against the Japs in the Pacific? Who wouldn't want to surround themselves with loved ones after suffering through all that brutality? But there's something pushing me beyond that. Or someone. *Her.*

Most of you won't believe this story, but it's true. The fact that I'm still here, that I'm able to write this down, should be proof enough for you that it happened. Some of you will probably chalk it up to jungle fever, or battle fatigue from fighting too long in the Philippines without a break, or some other psychobabble the shrinks throw out. But that doesn't mean it didn't happen to me. No matter how incredible it may seem to you.

Okay, now I'm the one who is starting to babble. I think I just need to start putting it all down on paper.

The first time we did it caused quite a stir. But the second and third times really put the fear in them. We could see it on every one of their Jap faces. Even their commanders. They were damn scared of those jungle trails after that. Nearly petrified to the point of inaction. I remembered seeing one of those Jap soldiers spot his buddy on the trail and his eyes went so wide I thought they were going to bug right out of that Jap's head. Another one of them pissed his pants on the spot, literally. Me and Greely could see the dark stain spreading across his crotch while he stood near the Jap body we just decorated.

Decorated. That's what we called it. We were decorating the bodies. Giving them a little extra something to distinguish them from the others. An embellishment, as it were. I don't even remember whose idea it was. Probably came up during a bullshit session with Greely. He was always pulling weird facts about the Japs out of the air. Well, he was right about this one. They were definitely scared of what we were doing. Real scared.

I thought I knew what fear looked like, especially because I still remembered the terrified looks on the faces of those punks we whacked in Hobart. We laid into those juvies real good for stealing from my Pop's store just before we shipped off to the war in the Pacific. Yeah, we put a real fear into those punks, or so I thought at the time. But I was wrong about what real fear looked like.

Those Jap soldiers out in the Philippine jungles, they were scared for real. Scared for their eternal souls, which was far worse to them than being scared about dying from a bullet from an M1 or a Springfield, or dying from the stabbing slash of a trench knife. The flesh and bone of your body eventually rots away to nothing no matter how you die, but your eternal soul goes on forever. Even their macho bushido code couldn't protect them from the everlasting dishonor and damnation from a vampire's bite.

We used nails the first time on a Jap that was dead a few days. We had to dress up the holes and smear some blood around them to give them that authentic touch, but they looked pretty good after we were done. We decorated him real nice. Greely was too scared to do it. He didn't have the stomach for desecrating the dead. Me? I didn't give a shit. Not after what those Japanese savages did to McDowd and Valentino. You ever see a man with his dick cut off and shoved into his mouth? I have. More than once. No, I had no problem at all picking up a rusty nail and stabbing a few holes into that dead Jap's neck to simulate a vampire's bite. No problem at all.

After we put the holes in his neck and smeared some blood on his throat, we dragged the Jap's corpse out on the trail and dumped it just off to the side of the muddy path. We left a foot hanging out of the foliage so his buddies couldn't miss him. The Japs were usually quiet and calm when they moved through the jungle, but that corpse really riled them up. We could hear them jabbering in excited voices when they found the body. We didn't know what they were saying, but it was clear they were agitated and maybe even a bit hysterical, and a whole helluva lot of scared.

The second and third corpses we decorated for them really put them on edge. They might have been able to brush off their first encounter with a vampire victim as a weird occurrence, but not two, not three. We really played up the vampire mythology well, too. A few of the Jap soldiers started wearing silver crosses, so we left them alone. We only went after the ones who weren't wearing crosses. We wanted them to really think a dark supernatural evil was targeting them.

The next couple of corpses we decorated with fake vampire holes in their necks really put them over the edge. We knew it did because the next patrol we encountered was packed with Japs wearing silver crosses. Every one of them had one dangling around his neck. Even their commander.

Heck, we even started wearing crosses ourselves.

You play around too much with this stuff and it starts to feel real, even when you know it's fake. I still remember how cool that silver metal felt on my fingers. I caught myself absently touching and fondling the cross all day long. It did give me a weird sense of comfort. Well, at least it used to, but I'm getting ahead of myself here.

What really got *us* scared was the body Greely found on the trail. None of us had left it there. Greely swears he didn't do it and I believed him. He was too jittery to even poke a few tiny holes in a corpse, let alone rip four gaping holes into a dead guy's neck. And that's what this corpse had in its throat. Four big savage holes the thickness of quarters, two on each side of his neck.

There were wild boar with some pretty nasty tusks in the Philippine jungles; we all knew that. Some big monkeys, too. But these weren't animal bites. These were too strategically placed to have come from a wild animal. Too neat. We wondered if the Japanese were screwing with us, trying to turn our own psychological warfare against us.

Turns out, it was a native screwing with us. But not the kind of native we all thought.

She showed up out of nowhere. I had no idea where she came from, or how she had gotten past our sentries, but she had. She just appeared in my tent one night, looming over my cot. I felt her presence more than heard it and opened my eyes to see the shape of her figure poised over me. A sliver of moonlight streamed in from outside, giving her obviously feminine form a soft silver glow.

"You are giving me a bad name," she said. Or at least that's what I think she said. I'm not really sure, but that's what it sounded like.

I fought back the urge to wet myself at the shadowy sight of this woman standing over my cot. I'm a light sleeper and usually wake up at the drop of a hat (you had to be a light sleeper in the jungle or you just didn't last very long), but I didn't hear her enter my tent at all. Not one footstep. Not one rustle of clothing. Nothing.

I really didn't know how to react. I supposed I should have reached for my trench knife or my Colt, but I didn't. I just lay in my cot, unable to move. It was if all of my training had suddenly been for naught. It's hard to explain the feeling now, but I remember it as being some sort of weird paralysis. It didn't last long, but I still remember just being unable to move that first time I saw her.

I knew she had spoken again but I wasn't able to comprehend the words. I just mumbled something back at her, but I can't remember what I said.

"You need to stop making me look weak," she said.

I was starting to feel more awake now. My eyes adjusted to the dim gloom quickly. Months of fighting the Japs in the Philippine jungles acclimated my body to quickly react to any situation, and that experience started to take over, pushing the weird paralyzing feeling away. She stood over my cot, staring down at me. Her skin was pale and smooth. It looked so damn smooth. Not a wrinkle on it anywhere. It was just something I noticed at the time. The only women I had seen recently were older Filipino women, and their faces were all severely shriveled and wrinkled from years of exposure to the sun and the elements. The pale smoothness of this woman's skin was in stark contrast to the tanned leathery skin of the natives.

She moved closer. "I need to show you something."

I sat up in my cot and just stared stupid at her.

"Out in the moonlight. Come."

She turned and moved out of my tent. I sat on my cot for a long moment, trying to understand what the hell was going on. I glanced up and could see the shape of her standing outside my tent. The moon was high and bright so it illuminated her dark form pretty clearly. I wanted to just stay where I was, but I knew there was no way I could deny her request. I got to my feet, forced myself to be steady, then moved out into the night.

"I want you to stop," she said.

I frowned.

"Stop putting those little holes in the necks of those men."

I opened my mouth to protest. Those little holes were definitely having an effect on the Japs. They were making them nervous. And nervous soldiers made stupid mistakes. Mistakes we could capitalize on. But she held up her hand, silencing me before I could utter my protest aloud.

"Stop giving me a bad name. I don't put pretty little holes in men's necks. I rip their throats out. If you are going to do it, do it right, Captain."

And then she showed me her teeth. Okay, not her

teeth. Her fangs. Her thick, sharp fangs. Two long, sharp fangs on the top row of her teeth, and two long, sharp fangs on the bottom row of her teeth. All the better to grip your throat with, my dear.

She also showed me something else I had never seen before. She showed me her tongue; it had a small opening at its tip, like the opening of a small mouth. It was like a suction hose that she used to take blood into her system. And I can't even begin to describe what it felt like when she took my cock into that mouth of hers. You haven't had your cock sucked until you've had a mouth within a mouth draining you dry and sucking every last drop out of your tip. But I'm getting ahead of myself again. That happened later.

She stood quietly for a moment, staring up at the bright circle of the moon. For a brief moment, she closed her eyes as if basking in the moonlight. "I am on your side," she said. She turned to look at me. I could immediately see the age in her eyes. Not in her face. Her face was pale, but smooth and creamy with no clear sign of age. It was her eyes that showed her age. They had a deepness to them; they were eyes that had seen many things. "I am from Chicago, if you can believe that. Well, not really Chicago. One of the suburbs. It's just easier to tell everyone Chicago."

And then she told me her story. Her name was Mary Linston. She was a Catholic candy striper, a volunteer nurse, except she wasn't wearing one of those red-and-white striped jumpers that resembled a candy cane that the candy striper women were known for. She was wearing a sheer gown that was nearly translucent; I still have no idea where she got that garment from. She came out to the Philippines to help the sick and wounded, and to help the natives learn about Jesus. But some thing, some creature, had attacked her one night and turned her into what she was now. She was certain it had been another vampire, but she never saw him, or her, again, so she couldn't say for sure. She had just woken up in a dark cave filled with bats, and realized she had a ravenous hunger for human blood. Simple as that. She just knew she needed human blood to survive. She admitted she had thought of killing herself, but that was too grievous a sin in her mind. Plus, she didn't really know how to kill herself in her new condition.

"Pretty ironic, right? Here I am coming out here to help spread the word of Christ and now I'm only spreading more death." Mary looked at him earnestly. "Can a vampire still believe in God?" she asked him. "Is that madness?" She softly shook her head. "Because I still do. I still think I am doing His work."

"If you are killing Jap soldiers, then you are doing good work," I told her. "These men are savages. You've seen what they've done to our soldiers."

Mary nodded. "That is part of why I have decided to help you. I can no longer sit idly by." She was quiet for a moment. "Do you know what else they are doing?"

I had no idea what she was talking about, and I told her so.

"It goes beyond soldiers killing soldiers," she said, but I still didn't know what she was talking about.

"Do you know what they are doing with the native women? With the young girls? And even some of the young boys?"

I suspected where this was going now, but I just listened.

Mary was quiet for a moment. "They call them comfort women. They give comfort to the men. And I don't mean they give them words of encouragement and a pat on the back."

I waited for her to continue.

"They use them. They use their bodies in all manner of... vicious ways. They even take some of the young men and boys for the soldiers who prefer that sort of thing." Mary was quiet for a moment. "I saw them visit a school once. They made all the girls get up on a stage and sing. They laughed and joked and clapped. It was like they pretended to have a contest to see who was the best singer in the group. There was a clear winner. She had a beautiful sweet voice. Strong, but very feminine. They clapped and whistled and cheered for her. She beamed back at them. I still can see her pretty smile."

Mary had a sad, wistful look on her face. I waited for her to continue.

"They told her they wanted her to sing for their commander. He would appreciate her very much. She was so excited to go. And that pretty smile. I can still see that smile. She was so happy. They took her back to their camp." She paused. "But there wasn't any more singing. At least not by her."

The rest of the story was brutal and ugly. The men took turns with the young singer, holding her down, forcing her body into all sorts of sordid positions. I suppose I should have been more surprised, but rape always accompanied war throughout history. Here was no different. It was abhorrent, but I certainly wasn't shocked by the news. I had seen the brutal desecration of American GIs, so a gang rape of an innocent Filipino girl didn't shock me at all.

Mary was gravely disturbed by it all, though. It was clear that something had happened to her in the past. Something similar that permanently scarred her. After she finished the tale, she looked at me. "We can work together."

I said nothing.

She was quiet for a moment. "Your war means nothing to me anymore. Once it did, but not anymore. There were wars before this one, and there will be wars after this one." She looked at me. "You want to kill them because they have mutilated your friends. I want to stop them because they are torturing and raping innocent girls and women. Together, we can do both."

I looked at her, not knowing what to make of her offer. Who the hell was she? What was she doing here? Was she really a vampire? I mean, come on. I had seen a lot of shit in the jungle, but a real-life vampire? I found that hard to fathom and frankly found it all rather unbelievable. I didn't have time to ask her any of those questions because right then we came under attack.

Gunfire and shouts and the sound of scrambling men filled the night. Off to my right, someone screamed and more gunfire rang out. I turned to look in that direction, then looked back to the mysterious woman who had come out of the night, but Mary was gone.

I moved back into my tent, grabbed my rifle, and stepped back out into the night. The ground spurted up dirt and leaves. I dove behind some crates, looking for any cover I could find. Bullets chewed up the slats on the crates. A few more bullets hit the ground near my feet. From the trajectory of the gunfire, I quickly realized it was a sniper, somewhere up in the trees near me. I cast a cautious glance up into the jungle canopy above me and nearly took a bullet in the head. The round pinged off the edge of the crate, sending tiny slivers of wood splattering against my cheek. One of the slivers shot in deep into my flesh, but all I could do was wince and push away the stinging pain.

I heard a fluttering sound and saw a few dark shapes flit past me. I don't really know how I heard their wings flapping amidst the gunfire and shouting and cacophony of chaos all around me, but I did. I heard their wings flapping, and then I saw them flying up into the tree towards the sniper. He stopped shooting and started screaming. Then I heard branches rustling heavily and cracking, followed by a loud dull thud as the Jap sniper's body hit the jungle floor. I cautiously raised up and glanced over the top of the crates. Several bats were hovering over the sniper's body. And then Mary was there, kneeling down over him. I couldn't see what she was doing at the time because her body had blocked my view, but I know now exactly what she was doing, as I am certain you do. She was feeding on the fallen Jap sniper.

The bats continued to hover over the scene. They were waiting for her to finish, waiting for their turn to feed on their fresh kill after their mother fed. Their mother. Their master. I don't know what they thought of her, but I do know they held her in reverence. They might have just been animals, but they still deferred to her in everything they did. Mary was their commander, there was no doubt about that.

I didn't know this at the time, but I quickly discovered it later.

Finally, Mary rose up away from the dead sniper. The hovering bats descended on the corpse. One of the bats landed on the dead sniper's chest and immediately started feeding on him, lapping at the spilled blood. A second bat landed on the dead Jap's leg and started to feed.

Another bat slowly descended to Mary's shoulder and perched there, folding in its leathery wings as it landed on her. At the time, I didn't know if they were communicating or not, speaking in some silent language only they understood, but Mary suddenly hurried away from the scene, moving deeper into the jungle.

I followed her. I had to. There was no way for me to resist the compulsion to race after her.

<hr />

I was able to keep up with her all the way to the entrance of the cave, but once she disappeared into the cave, I had to slow down. The cave was fucking dark. I mean really fucking dark. I couldn't see a damn thing. I waited for my eyes to adjust to the deep gloom.

The cave had the reeking stench of blood, but that didn't deter me from going in deeper. I was used to the smell of blood by then, sad to say. Many of our skirmishes with the enemy had led to close quarter combat and heavy volumes of both enemy and friendly blood had spilled in those fights.

I could hear retching in the distance. I moved towards the sound as my eyes continued to adjust to the darkness. I started to make out shapes. At first I thought they were stalactites on the ceiling, but of course they weren't. They were bats. Hundreds of bats. Thousands of bats hanging upside down from the stone ceiling of the cave.

Thousands of bats all under her command.

I found her hovered around a colony of young bats. They all had their little mouths open, eagerly awaiting what she was about to give them. She contorted her face, almost grimacing, and retched, regurgitating blood into their mouths. The young bats lapped it up eagerly as their mother fed them human blood. I understood later what she was doing. She was teaching them to understand the taste of human blood. She was teaching them to thirst for it. She was teaching them to crave it.

Of course, I learned all this after she taught me the same lesson. Never disturb a mother feeding her young. She doesn't like that. She doesn't like that at all.

I must have kicked a rock, or disturbed something on the floor of the cave that drew her attention. She snapped her head towards me and I heard a feral snarl as she leaped at me. I didn't have a chance to fight back. Hell, I didn't even have a chance to react. She moved too fast. She was on me in a second. I saw her mouth open wide and her four fangs extend, two on the top, two on the bottom. Once a vampire got hold of your neck with those four massive fangs, there was no escaping that grip.

But she must have recognized me, because she stopped before she sunk her fangs into me. Instead, her fangs withdrew, sliding back into her gums. But then she puked blood into my mouth. I gagged and sputtered, trying to spit it out, but she wouldn't let me. She clamped my mouth shut, forcing me to swallow a mouthful of the hot liquid. I wanted to vomit, but she wouldn't let me do that either. She kept her hand clamped tight over my mouth, not letting anything come back out from between my lips.

The transformation was painful. I wasn't this lowly caterpillar turning into a beautiful butterfly. That's not how it felt. It felt like my insides were crawling with cockroaches who had razor blades for legs. Every part of my body screamed in pain. I tried to claw at my flesh, tried to get the razor roaches out of my body, but she wouldn't let me. She held me tight through the whole ordeal, rocking me in her arms. For a candy striper, she had a damn strong grip.

And then it was over. I was like her. I was hers.

We continued what we started.

I watched one the Japanese soldiers come out of the comfort station. He adjusted the belt on his pants, a very satisfied grin on his lips. I sent one of my bats to urinate on him, marking him for later. Oh, he would try to wash it off, but he wouldn't get all of it. The bat urine seeps into the skin and lasts for about a week before it fades, no matter how much a man washes it. It was how we marked our prey. At least the ones we didn't want to forget about, or the ones we wanted to give special deaths to.

Special deaths. Those were turning out to be my favorites. It allowed the inner artist in me to come out. Plus it scared the piss out of the Japs. One of my favorites was when I pulled out a Jap's intestines and spelled out BANZAI in the dirt with their long stringy lengths. Maybe I am a little crazy now. Maybe I am a little bloodthirsty. That one still makes me chuckle, though, even though most of them probably couldn't read English anyway.

There were still four soldiers in the comfort station with the girl. I had to get her out safely first. I sent Drac in to do recon. Okay, I probably need to take a step back here. Drac was one of the bats I could now control. After Mary transformed me, I also had the same powers over the bats that she had. Any bat that I fed regurgitated blood to was a bat that I could now control. I could see through Drac's eyes. Don't ask me how I could do that because I don't know. Something in the transfer of blood connected us. When I regurgitated blood into Drac's mouth, something happened. Something connected us in the grand cosmic blood feast of life. I have no fucking idea. And do you really have to ask me where his name came from? It was the first stupid thing that came to mind and it stuck no matter how hard I tried to rename him.

Drac fluttered in, unnoticed by the soldiers who had the girl pinned down to the rickety bed in the corner of the room. One of the Jap soldiers held her arms down, two others had one leg each. The fourth Jap was mounted atop of her, thrusting away, his pants down around his ankles. The three holding the girl had their weapons in their holsters, but their hands were occupied so it would take them a few seconds to let go of the girl and grab at their weapons. That was really all the time I needed. It was amazing how a few seconds of distraction made all the difference in the world in a battle.

I set the attack in motion.

Drac stayed high up in the hut, waiting.

I charged towards the comfort station; three more bats accompanied me, circling above me like little dark moons orbiting my big head of a planet. Just as I was nearing the entrance, I gave Drac the mental signal.

Drac screeched a horrible screech from the corner of the hut's ceiling. This made the Jap men freeze for just a second, and that's all I needed. Our timing was perfect. I burst into the hut, firing left, hitting the man holding the girl's arms with a nice spray of bullets across his chest. I kept the gun moving, spraying the man holding the girl's right leg with the same burst, then spraying the man thrusting into her. Then I quickly fired a flurry of bullets into the man holding the girl's left leg down.

They didn't all die at once. One of the men made a grab for his pistol and Drac made a bee line for his hand, clamping his sharp little teeth down on the Jap's flesh. Drac ripped out a few chunks of Jap meat, then thrust his head back down for more. The Jap howled and tried to give Drac a whack, but I put another bullet in his head and the Jap soldier stopped howling. The Jap's body shook and trembled and he shit all over himself, but he stopped howling.

And then the comfort station became quiet. One of the Japs groaned ever so softly and I sent all the bats dive-bombing on his face and his moaning sound also stopped.

All the while the girl hadn't moved. I don't know if she was conscious or not. She had blood all over her and I thought I might have accidentally hit her with bullets. I moved over to her and checked her body for bullet holes, but I didn't find any. I thought about puking blood into her mouth and holding her tight while she joined the family, but for some reason I didn't. She was just too young.

I fed on some of the Jap soldiers, eating my fill. They all had silver crosses dangling around their necks, which I thought was hilarious. You would have thought by now they would have realized those had no power to save them, but they kept wearing them anyway. It's a real messy affair to eat humans. No matter how neat I try to be, I always get blood all over the place, all over my face. I'm still getting used to the odd sucking aperture on the edge of my tongue, too. I'm sure I'll probably get better as I get more experience.

Mary came in to the comfort station and stood over the soiled cot, staring sadly down at the girl. I thought for a moment she was going to puke blood into the girl's mouth and change her, but she didn't. She joined me, feasting on the dead men alongside of me.

It is amazing what feasting on human blood does for a guy's cock. I mean I swear I doubled in length and tripled in girth after I feasted. I'm not sure where it all went when she ate. It didn't go to her boobs. I mean, she had great boobs, but they didn't get any bigger after she feasted. It went to her loins, I guess, made her pussy lips a little puffier, made her wetter, not that she wasn't soaking wet already.

We fucked in the comfort station, right on the hard earth floor next to the unconscious girl on the cot who had just been getting gang raped. It doesn't seem right we did such a thing, but at the time it was so right. You just can't understand the feeling unless you've experienced it. Oh, you think you might understand raw lust, but you don't. You can't. You can't possibly understand it until you experience it directly for yourself. And this was raw lust of the most pure kind. We had to do it. We had to fuck right then and there. My body was engorged with blood and it felt like all of it had rushed to my genitals. There was no fighting it. Mary didn't even bother to try and fight it anymore, and I quickly learned it was pointless to struggle against it. You can't understand any of the allure, the hypnotic-inducing lust that feasting on blood causes, unless you've done it. And I have done it. Hundreds of times since then.

And then Mary did that thing with her mouth, with her tongue. She put her mouth over my cock and started sucking. Her lips went up and down my shaft at the same time her tongue-orifice was sucking on the head of my cock. It was the most deliriously ecstatic feeling I have ever felt. I never got tired of her doing that.

We got the girl safely back to her mother. And then we continued the fight, attacking when the opportunities presented themselves, spreading fear and terror amongst as many Japanese squads as we could. Finally, the war ended, and Mary disappeared back into the jungle. I haven't seen her since.

I'm back in the States now. I feel guilty leaving

Drac and his brothers and sisters behind in the Philippines. I wonder if they'll find me. I can still feel them. I can't see through their eyes, but I can feel a vague presence when I really concentrate. They are still out there somewhere. I wonder if they can find me like those lost pets that travel hundreds and thousands of miles to find their homes and owners again. Something tells me they will.

I'm not sure if Mary followed me. Or was she the one who sent me here? I keep coming back to that, but I still don't know. I don't know if I returned home because I wanted to, or because Mary guided me here. There is a lot of misery and abuse and rape happening in the States, too. Is that what Mary has sent me to fight? I don't know if anything I do is because I want to do it, or because she's guiding me. I think I want to be here. I think I wanted to go home. I mean, why wouldn't I want to go home? Why wouldn't I want to see my wife and daughter again? Why wouldn't I want them to feel what I feel? Why wouldn't I want them to learn to love the taste of human blood?

Besides, if my wife learns that tongue-orifice trick how hot would that be?

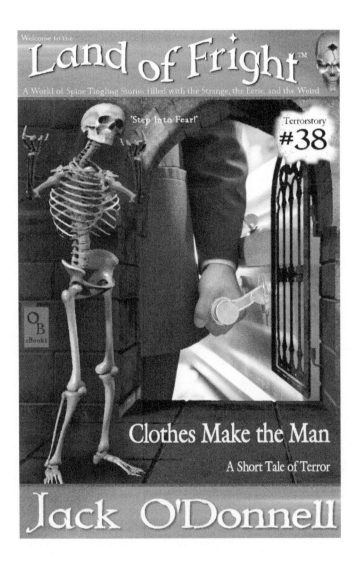

Welcome to the

Land of Fright™

A World of Spine-Tingling Stories filled with the Strange, the Eerie, and the Weird

'Step Into Fear!'

Terrorstory #38

OB eBooks

Clothes Make the Man

A Short Tale of Terror

Jack O'Donnell

TERRORSTORY #38
CLOTHES MAKE THE MAN

Blake Goldwin stared at the dead man in the casket, trying to figure out how he could get the suit off Robert's corpse without anyone finding out. How the hell *do* you get a suit off a corpse? Blake had no idea. But somehow he was going to figure it out.

Robert always had said that the suit was the real source of his wealth and his sex appeal. He had said it was indestructible. He couldn't rip it. He couldn't cut it. He couldn't even burn it (and Robert said he had tried). It was some kind of super suit.

The clothes make the man. The sentence kept rolling over and over in Blake's head like a tumbleweed rolling across a dusty western road. The clothes make the man. That's what his dad always told him. Thank God for Dad, Blake thought. Blake had hit some pretty hard times lately and his dad was there to pick up the pieces. He never in a million years thought he would end up back home, but a slew of bad jobs and some really bad investments left him in some financial hot water. He fell hook, line, and sinker for a lot of high tech companies that had made a lot of high-flying promises. Too bad his financial wings were made out of wax and he had flown way too close to the fucking sun. You'd think he would have learned after two hard crash landings, but no. Blake kept putting those wax wings back on and trying to soar high on those stock market jet streams. And he kept getting burned by the fiery rhetoric of aggressive brokers. He should've skipped the part about trying to fly and just jumped straight off a cliff. The end result would have been the same, but it would have been a helluva lot quicker to get it out of his system.

Blake's dad graciously, without scolding, without judgment, let him come back to the house and live in his old room until he could get back on his feet. With Mom gone, Blake thought Dad was probably lonely anyway. They never talked about it, but Blake could sense that his dad liked having him around again, even though Blake had proven himself a financial retard. Maybe especially because of that fact. Now Dad had somebody to take care of again.

Blake stared down into the casket at the suit. It was a black three-piece suit with a single-breasted jacket, a vest, and pants all made from some similar material. The suit had very thin, very faint pinstripes, giving it a touch of a gangster feel. The material did seem to have a soft sheen to it, a subtle glow. Maybe the suit would be his ticket. Maybe that would be how he got back on his feet. He was out of ideas. Blake remembered asking Robert where he had gotten the suit from, but Robert would never tell him. He knew Robert had come back with the suit after a mysterious business trip to Europe, but Blake had no idea what country Robert had gotten the suit from. Italy, maybe. Robert had given off an old school Mafia vibe when he wore it. There had been an aura of power, a hint of danger, and a smoldering sheen of promised sexual prowess around Robert when he strutted around in the suit.

Too bad Robert wasn't wearing the suit when the limo crashed, Blake thought. Robert had been on his way to take a vacation in Tahiti in one of those overwater bungalows when a sleep-deprived truck driver lost control of his rig and slammed into the limo, sending it spinning. The force of the truck pushed the limo right off the overpass, right through the concrete guard blocks and the fence. The long black limo smashed onto the highway below, right in front of 70-mile-an-hour traffic. It caused a thirty-eight car pileup. Robert had suffered fatal head trauma in the crash. He had bled to death before they could cut him out of the wreckage, bleeding all over the colorful Hawaiian-style shirt he had been wearing, coating the white flowers in a deep red stain.

Blake stared down at Robert's corpse. The head wound was invisible behind his full head of hair; the mortician had done some fine work. His friend did look peaceful. Friend? Blake scoffed at the thought. He wasn't a friend. Robert was just some guy he worked with. The suit still looked damn good on him.

Like it always did. Robert had been a woman whisperer when he wore that suit. No woman could deny his advances when he started strutting his stuff in that suit. His peacocking was obvious to every guy around him, but the women just seemed to eat it up. He banged chicks left and right, and backwards and forwards, and up and down. Robert always said it was the suit. The suit was a chick magnet.

Blake resisted the urge to reach down into the casket and touch the suit as he kneeled before the open casket. Robert had wanted to be buried in that suit; it was the first declaration in Robert's will. *That was pretty damn selfish of you*, Blake thought as he stared down at the pale face of the dead man before him. *Why keep all that… all that… magic… to yourself when you could have at least shared it after you died?* He thought of that one word that came to mind. *Magic*. Had he really used the word magic? Blake didn't believe in magic. That was just silly and stupid. But then he thought of the suit, thought of everything that happened to Robert when he wore the suit, thought of all the stories Robert had told him. It was impossible to deny the suit had some kind of… enchanted power built into its fabric.

There was only one way to find out. Blake had to put the suit on and see for himself. The wake would be over in a few hours. The burial was tomorrow. He would have to do it tonight or the suit would be lost to him forever.

There was only one woman left at the wake now. She had entered the room just as Blake was maneuvering himself into a hiding spot behind the vast array of funeral flowers that were positioned near the casket. He heard her approaching and ducked down behind a massive wreath just seconds before she entered the room. Thankfully, there were several other wreaths positioned on stands in front of the larger funeral wreath, so he was pretty confident he was well hidden from view. He was near the bottom end of the casket, so he could still partially see Robert's corpse lying inside the casket from his hiding spot.

The woman was very pretty. She had long dark hair and smoky eyes. Her face was perfectly mascaraed, her cheeks highlighted with a soft smear, her eyelids accentuated with a faint splash of color. She finished her silent prayer on the kneeler before the open casket and stood up. She glanced around the room, as if looking to see if anyone was watching, then did something that nearly made Blake gasp out loud.

She hiked up her short dress and slid her finger up between her legs. She closed her eyes for a moment, leaving her finger between her legs for a few seconds. Then, she opened her eyes and withdrew her finger. The tip of her finger glistened with wetness. She looked at her moist finger for a moment, then reached into the casket to smear it across Robert's dead lips.

Jesus, Blake thought. *Jesus Effin' Chrimey. The guy's getting chicks hot and he's fucking dead.*

The woman reached down and caressed Robert's cheek. A few tears trickled down out of her eyes, smearing some of her make-up. Somehow, that made her even more beautiful, Blake thought. The woman turned away and slowly walked out of the room.

Blake watched her leave, admiring her curves, then turned back to the casket to stare at the part of Robert's body that he could see from where he was hiding behind the funeral flowers. He could see the dead man's pale face, his hands folded across his chest. And the suit. He could see the suit. Blake gazed intently at the dark suit. The suit seemed to shimmer as he stared at it. *It's the suit. It's gotta be that fucking suit. I need that fucking suit.*

⊰⊱⊰⊱

The funeral home was finally empty. All the lights were out. All was quiet. Blake waited a few minutes longer after he heard the funeral director's car pull away before easing out of his hiding position behind the flowers. He really thought the funeral home director was going to spot him when the old man had closed the casket lid up for the night, but he hadn't. The old man did seem to be a little slow. His vision was probably as bad as his hearing.

Blake moved over to the casket. The room was dark, very dark. He turned on his smartphone and used it as a flashlight, shining it on the casket lid. He kept his phone in one hand and raised the top half of the casket lid with the other.

Robert lay peacefully inside, his hands folded across his chest. A crazy fear flashed through Blake and he imagined Robert's eyes springing open to stare at him. He kept the soft glow of light focused on Robert's face, daring him to open his eyes. But Robert's eyes remained closed. His face looked pasty white, glowing with a ghostly sheen in the phone's light. *He's dead, you idiot. Get on with it.*

Blake stared down at the corpse. He thought he vaguely smelled pussy. He forced the image of the beautiful woman and her farewell gift to Robert out of his head to concentrate on the task at hand. *How the hell am I going to get that suit off of him?* He knew he had to pull him out of the casket. He opened the bottom half of the casket, revealing Robert's entire body. Blake moved his phone over Robert's body, illuminating the length of his corpse. Robert was fully dressed, shiny black shoes and all.

Blake shoved his phone back into his pocket and reached under Robert's arms, getting a good grip on him. His skin crawled as he felt the weight of the corpse in his arms, but he forced himself to keep going. I need the suit. Blake started to pull the body from the casket, but felt the casket suddenly start to tip. He immediately stopped pulling and froze, fearing the worst. But the casket did not fall. He paused for a moment, willing his heart to stop pounding like a jackhammer in his chest.

He kept going. Robert's body suddenly felt light. *Probably because your heart is beating two-forty and adrenalin is pumping through your body. Just hurry up and get it done!* Another crazy image flashed in Blake's head, this one of Robert wrapping his arms around him and squeezing him tight against his dead body, squeezing the life out of him in a monstrous zombie bear-hug of death. Blake pushed the thought away and kept tugging, lifting Robert up and over the side of the casket.

Blake finished pulling the corpse out, holding Robert's body under the arms as he pulled the dead man over the edge of the casket. Robert's feet thumped against the ground, the carpeting muffling the sound. Blake paused for a moment, listening, fearing that somehow somebody had heard that soft sound and would come charging into the wake room to see what the hell was going on. Silence rang in his ears. He remained motionless for just a moment longer, still clutching the corpse under its arms, still listening. But he heard nothing. Blake laid the body flat on the carpeted floor between the kneeler and the first row of visitor chairs that were positioned several feet back away from the kneeler.

He took his phone out and shined the phone up to Robert's face to see Robert staring at him with one open eye. Blake started, pulling back sharply with a muffled yelp. His heart pounded in his chest, in his ears. He could almost feel the beat of his heart in his mouth it was pounding so fast. *Jesus. He's dead, man. Dead. You must have jarred it open.* Blake reached up and tried to slide Robert's eyelid closed, but it refused to shut. *Didn't they sew those shut or something? What did they use, cheap rubber cement? Fuck. Use super glue, you fucking idiots.* Blake pushed at the eyelid, moving his finger quickly over the dead flesh, not wanting to linger too long on the dead skin. Robert's eye stayed open. Staring. Staring right at him. *Just get the goddamn suit and get the fuck out of here.*

Blake turned away from the staring eye and set his phone down on the carpeting next to the body. The light from the phone illuminated a small area around him in a pale white glow. He fumbled at the suit buttons, undoing them with shaking fingers. He managed to get one arm out of the suit, then had to lift and roll the body to get the other arm out of the suit. But he did it. He managed to get the suit coat off

Robert's corpse. He held it up; the light from the phone made it seem like the suit was almost glowing. Blake felt a tingling in his hands as he held the suit coat. Was that its power? Something told him that it was. It was like the suit did have some kind of energy source, some kind of dark power to it. He felt a thrill racing up his spine. *It did have power!* He could feel it. He could fucking feel it. He gently set the coat down next to him on the carpeting.

He repeated the same procedure to remove the vest from Robert's corpse, rolling the dead body this way and that, maneuvering the vest off the deceased man. Blake set the vest down next to the suit coat and stared at the two pieces of clothing. There was definitely something mesmerizing about them. He continued to stare at the black cloth, the subtle pinstripes, feeling their power.

Get the pants, asshole. Get the pants and get the fuck out of here.

Blake fumbled at the shoelaces on the corpse's shoes, untying them with excited, trembling fingers. He pulled off one of Robert's shoes and stared at it. *Are the shoes part of the suit?* He wasn't sure. *No, it's just the suit.* Robert never talked about the shoes. Only the suit. The coat and the vest and the pants. That's all he needed. Blake set the first shoe down and quickly removed the second shoe, setting it down next to the first.

He moved back up from Robert's feet to his waist. He reached for Robert's belt and undid it. Blake unbuttoned the pants and pulled the zipper down, hoping against hope that he wouldn't accidentally brush up against Robert's dead dick. He thought he might have felt a bump, but he didn't stop. He finished unzipping the pants and sat back on his haunches. *Shit, my knees are killing me. I can't sit like that anymore.* Blake worked on the pants, shimmying them this way and that, working them down Robert's pallid legs. Finally, he managed to get them completely off. "Yes," he said aloud in a hushed whisper, feeling amazingly triumphant. *You realize you are stealing the clothes off a dead man, right?* He squelched the questioning voice and continued to relish in his triumph.

What about the tie? Do you need the tie? Blake stared at the thin piece of fabric tied around Robert's neck, doing his best to avoid looking at the one open eye that seemed to be staring accusingly at him. No, Robert wore different ties with the suit. Blake was confident the tie wasn't part of the magical suit. *Magical suit. Listen to yourself.* He felt a sudden urge to giggle, but the sound of a door opening in the distance made Blake freeze, squashing any feeling of glee he still felt. He quickly flipped his phone over so it was face down on the carpet, but some stray light still managed to seep out from around the edges of the phone. Blake huddled in the near darkness. He knew he should click off his phone and completely kill the light, but he was too afraid to even move, too afraid to make any sound at all. He heard footsteps outside the room. *Who the fuck is that?* Blake fought to control his pounding heart. *Was that the funeral director? Did the old man come back? Was he going to work on Robert?* The light oozing out from beneath the phone looked like a dazzling bright spotlight to Blake, but he was still too afraid to reach for it, too afraid to move.

The ugliness of what he was doing struck Blake hard. He was stealing a suit off a dead man! How fucking sick was that? *But you need that suit. You need to know.*

And then the footsteps came closer, passing by the door to the wake room. Another door opened and closed.

Blake waited in the ghostly gloom, feeling a tightness in his chest, fearful that his scared breathing sounded like the panting of a dog in an echo chamber. He thought of scurrying back behind the flowers to hide there again, but almost laughed out loud. There was a dead body lying half undressed on the floor in front of the casket. Hiding behind a row of funeral wreaths wouldn't do him any good at the moment.

Then he heard a car starting up, and within moments the sound of its engine receded into the distance. Everything became… deathly quiet.

Blake waited several more very long minutes to be sure whoever had returned was now gone. He folded the suit coat and vest and pants neatly into a bundle, tucking them under his arm as he rose to his feet. He picked his phone back up for the light and the beam caught Robert's body lying on the floor. All Robert had on now was a black shirt, white underwear, and some black socks. Robert's lone open eye stared directly at Blake. *You can't just leave him there like that. You want his family to come back tomorrow and see him like this?* Would they come back? Blake wasn't sure. When was the wake officially over? He couldn't remember. He vaguely remembered there was additional viewing time in the morning. Or had that been for today? Fuck, he didn't know. *It doesn't matter. You can't just leave him there like that. You can't.*

⧸⧸⧸⧸⚜️⧹⧹⧹⧹

Blake searched the funeral home, moving carefully through the building because he didn't know the layout, shining his smartphone before him like a flashlight. His battery indicator was low so he knew he didn't have much juice left in it. He needed to find a suit and put it on Robert and get the hell out of there.

But he didn't find a suit. There were no spare sets of clothes anywhere that he could find.

And then he realized he had a suit close at hand. His suit. It was black, like Robert's, but it was a different style, with different buttons, a different pocket, and there was no vest. Would anybody notice? *Fuck, what choice do I have?*

⧸⧸⧸⧸⚜️⧹⧹⧹⧹

Blake stood in his shirt and underwear, staring down at Robert in the casket. He had buttoned the jacket all the way up, then tugged and twisted the collars to hide the lack of vest as best he could. *Not bad,* he thought. *Yeah, Dad would be real proud of this moment. You're a real winner.* Blake pushed that unpleasant thought away and studied the dead man. Blake was taller than Robert, but luckily they were close enough in height and weight for his suit to fit well enough on Robert. It had been relatively easy to put his suit on Robert, but it had been a fucking bitch to get the dead man back into the casket.

Blake couldn't remember if Robert's right hand had been folded over his left, or vice versa, so he just guessed and put Robert's right hand over his left. He wanted to touch Robert's actual flesh as little as possible, so he moved the dead man's hands by picking up the suit's sleeves and maneuvering the hands that way. He still couldn't get the eye to close and it watched him while he worked. He did his best to put all of Robert's body parts back in the position they had been in before he had removed Robert's suit from his dead body, but the damn eye would not close. Blake stared down at the dead man. The eye stared back. He looked down at his own suit that Robert was now wearing. He wondered again if anybody would notice the change in clothing. *Of course they would, you dumb ass. It's a completely different suit.* But would anybody really say anything, or would they just shrug it off and let it go? Who's going to ask if a corpse is wearing a different suit? *Whatever. It's done.*

Blake turned away from the casket and stared at the suit waiting for him on a nearby chair. Robert's suit. *The* suit.

Blake thought the suit would reek of embalming fluid, but it smelled good, fresh, strong, manly. It fit him very nicely. Almost as if it were specifically tailored just for him. It should have been too short in the arms, but it wasn't. It was perfect. The vest fit quite well, also. Blake knew from past experience that vests could be a surprisingly hard garment to fit properly. One tailor he had gone to had insisted on making at least a shirt and a jacket for him to familiarize himself with Blake's measurements and proportions before tackling the vest. The pants also should have been too short since he was taller than

Robert, but they also fit well. Perfectly. As if the pants had suddenly grown out an inch. But he knew that was impossible. Or was it? It was *the* suit, after all. The, dare he say it, magical suit.

Man, do I feel good! I feel like I just snorted a line of coke. I feel like partying big time. He glanced at his watch, but couldn't see the dials because it was too dark. He checked his phone. It was just past midnight. *The night is still young! The Whirlwind is waiting for me.*

<hr />

The Whirlwind wasn't waiting for him. The party had already started without him. As it always did on Friday night. But the party did pause when Blake entered the club. The music seemed to fade ever so slightly, the lights flared just a touch hotter, the patrons felt their gazes being pulled towards the guy entering the club. Everything seemed to slow down just for a brief moment. Blake took a few steps deeper into the club. Eyes focused on him. Gazes swiveled to track his movement. And then everything picked right back up where it was before Blake had arrived on the scene. Music pounded and throbbed. Lights splashed and pulsed. Heads turned back to continue with what they were absorbed in before his entrance.

Blake saw it and felt it. His own body pulsed and throbbed. He felt an exhilarating energy coursing through him. It was as if the suit was electrically charged, juicing him up like a fresh battery juicing up a phone. He was full of life and ready to party.

Blake scanned the room and saw the woman immediately. She was sitting at a small table near the back of the room, nursing a drink in her slender fingers. His gaze pulled on her, causing her head to lift up, drawing her stare to his. It was the woman he had seen hours earlier at Robert's wake. The woman who had smeared herself across Robert's lips. She held his stare and returned it, giving him an obvious invitation to come over and join her.

He joined her. And then Blake fucked her. Many times into the wee hours of the morning. Their first fuck happened in the women's bathroom at the club. She had pulled him into a stall, dug his cock out his pants, hiked up her skirt, slid him all the way deep inside her, and fucked him right then and there. He pounded her hard, pressing her back up against the bathroom stall as he pumped into her. He felt like the suit had somehow bestowed a few extra few inches to his length. He had never felt so thick and so hard, either. He could feel the entire length of his cock, as if every inch of the shaft was as sensitive as the head. Even though this first lusty session didn't last long, he had the most intense orgasm he had ever had.

And then he learned her name was Marjorie.

Blake and Marjorie both missed the funeral because they were still in bed going at it again. They missed the priest's final prayers. They missed the mourners paying their last respects. And they missed the casket being lowered into the ground.

Blake felt bad, but he also felt relieved. He hadn't really wanted to attend Robert's funeral. He didn't even want to know if any suspicions had been raised by Robert's sudden change in appearance. Or his open, staring eye. Ignorance was indeed bliss in this case.

He fucked Marjorie again.

The suit was lovingly draped over a nearby chair, a quiet sentry keeping watch over its new owner.

"So are you interested in this position?"

Blake grinned. It was his third job interview since putting on the suit and each business he went to wanted to hire him on the spot. The woman about to be his future boss was bent over her desk, baring her delicious ass to him. She was offering him the job and her luscious body all with one simple question.

He took her, and the job.

I love this fucking suit!

Blake wore the suit as often as he could handle it. The suit was like crack. You could take a hit of it, but you couldn't keep it on 24/7. He put it on for special occasions. He closed four deals when he was wearing it, sealing the deals faster than anyone in the history of the company. He wore it to score with other women at work. He wore it to score with women outside of work. He wore it to score with women anywhere he went with the suit.

Man, these contacts suck, Blake thought. He was in his car, coming home from the fitness center. That fucking quack of an eye doctor gave me a bad prescription. I should have just stayed with Lenses for Less. Blake squinted, but his vision stayed muddled. Driving at night was even worse. He could barely see the road a dozen feet beyond the hood.

He took his right hand off the steering wheel and shook his wrist. His fingers felt numb. Probably working out too hard, he thought.

<hr />

"What'd you say?" Blake asked.

His dad laughed. "You going fucking deaf, Blake? That's supposed to happen to me, not to you."

Blake looked at the volume level on the television. He used to have it at 22, but now he had to put it up to 28 just to hear it. What the hell? What was going on?

Blake was sitting on the couch in the living room of his boyhood home, dressed in jeans and a t-shirt. He was still living with his dad, but he was on the verge of moving back out and getting his own place again. His job was going like gangbusters. His bank account was filling back up. Even his investments were doing quite well. He was nailing chicks left and right. He needed his own place again so he could really strut his stuff.

But something felt wrong. Something felt off with his body. His vision was definitely getting worse, and obviously so was his hearing if even his old man was making fun of him.

Blake pulled at the skin on his arm. It had a weird, withered look to it. Almost like a decayed look. Is that a blueish tint to my skin? *Do I have some kind of disease? Maybe I picked something up from one of those women? You should have used a condom all the time. Yeah, but I didn't. I hate those damn things. Yeah, now you're paying the price. You probably got Ebola or something. Or cancer. Maybe you got cancer. Mom had it, so why not you? Maybe you'll die young just like she did.*

Blake shook his head. He knew he didn't have cancer. He got yearly cancer screenings because of what happened to his mom. His last check-up was clean. Completely clean. Yeah, but that was before you put on the suit, a voice inside him said. *Before the suit.* No, the suit had power. The suit was magical. The suit was giving him everything he ever wanted.

He pinched at his skin. He didn't feel anything. He pinched harder. Nothing. He pinched even harder. He felt that, but just barely. What the fuck was going on?

⊰⊱⊰⊱⊰⊱

Blake's vision continued to decline. His hearing continued to get worse. The blueish tint to his skin became darker. He felt a constant weakness in his arms and legs. It was hard to open any jar without seriously struggling with it. Going up the stairs to his bedroom was getting more and more difficult; he found himself needing to grab the handrails to make it up to the top. Other weird discolorations started to form on his flesh. His teeth started to turn brown.

⊰⊱⊰⊱⊰⊱

Blake stared at the tiny label on the suit. He hadn't noticed it before. It was just a tiny tag on the inside of the suit, attached near one of the inner seams. He read the words on the label. Vittorio Coniglioni.

There was a phone number next to the name on the label. He dialed it.

"Hello, Robert," the voice answered. The voice had an Italian accent, rich and heavy. Old. Ancient. Powerful.

Blake froze for a moment at the mention of Robert's name. "This isn't Robert," he said. "This is Blake."

There was a long silence. "Blake." There was more silence. "Where is Robert?"

"He's dead."

More silence.

Blake felt like he should say something, but he really had no idea what to say. The silence lingered. He stared at the suit laid out on his bed. "Did you make the suit?" he finally asked.

"Yes," the voice answered.

"You are Vittorio?" Blake asked.

"Yes. I am Vittorio Coniglioni."

There was more silence.

"Why are you calling me, Blake?" the deep voice asked.

"What is the suit? Where did it come from?"

"I made it. For Robert."

"But what is it? How does it work?"

Silence. "It is a suit, Blake," Vittorio said.

"I know it's a suit," Blake said. "But where does it get its—" He wanted to say magic, but he finished with "—power?"

There was a very long silence on the other end of the phone. "Did you put the suit on Blake?"

The question sent a cold chill racing up Blake's spine. For a moment, he couldn't find the energy to speak. His mouth felt frozen. "Yes," he finally answered. He started to pace alongside the bed, moving up towards the headboard, then turning and pacing back down towards the foot of the bed.

"Did Robert give you the suit?" Vittorio asked.

"What?"

"Did Robert willingly give you the suit?"

Blake paused. He pushed his fingers through his hair. "No." He pulled his hand down and saw several strands of his hair dangling from his fingers. Blake frowned and quickly shook his hand, dislodging the hair from his fingers.

"How did you get the suit, Blake? Tell me true or I will not be able to help you."

Blake hesitated. He glanced at the suit on the bed, then looked away from it. He felt compelled to tell this deep voice the truth. "I stole it."

Silence.

"I stole it from his corpse," Blake said.

Silence.

"He was already dead," Blake said, feeling a strong need to clarify what happened.

More silence.

"I didn't kill him, if that's what you think," Blake said. "He was already dead."

Then the enigmatic man on the other end of the phone spoke. "That is a bad thing you did, Blake."

"Tell me how to stop it!" Blake said, his fear erupting out of his mouth. "I think I'm fucking dying. I'm withering away here. Tell me how to stop it!" Blake started pacing again, moving quicker now.

"I cannot stop it," Vittorio said.

"What do you mean you can't stop it? You made this fucking thing. How do you stop it?"

"It   cannot   be   stopped.   The   fabric   is indestructible." Vittorio paused. "You know that."

"What if I just stop wearing it?" Blake asked. "Will that make all this stop?"

"No. You are the new owner of the suit. You stole it from a dead man. The suit will only bring death now. The slow decay of death."

Blake stopped pacing and clenched his phone tight against his ear. "Bullshit! Tell me how to stop it!"

"You are the owner of the suit. You took its power."

"I don't want its fucking power!" Blake shouted into the phone. "I want to get rid of its fucking power!"

"Then you need to find someone who wants it."

"Who the fuck wants a used suit from a dead man?"

Silence. "You did." More silence. "Goodbye, Blake," Vittorio Coniglioni said.

The phone went dead.

Blake stared at the suit. The fabric still shimmered, but now it looked more like a hellish glow than an angelic shine. *How the fuck do I get rid of this thing? I can't burn it. I can't rip it.* And then it came to him. Blake smiled. It was such an obvious solution.

<hr />

"Hey, Blake, check it out."

Blake heard the happy cheer in his dad's voice and he stepped out of the kitchen to see his dad coming in the front door.

"You ain't got nothin' on your old man, now," his dad said.

Blake's heart seized in his chest. No, not him. It

wasn't supposed to be him.

"Pretty sharp, huh?" His dad twisted and turned, showing off his new attire.

Blake stared hard at his dad. It wasn't supposed to turn out this way.

"I got it from that Goodwill store in town," his dad said. He continued to strut, still twisting and turning, showing off his new clothes.

Blake felt a lump rise in his throat. "Yeah, that's a great suit, Dad. A really great suit."

TERRORSTORY #39
MEMORY MARKET

The black market for memories was a scary place. What was really scary to Paulo was how pristine and pure the whole place looked, despite what was being sold here. Everything was polished and shiny, chrome and whiteness, gleaming with cleanness. Yet he knew many of the memory sticks sold here contained dark and horrible things, twisted and macabre activities, heinous events and horrid crimes, terrible tragedies, and the pain-filled end to many lives. *So what are you doing here?* he wondered again. God, he hated this business. He hated everything about it, yet he couldn't stay away. Nobody could stay away from the memory sticks anymore. Everyone in the world seemed addicted to them. *Yeah, but most of them stick to the legal memories.* The happy family memories. The adventurous travel memories. The triumphant sports memories. The movie star memories. The sex memories. *Oh, but not you. No. You're never happy with what normal people do. You always gotta have more. You're here because you are a sick, twisted fuck.*

Paulo couldn't help himself anymore. He used to fight it, but he gave in long ago. He thrived on the thrill of it all. Last week, he uploaded the memory of a failed bank robbery from the POV of one of the henchmen. The guy got a bullet from a security guard right in the knee, then another bullet in the chest. The guy bled out on the floor of the bank, staring right up the dress of a teller through his ski mask. The woman teller couldn't move because another one of the bank robbers had a gun to her head. She had white panties on. It was the last thing the guy bleeding out on the floor saw when he died; a vision of white panties and a hint of black pubic hair sticking out the sides of the woman's underwear. You could even see the curling folds of her cunt lips pressed up against the fabric because the panties were so tight. It looked like they were a little wet, too. Paulo didn't know if it was because she peed herself a little because a gun was to her head, or because she was excited by the whole thing.

The week before that Paulo uploaded the memory of a skydiving accident where the parachute didn't open. That was a rush. Seeing the ground racing up to meet you just seconds before you got splattered across a hundred yards of rocky ground.

The week before that was a massive multi-car pileup during a violent thunderstorm, extracted from the Memsphere of the fat guy who had been driving a motorcycle in the middle of it all. He hit the back of a stretch limo and went flying end over end over the entire length of the big black sedan, bouncing over and over along the long roof. Hot flashes of lightning ripped the sky as the guy went tumbling and you could see the jagged forks of lightning reflected in the limo's roof as the guy went tumbling over it. You couldn't have created better CGI special effects on a computer if you had tried. Then, the motorcycle guy ended up staring at the front grill of a truck on the other side of the highway speeding straight towards him. Lightning lit up the truck's grill just as the guy was about to get hit by it, and thunder blasted at the exact moment the big rig splattered the guy. Watching the last moments of the motorcycle guy's life play out from his point of view really was visually spectacular.

"Why take the risk?"

That was their message. You saw it everywhere. They played on people's fears and they did a damn good job of it. Why take the risk of imploding your inner ear on a deep scuba dive to an ancient wreck? Just buy the memory of the experience. You'll re-live it like it was your own. Why take the risk of a parachute not opening and leaving you splattered on the ground? Just buy the memory of sky diving. Why take the risk of driving a race car two hundred miles an hour around an insanely hard off-road course? Just buy the memory of it and you can experience that thrill of speed safely from your favorite chair.

The problem started with the most popular memories. Okay, it started with human nature, with some people having the unquenchable desire to have things that no one else has so they can strut their superiority, but that's a discussion for another day. The popular memories spread across the entire world in a matter of days when they hit big. They went cranial. That's what they called them when everybody had them. Cranial. Everybody wanted them uploaded into their craniums. The crazy daredevil actions. The wild sex memories of movie stars. They became so popular that everyone just had to have them. Everyone had the memory of the first Mars space flight. Everyone had the memory of the guy getting sucked up by a tornado and getting dropped harmlessly into a backyard pool. Everyone had the memory of the Indy 500 crash where the car rolled a hundred times but the driver walked away unscathed. Everyone had the memory of the archaeologist discovering a brand new city in the Florida swamplands that proved the Romans had reached the Americas centuries ago. All the popular memories were shared by everyone. Nothing was unique. No one was unique.

For most people, it was okay that everybody seemed to have the same shared memories. They had something in common they could share and talk about with their neighbors and co-workers. But for a few others, that wasn't good enough. The shared memories lost their luster. They were too popular. Sometimes, Paulo felt everyone else was just the same person on the inside but with a different body on the outside. Too many people shared the same experience. Some people, others like Paulo, wanted something different. They wanted something exclusive. But exclusive demanded a premium. A very high premium.

That's where the black memory market came in.

And when the hidden power of the Memsphere was tapped, that really stirred things up.

<hr />

Paulo thought about the memory cloud. It had been given dozens of different names before one seemed to stick. Cloud ten, sky cloud, eighth heaven, the memory realm. The Memsphere had at first been called the Neural Nebula, but most people weren't so keen on that name; that was too cerebral sounding. They tried to rebrand it as the Memory Mantle, but that lame name lasted about an hour. Some newscaster made some word play on the cloud and stratosphere and memory, and started calling it the Memsphere. That word just stuck and so the Memsphere was born.

The Memsphere is where everyone's memories are stored. It had supposedly started off as an experiment to preserve some billionaire's consciousness for all eternity in the Memsphere, but that hadn't worked out. The human brain was still too complicated. But they did manage to learn how to capture and store individual memories during their attempts to replicate the billionaire's consciousness.

Naturally, someone figured out a way to profit from this knowledge. And so they started selling space in the Memsphere for people to use, for people to upload the memories they wanted to preserve. The wealthy and famous used it first, but then, as usual, the prices came down and soon everyone could afford it.

Of course, if you could upload memories, you needed to be able to download and retrieve them. Otherwise, what was the point of storing them? Some entrepreneurial genius came up with the idea of selling other people's memories, hawking the memories to those who could never experience the same things the rich and famous did but desperately wanted to. It was easy to sell movie-star memories, the walk on the red carpet, the winning of an Oscar, the lavish parties, all the glitz and glamour of being a movie star. Pop star memories were very popular at first, too, especially the live concert memories of lead singers. Fans could experience all that adulation first-hand and get a true taste of pop star glory. Then the travel memories hit it big, bringing people to places they had never been, and allowing them to experience sites they knew they would never have the money or the time to visit.

The death memories were really an accident. No one had really planned to store them. One of the side effects that caught the developers off guard was that the fail-safe of the upload chip, a chip that nearly everyone now had implanted in their necks at birth, would automatically dump the entire contents of the memory chip into the Memsphere as a safety back-up measure when the chip detected a problem. Of course, the last memory people had was of their deaths, which the chip detected as being a problem. Imagine that. Death being a problem. Anyway, the Memsphere soon filled up with death memories being uploaded via the back-up failsafe built into the chip.

Not everyone knew the Memsphere had been

hacked, but Paulo did, as did thousands of others privy to this underground world. Of course, this information was kept tightly under wraps and out of the public's data stream. Could you imagine your own personal lovemaking memories exposed for all the world to see? Or your child's memories stolen by some pervert for their own sick amusement? No, this was information no one wanted to get out. Even the black market memory thieves were vigilant about keeping this information secret because they knew if it went too far public the government might take down the Memsphere entirely and that would be the end of their business. No, everyone had a vested interest in keeping the secret, and so the black memory market continued to exist.

The death memories were exhilarating. It was such a weird thing to think, but it was true. Nothing made Paulo feel more alive than experiencing someone else's death. Not sex. Not drugs. Not actual physical vacations to exotic lands. Nothing. Nothing else fired up his neurons like experiencing the last moments of someone else's life, then coming out of it still alive and kicking on the other end of the memory. Man, what a rush!

They were addictive. And Paulo knew he wasn't the only one addicted to death. Not by a long shot. The death dreamers (which he preferred over deathnauts) numbered in the thousands all across the world. And the sick beauty of it all is that they would never run out of supply. Never. Never ever. People were dying horrible deaths all the time. Every fucking day. Every fucking minute. Every glorious second. Paulo sometimes got giddy just thinking about the sheer quantity of death sticks available in the black memory market. So many to choose from. So many more yet to come in the future. Death was so unpredictable; he knew there would always be unique death experiences to purchase. Always.

The death memories were all illegal in the United States, of course, but when did that stop anyone in the human race from pursuing their passions? Besides, what was legal in one country, like marrying and banging a twelve year old, was considered immoral, highly illegal, and mentally disturbed in another country. Just because some holier-than-fucking-thou politicians decided it was in the country's best interests to ban death sticks and make them illegal, didn't make it right. I didn't even vote for the fucks, Paulo thought. Yeah, sure I live here. But I was born here. That mean I gotta follow every fucking rule these fat cats dream up? Umm, no. Who the fuck are they to tell me what's right and wrong? I know what's right and wrong. Uploading death sticks into your head is wrong, you dumb ass. Yeah, I know it's wrong, but it's my fucking choice, ain't it? I'm not bothering anybody. Just leave me be to do what I want to do. That's what a real free country does. Hell, some Canadian province legalized death sticks two years ago. They regulate them and tax the shit out of them. Now, *that's* how to run a fucking country. Keep making money off your citizens for as long as you fucking can, even after they get put six feet under. Geniuses up there. Then why don't you move up there, jackass? Fuck that. Canada's too damn cold.

"Hey, Paulo, how are you doing today?"

Paulo looked up to see Guidor smiling gaily at him. For a guy dealing in death, Guidor was sure quick and easy with his grin. "Good," he said. "How about you?"

"Good, good." Guidor pumped his head up and down in affirmation. He was a tall, thin man with a long, narrow chin. The skin on his face was smooth; he had obviously had all his facial hair removed with lasers long ago. His smile widened even further. His white teeth gleamed as brightly as all the polished chrome trim that rimmed the counters.

Paulo looked at him curiously. Guidor had a sly grin on his face that Paulo knew hid a secret that Guidor was just aching to tell him.

"I got something for you," Guidor said.

Paulo stepped closer to the counter, instantly intrigued. He waited for Guidor to continue.

Guidor pointed at him. "You wait right there, yes?"

Paulo nodded. He actually felt his pulse quicken.

Guidor disappeared into a back room, then came right back out a few seconds later. He clutched a black memory stick in his thin fingers. It was a black stick with a red cap. He waved it in the air in front of Paulo. "You know what this is?"

Paulo didn't answer. He thought he might know, but said nothing. He just waited for Guidor to continue.

Guidor leaned in closer for a conspiratorial whisper. "It's a murder stick."

Paulo was taken aback. But just for a second. Murder sticks were also illegal, very illegal, but they still existed. They were the cream of the crop. The ultimate death stick. You didn't experience the death. You caused the death. You actually took a human life and snuffed it out. Paulo leaned back in towards Guidor. He'd never uploaded a murder stick before.

He always told himself he wouldn't take that step. After a murder stick, there was nothing left. That was the height, or depth, of depravity, depending on how you looked at it and who you asked. "Who is it?"

Guidor shook his head. "That ruins one of the best parts. I can't tell you. I'm no spoiler."

"Can you tell me anything about it?"

Guidor shook his head.

"How long is it?"

Guidor shrugged. "I don't know exactly."

"You didn't upload it?"

Guidor shook his head. He looked at Paulo. "It's an exclusive."

Paulo couldn't believe what he had just heard. An exclusive? That was just a myth. Such a thing didn't really exist. They were just fairy tales. Exclusives were one-time sticks. Once you uploaded it, the stick wiped itself clean and wiped the memory from the Memsphere forever. A permanent deletion. Not even the technauts could bring back a permanent deletion. It was gone for good. No one else could upload the memory. No one else could retrieve it from the Memsphere. Only the buyer would experience it, no one else. It was the rarest memory of all. An exclusive was unlike all the other memories for sale that were shared by millions, if not billions, of people all over the planet. It would be his and his alone. He couldn't even upload it back up to the Memsphere. Exclusives were locked in the brain of the person who uploaded them. Or so the rumors went. An exclusive. Wow, unbelievable. That would really separate him from the sheep of humanity content to experience the same things as everybody else.

"Where'd you get it?" Paulo asked.

Guidor shook his head. "You really think I'm gonna tell you that?"

Paulo stared at the small black stick, his gaze fixating on the red cap. "How do you know it's a murder stick?"

Guidor looked at him with a serious expression. "I know."

Paulo left it at that. He suspected there was much more to it than just that, but he really didn't want to know.

"If it's not, I'll give you a full refund, plus twice the purchase price."

Paulo stared at the murder stick. "How much?"

Guidor told him.

"Whoa. That's crazy," Paulo said. That would be one hefty refund.

Guidor shrugged. "I got no problem getting rid of these. I just thought you might be ready for one." Guidor put the black stick with the red cap into his pocket.

Paulo looked at Guidor's pocket, then back up to his face. "How do I know it's exclusive?"

Guidor cocked his head very slightly. He almost looked insulted by the question. "It's exclusive." The conviction in his words was undeniable.

Again, Paulo knew there was more to this that Guidor wasn't going to share with him, but he really didn't want to pursue it. A murder stick. No, not just a murder stick. An exclusive murder stick. How many more chances like this would he get? It might never happen again. This could be his one and only chance. A murder stick. He felt an undeniably dangerous thrill race through him. Damn if goosebumps didn't pepper his arms.

Guidor pointed to some other black memory sticks under the display case glass. "I got some other ones for you." He reached into the display case and pulled out a stick. "Here's a guy dying having sex with a supermodel." He tapped his own head. "It's hot. I uploaded it last week. Just as he was squirting his load into her cowgirl style, his ticker gave out. Coming and going all at the same time." Guidor laughed at his own wittiness.

Paulo didn't take the stick and Guidor put it back. The memory merchant grabbed another black stick and pulled it out. "Here's a kid getting run over by an ice cream truck. Not my cup of tea, but maybe you'd like it."

Paulo shook his head. "I'll pass." He didn't like the ones with kids. He still had the one with the kid who died falling off the swing set stuck in his head. He wished he could get rid of that one, but once the memories were uploaded, you were stuck with them. They became a permanent part of you. You had to choose carefully. Someone really needed to invent a memory eraser, Paulo thought. Whoever did that would make billions. Tons of people probably had memories they wished they could be permanently rid of. He knew he did. He could still taste that trannie's cum in his mouth and see his big dick waving in his face. That was a memory he didn't want anymore. It was just a one-time experiment to see if he grokked that kind of thing, but he had found it incredibly distasteful and not arousing whatsoever. To each his own, Paulo thought, but that just wasn't for him and he wished he had never downloaded that memory.

Guidor moved to a different section, grabbing for some green colored sticks. The green symbolized nature memories, outdoorsy kind of stuff. They didn't involve any deaths. They were much more pleasant. Mountain climbing. White water rafting. Nature hiking. Jungle safaris. Guidor pulled out a green stick. "This one's really popular. An encounter with a herd of elephants in Africa. Very pleasant. Not too many elephants left in the wild."

Paulo shook his head. "Nah, not in the mood for that." Plus, it struck him as being too sad. There were probably only a few hundred elephants left in the entire world. He wasn't in the mood for sad nature memories.

Guidor moved to the pink, flesh-colored sticks. The sex sticks.

Paulo quickly shook his head. The sex sticks didn't do it for him anymore. He couldn't really explain why. They just didn't.

Blue was for flying adventures. Hang gliding. Sky diving. Blue-green was for ocean adventures, snorkeling, scuba diving, river adventures. Silver was a bit more rare in that there weren't that many different ones available. Those involved astronauts, space shuttle excursions, outer space type stuff. Paulo had uploaded a few of those and enjoyed them, especially the spacewalk near the International Space Station. The view of the Earth from up there was amazing, but he wasn't in the mood for that either right now.

Paulo glanced back at the case of black death sticks, thinking of the exclusive in Guidor's pocket. It was damn expensive. Yeah, but it was exclusive. It would be yours and no one else's. How many people could say they had exclusives? And a murder exclusive to boot? He still found it hard to believe that Guidor actually had one of those to sell. No one in his group had ever uploaded one, let alone even seen a real one. Sure, Morganthal said he had one, but no one believed him. He was just a chronic bullshitter. No one really believed anything he said.

This might be a once in a lifetime opportunity, Paulo realized. When would he ever get another chance like this? Probably never. He had the money for it. It would set him back a few months, but he had it. "I'll take it," he blurted out.

Paulo got himself ready. The room was softly lit. His lounge chair was set in the slightly reclined positioned that he liked the most. A glass of ice water waited on the table next to the chair. Classical music played softly in the background, so soft he could barely hear it, but that's how he liked it. Just a hint of The Planets by Holst filtered into the room.

He dressed in comfortable jeans and a plain grey t-shirt. Thick socks adorned his feet. He liked having warm socks on. There was something comforting and reassuring about wearing thick socks.

Paulo sat in the recliner and stared at the black stick in his hand. He fingered the red cap. He finally had one. An exclusive. He had it for five days now, waiting for Saturday morning before he uploaded it. It had been one of the longest, but most exciting, weeks in his life. He could barely focus at the office and Mitch had to berate him a few times for fucking a few things up. But right now he didn't care. He had a black stick. A murder stick. A black stick with a red cap. An exclusive murder stick.

Paulo extended the dongle and hovered the stick

over the slot in the back of his neck. And then he slid the death stick into the slot and closed his eyes. He was ready to murder someone.

When Paulo opened his eyes, he was in the memory. He was in the head of someone else, seeing what they had seen before they murdered someone. Paulo was just a passenger now. He would go where the man went, see what he saw, feel what he felt. He couldn't control any of the man's actions. The memory had already happened. It was like watching the greatest movie of all time because he was actually in it, re-living it. Paulo knew he was in the memory of a man immediately because he could feel his raging hard on. The man glanced down and Paulo saw his cock was stiff and at full attention. For a moment, Paulo felt cheated. Was this just a sex memory instead?

The man whose memory Paulo was experiencing looked towards a king-size bed that filled most of the room in what was obviously a bedroom. Paulo looked at the man and the woman in the bed. Paulo recognized the bed. It was his bed. Paulo recognized the man on the bed. The man was his brother Dillon. And Paulo recognized the woman. She was his wife Marcy. They were both naked. And they were fucking. His brother was fucking his wife in his bed. And they were obviously enjoying every minute of it. Marcy had a look of pure bliss on her face as Dillon thrust her into an orgasmic state. She gripped the sheets with her fingers and held on tight as she gasped and panted under Dillon's pumping cock.

Paulo just stared through the eyes of the man whose memory he was re-living. His wife and his brother were so absorbed in their fucking they didn't even notice him. Yet. Paulo saw the gun raise into view, gripped in both hands. The gun was black and shiny, obviously a new weapon. The first shot went right through Dillon's pumping ass, then came exploding out of his belly as the bullet careened around inside him and found an exit in his gut. The second shot hit Dillon in the shoulder, blowing out chunks of flesh and bone that splashed against the headboard. Somehow Paulo knew that second shot had been intended for Marcy's head but Dillon's shoulder got in the way.

Marcy screamed after the second bullet struck Dillon. Dillon just collapsed on top of her, blood and guts and piss and shit covering her lower body. The third bullet hit the headboard, just missing Marcy's screaming face, sending splinters of wood flying about. The fourth bullet hit Marcy right between the eyes, just above her nose. She went silent forever.

Paulo heard panting noises. It was coming from the man with the gun, from the man who had just put bullets into his wife and his brother. No, he wasn't just a man, Paulo thought. He was a killer. A murderer. Paulo heard the murderer panting.

There was a mirror near the dresser on the left side of the bed. The murderer looked up into the mirror. And Paulo stared back at his own face. He had killed Marcy. And he had killed his own brother.

Someone *had* invented a way to erase memories. And Paulo had a sickening revelation that he had used it on himself to forget. To forget that he had committed two horrible acts of murder against the only two people he had ever really been close to in his whole life.

Paulo never felt more alone.

<hr>

"People think they are just buying memories," Guidor said to Oliver, the young man sitting across from him.

Oliver was a new employee of Guidor's, a young kid just hitting his mid-twenties, just starting to learn the tricks of the black market memory trade. They were in Guidor's shop, sitting in lounge chairs in the back room, enjoying a cold beer together after hours. Memory sticks of all different colors lay scattered about on some tables nearby, waiting to be organized and priced for sale.

"But they aren't," Guidor continued. "We're lacing the sticks with more than just memories. We're planting the desire to experience more memories. A craving. A lust for them, if you will. Every memory stick has that built into it. Every single one. A little bit of code that creates the desire for more sticks. All it takes is a single planted thought to create the desire." Guidor laughed. "It's so fucking easy. That's one of our secrets, kid. The sticks are addictive as hell because we make them that way." He took a drink. "You picked the right business to be in, kid. We'll never run out of customers and we'll never run out of supply."

Guidor paused. Oliver waited for him to continue. Guidor looked at him curiously. "You were telling me about that guy…" Oliver prompted.

Guidor squinted, then nodded his head. "Right,

right." Then he laughed. "I need to sell myself my own memory sticks." He tapped at his head. "Getting fucking old in there."

Oliver smiled a soft smile.

"When he first came looking for the memory eraser, I just knew he had done something bad," Guidor said. He shook his head softly. "That Paulo didn't hide his guilt well. He was a good customer, but a real nervous Nellie. I wasn't sure what he did, but I knew he had done something terrible. His face looked like it was stuck in a permanent state of shock. He was all wide-eyed and trembling and shit." Guidor paused to take a drink from his beer. "Here's the beauty of it," he said. "I sold him a memory eraser last week, but I set it so he wouldn't know that he bought it." He laughed. "Shit, I set the stick so that he wouldn't even know memory eraser's existed at all. I wiped all traces of their existence right out of his head."

"You erased the memory of the memory eraser?" Oliver looked at Guidor with profound respect. "Damn, you're good."

Guidor nodded. "Not only that. I set the stick so it would give me a download dump of his latest memories. He was so freaked out I just had to know what he did. Figured I might be able to use that information later, and boy was I right. That's how I knew he killed those two."

"Who were they?"

"His wife and his brother. She was cheating on Paulo with his own brother."

"Damn," Oliver said under his breath. He took a long drink of his beer.

Guidor nodded. "It's a good stick. Sold half a

dozen already." He pointed to a pile of red-capped black murder sticks on the table. "I'm pretty sure I can move all those in another week or two."

"So it wasn't really an exclusive?" Oliver asked, hesitant to say the question aloud but his curiosity got the better of him.

Guidor squinted at Oliver. "Exclusive? Come on, kid. They don't exist. Everything can be hacked and duplicated. Everything. Some slick just made that exclusive shit up to charge more for death sticks. It's another little fake nugget of info we plant in the sticks, so when people hear about an exclusive they think it's a rare fucking thing and worth the extra price." Guidor raised his bottle. "Here's to whoever thought that one up. Helped make me a ton of money." Guidor paused to take another drink. "Now this is the best part of the Paulo story."

Oliver waited for Guidor to continue.

Guidor grinned like a Cheshire cat saying cheese. "Then I sold him his own murder stick back as an exclusive. For a big fat chunk o' change, too."

Oliver whistled softly through his teeth. "Man, you played that Paulo guy through and through," Oliver said.

"I puppet mastered him big time, yeah, "Guidor said, nodding his head. "I been at this a long time, kid. Just keep your eyes and ears open and you'll learn a lot."

"So this Paulo guy is in jail?" Oliver asked.

Guidor nodded. "Yeah. He broke down and confessed. Gonna be executed next week."

"You gonna pick up a copy of that?" Oliver asked.

Guidor frowned at him and narrowed his eyebrows. "Now that is a stupid question."

Oliver took a swig of his beer, clearly embarrassed by his own inexperience and his naive question.

Guidor slapped his thigh and hooted. "God, I love this business!"

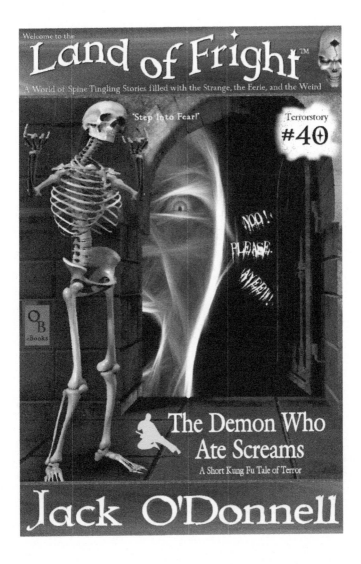

TERRORSTORY #40
THE DEMON WHO
ATE SCREAMS

You may have heard parts of this story before.
It begins with a young martial artist forsaking violence
for a peaceful way of life. He has a hot temper, and
this always seems to get him into trouble, so the
young man goes to the temple to study under the wise
monks to learn their simple ways, and to learn how to
keep his anger under control. The young man
continues to train in the martial arts, of course, as that
is part of his holy life. He uses kung fu to keep his
body as fit as his mind. He struggles to remain chaste

and pure, doing his best to ignore the sweet advances of a young woman he sees in the village on his rare visits into town (but fails — several times).

As you are probably aware of the tragic plights that befall most of these young men, then you know something always happens to rip the young martial artist out of his peaceful life. Always. Either his sister gets murdered, or a monster made of straw nearly decapitates him, or the village he grew up in gets destroyed, or a one-eyed dragon stalks him, or an ancient warrior made of stone attacks him, or a demon torments him, or his brother monks in the temple get slaughtered, or a skeleton army assaults him, or an entire school burns down with the children still inside. Something bad always happens to rip the young martial artist away from his idyllic life in the temple, forcing him to embrace the violent creature that exists deep inside himself.

Usually, though, not all of those horrific things happen to the same guy. Except this time they did.

The catalyst for all these dire events was a demon in human form named Drog Kuhn. And he was a vicious motherfucker, a heinous villain with a deadly appetite. Drog Kuhn didn't drink blood. He didn't dine on the dead flesh of his victims. Drog Kuhn fed on the sounds of misery. That's what fueled him. That's what gave him sustenance. That's what he craved more than anything else in the world. He feasted on the sounds of tortured victims screaming in pain, the sounds of them begging for mercy, the sounds of them crying out for help. Their lamentations were food for his twisted psyche. Just taking one of his long clawed fingernails and thrusting it into a hapless victim's chest brought Drog Kuhn no joy, not if they just died instantly on the spot. But if they shrieked in pain, if they died jabbering loudly in frenzied agony, then he felt satiated as he fed on the sounds of their fear and torment.

Each type of human cry satisfied Drog Kuhn in different ways. A soft whimper of pain was like an appetizer, a delicate morsel of sound that tickled his ears. An agonized shriek when he snapped someone's arm in half was like a quick snack. When he slowly tortured someone to death, their pitiful cries for mercy and their terror-filled screams of pain were much more like a full course meal, and obviously much more satisfying to the demon.

Drog Kuhn was big, at least in relation to most of the villagers in a country where a six-and-a-half-foot tall man was seen as a giant. His skin was a deep brown now, but not as deeply brown as it got when he was out feeding in the world. The months he had just spent in his cave going through his cleansing ritual had drained some of the dark color from his skin.

And you might have thought a demon who fed on the sounds of misery would have overly large ears, but that was not the case. His ears were relatively normal in size, if even not a tad small for his head. They were richly grooved, with more additional curvatures and slopes inside them than a normal human had in their ears, but you couldn't really see those unless you were up close to him. And if you were close enough to Drog Kuhn to see those grooves in his ears, then you were probably about to die.

He sat cross-legged in utter solitude on a soft wool mat in his dark cave, his ears plugged with chunks of wax. He could hear nothing. It was a purifying ritual Drog Kuhn went through every year. Cleansing his mind. Cleansing his body. Cleansing his soul. Cleansing his palate. His hands were pressed flat against the rocky floor of the cave, absorbing the energies that flowed up from the depths of Hell. The cleansing ritual served another purpose. It also recharged him, refueled him with the dark powers of the underworld he needed when he walked amongst men.

Drog Kuhn raised his arms above his head and stretched. His cleansing ritual was complete. He felt refreshed and rejuvenated. His body tingled with power. Now it was time to visit the world of men again. He gently removed the wax from his ears. It was time to feed.

Just outside his cave entrance, visible a few dozen yards behind Drog Kuhn, the sky was dark with clouds as black as burnt trees after a forest fire. Fat raindrops poked at the earth like an obnoxious group of children poking at an obese blind man's belly. The heavens grunted thunder in a few short bursts of noise, sounding like a constipated dragon making guttural noises as it tried to push out the remains of the half dozen cows it had consumed earlier. The stalactites jutting down from the cave's ceiling high above the cave floor shook ever so slightly. Then a long, deep rumble rolled across the sky as the thunder found full release.

Drog Kuhn listened to the sounds of the storm outside for a moment. The harsh sounds of the weather didn't fulfill the need that ached inside of him, but he was still able to enjoy them. To him, the effects of the rough and violent sounds of nature were like a human tasting wine on the tip of his tongue, or tasting a spice with the tip of his finger. Tantalizing, yes, but far from fulfilling any need. The angry sounds of nature simply tickled him, no more than that.

He looked at the maps affixed to the cave wall before him, the weathered parchments illuminated by several candles burning brightly on stones nearby. Several maps were full of markings, all of the villages already crossed out with a big X through each area. He had already passed through those villages, feeding on the lamentations of their residents. His gaze moved along the maps, slowing as he reached a fresh, unmarked map, then coming to rest on the name of a village near the Yangtoi River. Fallen Rocks. Drog Kuhn stared at the name on the map, remaining completely motionless for a moment. Fallen Rocks. And then he nodded. Yes, he would pay the villagers of Fallen Rocks a visit. The area was weeks of travel away from his cave, but he remembered hearing talk of a new school being planned for the village. It was most certainly finished by now. Drog Kuhn stroked his ear, gently running his long fingers along his earlobe, careful not to scratch himself with his long, sharp fingernails. The school would certainly be filled with noisy children. He smiled. Children always screamed the loudest. They got so afraid. So very afraid. His smiled widened. This would be a true feast.

Drog Kuhn lowered his hand away from his ear as he noticed something else on the map. It was another name written on the map, written in much smaller letters than the name of the village. The candle light flickered over the name. HungYao Temple. It was located just north of Fallen Rocks, near the cliffs that bordered Fallen Rocks. He sighed. He would have to take care of that potential problem first. Monks always became a very troublesome nuisance if he didn't take care of them first. They would try to stop him with their Tiger Claw strikes or their Praying Mantis kicks or their Monkey Fist punches. And he knew exactly which spell he would invoke. The spell of the Goilemi. The spell that brought inanimate objects to life. That would keep the meddlesome monks busy for a while.

Outside, lightning carved a jagged scar into the face of the sky and thunder wailed.

The young martial artist's name was Chaki To. Chaki was a slender young man, but full of muscles. A lifetime of martial arts training had turned his entire body into a lean mass of muscle. Chaki was ripped with a wall of ridged abdominal muscles that made every other brother monk in the temple jealous, despite jealousy being frowned upon as an unhealthy emotion for any brother monk of the HungYao Temple. He had a smooth face, young and clear. He had straight black hair that just reached his deeply tanned shoulders, the edges of his hair curling just ever so slightly. Most of the brother monks had cut their hair short as part of their austere lifestyle, but Chaki hadn't worked himself up to that point yet and the elder monks had let him maintain his long locks, at least for now. He often wore a bandanna around his head to keep his thick hair out of his eyes, and today was no exception; he wore a tight ring of white cloth around his forehead.

Tomorrow was a special day for Chaki. His sister was going to be wed. Abbot LeeChan, the head brother monk of the HungYao temple, was graciously allowing Chaki to skip a few hours of training and prayer later in the afternoon to attend Zhang Li's wedding ceremony in Fallen Rocks, the village near their temple.

Chaki increased the intensity of his efforts, knowing that the few missed hours of training could never be replaced; he practiced every day for hours at the temple to keep himself in top physical condition. He was in the Sea of Salt Chamber (named for the salty taste of sweat that touched the corners of a brother monk's lips during a vigorous workout) in the basement of the temple, surrounded by all manner of equipment that helped keep his mind and body strong. He often practiced outside in the hot sun, but today had brought a strong storm, and the rain and wind howled mightily outside, so Chaki remained indoors in the Sea of Salt Chamber for his training.

Several other brother monks were also present in the practice chamber, the young men hard at work keeping themselves in fit physical condition.

Brother Hammo was fat, but quick. It was somewhat astonishing how quickly he could move for a man of his girth. It was also odd how the man never seemed to be hungry at their communal meals. Brother Hammo would sit at the communal table in the Hall of Nourishment, his lumpy arms resting on the gleaming wooden table, and watch everyone else eat with just the hint of a smile on his lips. Chaki wondered if Brother Hammo was having dumplings and sweet bread smuggled into the temple from the village.

Brother Chupang was young, not yet twenty. Brother Chupang was a very handsome young man, almost to the point of being pretty with his big eyes and long lashes. There were questions about his sexual preferences, but those whispered questions went unanswered. Brother Chupang had never propositioned Chaki, nor made any odd advances towards him, so Chaki discounted any of those rumors.

Brother NiJow might have been an actual idiot. Chaki wasn't sure if it was an act, or if he really was that dumb. His buck teeth and foul breath didn't help his social standing any. There just seemed to be an unnatural lack of cleanliness about the man no matter what he did. Brother NiJow could step out of the river after bathing in the cool fresh water and still reek like a dog that had just rolled in its own excrement a mere few minutes later.

But they were all brother monks just like him, and Chaki had come to enjoy their company and their camaraderie. The three men had all lived longer at the temple than Chaki had, and they all had shorn their locks down to near baldness. They so loved to tease Chaki about his girlie long hair. They had a running bet as to how long it would take Chaki to succumb to the peer pressure of cutting his long hair to fit in with all the other brother monks living in HungYao Temple. Everyone eventually succumbed; it was just a matter of when.

And they loved to tease him about his sister Zhang Li; she was very beautiful, even Chaki would have to admit that. But his friends really loved to tease him about Wei Lin, a girl who lived in the village who had obvious affection for Chaki. Their teasing him about the girl got annoying after a while, but his irritated reactions to their taunting him about Wei Lin only seemed to provoke them more, so Chaki stopped fighting it and just went along with their teasing.

Chaki thought about Wei Lin. Despite their troubled past, Chaki could still not stop thinking about her many times throughout the day, and especially at night when he was alone in his bed. Her smooth pale skin. Her long, straight legs. Her softly pointed chin. Her big brown eyes; Wei Lin's big brown eyes always seemed to sparkle with a delighted mirth when he looked at them. Those delicious red lips. He was a brother monk, so he was supposed to be chaste, keeping his mind and body pure, but Wei Lin was too much for him to resist. He fantasized about fucking her hard again, imagined bending her over a stack of rice bags, like he had done the last time he saw her, and pumping deep inside of her. He wanted to grip her tight little ass and pound his cock into her tight cunt from behind. And those little gasps he knew she would make when he put his entire length in her would be music to his ears. He looked forward to seeing her again at the wedding. Chaki knew Wei Lin would look beautiful no matter what she wore. And she would look even more beautiful with nothing on later that night when he knew they would rendezvous for some furious lovemaking. He forced himself to stop daydreaming of Wei Lin, and returned his concentration to his training.

Sweat glistened on Chaki's brown-skinned upper body as he exerted himself against the straw man. The straw man was a practice dummy in the shape of a man. Its torso, arms, and legs were made of thick poles of wood. The straw man was dressed in a burlap shirt and pants, the interiors of the shirt and pants stuffed full of straw. The practice dummy's head was made from an old rice sack, but also stuffed full of straw, not rice. The straw man had a crude face painted on its rice sack head; two beady black eyes, a button-size black nose, and a slash of red for a mouth made up its crude face. Chaki made quick chopping motions towards the dummy's head and neck, stopping the momentum of his strikes just a hair's breadth away from the dummy itself. It took just as much concentration and control to barely miss the straw man as it did to strike it, if not more.

Thunder boomed in the distance, shaking the walls slightly, making the flames from the torches burning in their wall sconces flare up and flicker brightly for a second. Chaki paused and glanced upwards, not really seeing the stone ceiling above him. It sounded nothing like the incredible storm that had passed through the village weeks ago, when the sky had turned as black as coal, but he frowned nonetheless. He said a quick prayer to the lords of the weather, wishing for pleasing sunlight and the music of a soft breeze for his sister's wedding. Zhang Li deserved a nice wedding. She was a demure, peaceful woman, always willing to help those in need. His sister had devoted years of her life to getting the school near the village built, and now the children finally had a safe place to go and learn about the history of their people, and learn of the great world all around them.

Chaki lowered his gaze and turned towards a weapon rack positioned on a stone wall near him. The elderly brother monks who commanded the temple frowned at the use of weapons against other men, but they understood that their use greatly improved hand eye coordination, which strengthened the mind, so they encouraged the young men in the temple to practice with them. Chaki grabbed a spear and twirled it in his hands, hefting the weapon, gauging its weight. Some of the spears had supple shafts, making them flexible and easy to bend, whereas other spears had solid shafts made of very sturdy wood. He had chosen one of the spears with the solid shafts. He wanted to practice his lunging moves and he preferred the precision the hard-shafted spears gave him over the flexible shafts.

Chaki moved into a slightly crouched position, clutching the spear, aiming it towards the straw man. He jabbed the spear forward, just barely missing the straw man's torso, the blade of the spear nearly scraping the burlap shirt the dummy wore. Chaki pulled the spear back and jabbed again, this time driving the spear just past the straw man's cheek. The edge of the spear grazed the straw man's cheek and Chaki frowned, berating himself for his lack of precision. He hadn't meant for the spear to touch the straw man at all; he had been going for a near-miss. He lowered the spear and glanced down, shaking his head softly, disappointed in himself.

Chaki lifted his head and readied himself for another strike, crouching low and gripping the spear with two hands, but then paused. He looked closer at the straw man, not quite sure he could believe what he was seeing. Chaki straightened, lowering the spear. He narrowed his eyes, staring with a growing confusion at the blood trickling down the straw man's cheek; the red droplets oozed down from where the edge of the spear had cut a very thin slit in the surface of the rice sack that comprised the straw man's head.

When the straw man came alive and grabbed the spear out of his hands, Chaki knew he was in for a long day. A very long day, indeed.

❦

Drog Kuhn took his hand off the temple wall. That should do the trick, he thought. The spell of the Goilemi would keep the brother monks of HungYao Temple quite busy. He knew the spell would spread through the temple walls in a matter of moments, bringing all manner of objects to life, objects whose sole purpose would be to destroy human life.

Drog Kuhn was dressed in a flowing robe, the colors very bright and garish. The cloth was still wet from the recent heavy rain so, even though the fabric was light and silky, the robe hung heavily on his large frame. The sky was still dark, but the storm had lessened and the rain fell in a soft drizzle, barely enough to be noticeable now. The storm seemed to have followed him all the way from his cave to the temple. Drog Kuhn shrugged at the thought. Who was he to question the ways of the universe?

A soft whimpering sound made Drog Kuhn close his eyes and smile. He turned away from the temple wall and glanced down at the monk trying to crawl away from him.

The monk scratched at the wet earth with mud-streaked fingers, desperately trying to pull himself along the ground away from the demon. A smear of blood trailed behind the monk's feet as he pulled

228

himself forward inch by inch, the light rain not strong enough to wash the blood completely away.

Drog Kuhn crouched down near the monk's face and lowered his head closer to the monk, tilting his ear closer to the monk's mouth, feeding on the grunting, wheezing sound coming from the monk's lips. The edge of Drog Kuhn's earlobe and the interior folds of his ear turned a deeper red as he fed, the ridges pulsing ever so slightly. The whimper was quite delicious. Such a delicate morsel. Casting a spell always made him hungry, as the effort of expending his dark powers required quite a lot of energy and some extreme exertion.

Drog Kuhn extended one of his fingers, hovering his sharply pointed nail over the monk's back. And then he thrust his sharp nail into the monk's flesh, pushing it right through the monk's robe and sinking it deep into the man's body. The monk cried out in pain, grunting and screaming as Drog Kuhn pushed his finger in deeper and twisted it. Drog Kuhn snatched the monk's cries out of the air like a frog catching flies with its tongue. To Drog Kuhn, the screams had physical substance. He could actually see them in the air. The tiny hairs in his ears shot out of his head and plucked the sounds out of the air, pulling them back into his ears so he could feed upon them. No human could see this as his hairs were so thin as to be invisible to the human eye, nor could the humans actually see sounds as he could. But that is how the demon fed. That is how Drog Kuhn ate screams.

Drog Kuhn stared straight down at the screaming monk, both of the demon's ears now pulsing a deep red. He twisted his finger again, feeling the monk's flesh rip and tear as he violently moved his sharp nail about inside the man. The monk howled in agony. The demon closed his eyes again, feeding deeply.

<hr/>

Chaki ducked and the spear whipped past over his head as the straw man attacked him. Somehow, the strands of the straw acted like thin, hooked fingers, allowing the straw man to grip the spear. Chaki felt the blade of the spear part a few hairs on his head. He dove to his right, rolling over on his shoulder, moving behind a rack of cast iron kettlebells the brother monks used in their weight training. The straw man couldn't possibly be alive, but Chaki had no time to think about that. He was too busy fighting to stay alive himself.

Chaki grabbed one of the heavy kettlebells with both hands. The kettlebell looked like a cannonball with a metal handle so it was easy to grab, but it was heavy so it took two hands to swing it with any force. Chaki quickly rose up and hurled the kettlebell at the straw man. The kettlebell hit the wooden post that made up the straw man's torso with a loud thunk. The blow staggered the straw man and it stumbled backwards on its wooden post legs. Chaki attacked, jumping forward to deliver four solid punches to the straw man's mid-section. But he immediately regretted that as intense pain flared through his knuckles. It was like punching a tree trunk.

The straw man tilted his rice-bag head down and looked at Chaki with its beady black eyes. Its slash of a mouth was distorted up into a twisted grin. It swung the spear handle around, catching Chaki under the chin, sending him flying into the kettlebell rack. The heavy metal balls dug into Chaki's back as he slammed into them. He fell to the ground, grunting heavily. One of the kettlebells fell off the top row and the heavy metal ball crashed to the ground a mere inch from Chaki's head. Chaki stared at the black ball of metal with wide eyes, but didn't have time to continue looking at it as the straw man came after him with another spear thrust. Chaki rolled away just in time, the spear tip thunking into the wooden floorboards where his head had just been.

Chaki scrambled to his feet, moving into a defensive crouch. Behind him and all around him, Chaki could hear other brother monks shouting, fighting. The other three straw men dummies in the training room had also somehow come to life and the other brother monks were busy fighting off their attacks. Chaki caught a glimpse of a brother monk lying dead in a pool of blood, and another brother monk clutching at his bleeding side as blood oozed through his fingers.

Brother Hammo and Brother NiJow stood side by side, fighting one of the straw men. Brother NiJow reached out and attempted to grab the straw man, trying to put it into a grappling hold, but all he came up with was two hands full of loose straw. Brother NiJow stared stupidly at the clumps of straw in his hand, momentarily befuddled. The straw man raked at Brother NiJow's face with the sharp edges of its straw fingers, creating four rows of slits in his flesh. The cuts in Brother NiJow's cheek would have been far deeper if Brother Hammo hadn't reacted with his incredible speed and yanked Brother NiJow back away from the slashing straw digits.

Chaki didn't spot Brother Chupang and feared the worst for his friend, but then he saw Brother Chupang holding a spear, battling another straw man, holding his own. For now.

Chaki scanned the room, searching, trying to think of a way out of this madness. He needed to help his wounded brother monks, but he needed to stop the straw men first. That's when he focused on one of the torches burning in its sconce on the wall.

⚜

Drog Kuhn finished urinating on the dead monk and stuffed himself back in his pants. His urine was very acidic and it melted away the portion of the monk's skin that his excess bodily fluid struck. He once thought it odd that the more he fed on the sounds of misery and pain and death, the more he had to urinate and expel the leftover remnants of sound that his body did not need, but he realized the waste had to go somewhere. It was simply how his body processed the excess and flushed it out. Was he once a man? Is that why he had vestiges of human functions? Is that why he had human form? Drog Kuhn often tried to think of his past, tried to remember where he had come from, but it was always clouded in an impenetrable haze. No matter. Who was he to question how the universe had created him? He was as he was.

Drog Kuhn glanced down into the valley below. The village of Fallen Rocks awaited his arrival.

⚜

The straw man burned. Chaki clutched the

flickering, crackling torch in his hand, watching. The straw man had no lips to open, so it couldn't scream, but Chaki had a feeling this hideous monstrosity wanted to scream as fire engulfed it. The straw man spun about madly, moving its burning wooden post arms up and down in futile gestures, as if it were a giant bird trying to put out the flames on its burning wings.

The other brother monks had followed Chaki's lead and the remaining straw men were also now going up in flames. The burning straw men still struck out, still desperate to destroy any human life they could, but the monks easily evaded their strikes, staying far clear to let the straw men burn away into ash. Several small fires burned here and there in the chamber, but the brother monks quickly stomped them out, or patted them out with their hands.

Chaki looked around the chamber. The straw men had slain two brother monks, and a third was severely wounded. Brother Hammo was bent down near the wounded man, working hard to save him, but Chaki knew the wounded brother monk was going to die; he had lost far too much blood. Brother Chupang rubbed his left shoulder absently, clearly trying to work away some manner of pain. Brother NiJow's flurry of scratches running down his cheek still oozed blood, but otherwise he looked to be okay; he had a slack-jawed and stunned expression on his face, but Chaki knew that was normal for Brother NiJow and didn't necessarily mean he was in shock.

Chaki glanced around the room. Despite the tragic deaths, the damage the straw men had caused was slight — at least compared to the carnage the stone statue man and the bronze dragon caused in the Hall of Ancient Relics.

Drog Kuhn neared the village of Fallen Rocks. The village was nestled between large cliffs on three sides. The main dirt road leading into the village, which was the only way in and out of the village, was lined with huge boulders. These large stones had fallen off the cliffs nearby, and over the years the villagers had dragged them into place as decorative markers. Most of the rocks were painted now, decorated with paintings of animals, nature, some abstract works, and even some childish scribbles and scratches. The last rock closest to the border of the village was the biggest of them all, and the words etched into the rock's surface welcomed all travelers to Fallen Rocks with great enthusiasm.

Drog Kuhn paused at the welcoming stone. He put his hand on the rock. The surface was still slightly damp from the storm. Just as he could push his energy into inanimate objects with his power, Drog Kuhn could also absorb energy from them. The welcoming stone radiated energy. Each time a traveler, or a native villager, or anyone, touched the stone they gave it a little bit of their energy. So many travelers had touched the welcome stone over the years that it practically glowed with energy to Drog Kuhn's demon eyes. Whereas the sounds of pain and misery and death fed him, the energy he absorbed from the welcome stone replenished his stores of dark earth magic. Drog Kuhn glanced into the village as he felt his well of power re-filling up inside him.

A blacksmith was busy in his open air shop that

was situated off to the right side of the village, a few dozen yards beyond the welcoming rock. The blacksmith hammered at a red-hot piece of metal, smashing the softened material into what looked like the shape of the blade portion for a shovel. An apprentice worked the furnace nearby, squeezing a bellows to push air into the red-hot coals.

Drog Kuhn stared at the hot coals. Those would be very useful. The humans did not like having their hands thrust into hot coals. That made them scream very loudly. And putting their face into the hot coals… that took their screaming to a whole new level. Drog Kuhn smiled.

Behind the blacksmith's shop, Drog Kuhn could see part of the open village square. It appeared some sort of ceremony was being prepared. A large wooden platform was being positioned in the middle of the square, with numerous men pushing the flat square structure into place. Several women milled about, positioning wooden slat chairs near the stage. Other women carried strings of flowers and began placing them throughout the area.

Drog Kuhn had a decision to make. Start feeding now and cause quite a disturbance in the village, or seek out the school and start the feast there. He thought about the screaming children and the decision was quite simple to make.

He glanced farther over to his right and saw the tombstones of the village cemetery dotting a wooded area that lined the eastern edge of the village. Drog Kuhn smiled. Yes, a distraction was in order. Something to keep the villagers busy while he attended to his business at the school.

Chaki and the three surviving brother monks from the Sea of Salt practice chamber moved up out of the stairwell and into the Hall of Ancient Relics, one of the main hallways of the temple. Chaki held a crackling torch in his right hand, illuminating their way. Brother Chupang and Brother Hammo were right on Chaki's heels, with Brother NiJow bringing up the rear. Brother NiJow kept looking back over his shoulder, protecting their rear from any potential attack from the straw men. They believed they had destroyed them all, but they still knew they had to be vigilant.

Chaki immediately held up his hand as he reached the floor of the Hall of Ancient Relics, motioning for the others to stop. Brother Chupang and Brother Hammo stopped, both crouching low. Brother NiJow backed into them, as he was still looking back over his shoulder when Chaki signaled them to stop, and collided with Brother Chupang, nearly sending him toppling to the floor. Chaki hushed them and raised the torch up to illuminate the area before them.

The Hall of Ancient Relics was aptly named for what the long narrow passageway contained. Ancient relics. Several paintings depicting scenes from long ago in the temple's history adorned the stone walls. Many items that had an important place in the temple's history were on display here. The simple wooden bowl that Brother JianYu ate his simple meals of rice from sat on a simple wooden pedestal nearby. Beyond that, an aging parchment that held the wisdom of several of the original brother monks who formed the HungYao temple brotherhood was encased in a frame, the frame tilted on a stand to make it easy to see the contents. The robe of Brother Boqin hung on a stand near the parchment case.

The four men stared with widening eyes at an empty stone pedestal, a stone pedestal that was once the base for a large stone statue of the great Brother Monk Kwan MandaKi. Kwan MandaKi was a legendary fighter, the man who had led the HungYao temple defense against the attacks of the brutal warlord Gengol Chu.

Centuries ago, Gengol Chu had wanted to destroy all the temples and murder all the brother monks because he felt their influences were a threat to his growing power. The warlord had been right. The monks were a threat.

It was ironic that the men of peace destroyed the man of violence with violence, but that is how the events played out. Kwan MandaKi defeated Gengol Chu in an epic battle of kung-fu and swordplay that resulted in Gengol Chu's death by decapitation from a killing strike delivered by Kwan MandaKi. Kwan MandaKi was forever immortalized in stone for his heroic deeds and given a place of high honor in the Hall of Ancient Relics. And now his statue was gone. Somehow stolen by thieves.

"Where is everyone?" Brother Chupang asked, keeping his voice barely above a whisper.

No one answered.

The quiet in the Hall of Ancient Relics was eerie, ominous. Where were all the brother monks? Usually, the hallway held at least a few brother monks traversing its length, if not dozens moving through it as the holy men went about their business of the day.

Chaki quickly turned to his left and raised the torch even higher. The light illuminated another empty pedestal. This was a large bronze pedestal that was once the base for the bronze dragon Firelord. There had never been a real dragon, not as there had been a real man named Kwan MandaKi. Firelord was just a fictitious creature fabricated for amusement; the dragon was somewhat of an unofficial mascot of the HungYao Temple. The early builders of the temple had a thing for dragons. But now the statue of Firelord was also gone, stolen by the same gang of vile thieves who had somehow penetrated the temple. Chaki stared at the huge empty pedestal. How could they have gotten the statue of Firelord out of the temple? The statue was very heavy. It would have taken half a dozen thieves just to push the huge, heavy sculpture.

A shimmering coming from the temple floor pulled Chaki's gaze. He took a hesitant step forward and the light from the torch revealed a most gruesome sight. A massive pool of blood filled the temple floor. Chaki raised the torch higher and the flickering light washed over a gruesome scene. Nearby, half a dozen dead brother monks lay in a heap, their bodies torn and ripped apart. Several of the bodies were missing legs and arms, and two of them were missing their heads.

No one said a word. They had found their brother monks.

⚜

Drog Kuhn moved through the cemetery, putting his hand on tombstones, pushing his dark energy back down into the earth and into what lay just below the surface. After touching a dozen or so tombstones, he nodded in satisfaction. That should suffice.

Drog Kuhn headed out of the cemetery, not even bothering to look back as the sounds of shifting earth and the clacking of bones started to fill the air in the graveyard behind him.

The school awaited him.

Chaki and the three brother monks moved slowly through the hallway. They had no choice but to walk through the spilled blood of their brothers as the blood filled the hallway from wall to wall.

They came across more brother monks, all of them dead, all of them battered and torn. Chaki froze as the torch light flowed over the face of one of the dead brother monks. Chaki knew the face. It was Brother Tong. His teacher. His mentor. His friend. Tong's right arm was missing, viciously torn out of its socket. A pool of blood shimmered where his right arm should have been. Chaki bent down to one knee over Tong, ignoring the blood that seeped through his pants. Chaki's timing was fortuitous as that is the moment the stone statue of Kwan MandaKi loomed out of the dark shadows and swung his blade and sliced clean through two of the brother monks standing near Chaki. Chaki felt a thud against his back as the upper torso of brother Chupang fell atop him. A shower of blood cascaded down all around Chaki. The upper torso of Brother NiJow hit the floor right next to him, the dead monk's face frozen in his stupid buck-toothed expression.

Drog Kuhn heard the sound of laughter and winced. It stung him and he covered his ears with his large hands. It was such an unpleasant sound. He looked up again at the school filled with the children of Fallen Rocks. Maybe this wasn't such a grand idea after all. But then Drog Kuhn thought of the sour laughter turning into sweet wails of anguish and terror, and this rekindled his enthusiasm for what lay ahead.

Chaki shrugged the bloody chunk of Brother Chupang's body off his back and rose up quickly. The stone statue of Kwan MandaKi had Brother Hammo impaled on the end of his long, curved sword. Brother Hammo opened his mouth to speak, but only blood came out, spilling out from between his lips, running down his chin like drool, splashing onto his protruding belly. Brother Hammo's body sagged and then went limp. The stone statue of Kwan MandaKi dipped his sword down, and the corpulent body of Brother Hammo slowly slid off the blade, the slurping sound of his descent echoing faintly in the hallway.

Chaki knew the torch in his hand was useless against this stone monster, but he still kept it clutched in his fingers. The light from the flames flickered across the stone visage of Kwan MandaKi. His eyes were cold grey stone with no other color to them. His skin was grey as well, as was the robe that was carved over most of his body as an outer shell. The stone man's head moved, but Kwan MandaKi's face remained the same as it was when the statue was first carved centuries ago. Grim.

Kwan MandaKi thrust his blade straight at Chaki's chest. Chaki instinctively blocked downward, using the burning torch in his hand to deflect the strike. Sparks flew off the torch as the burning wood and the bloodied steel struck each other. One of the sparks hit Chaki in the face, burning his left cheek; he ignored the searing flash of pain.

Chaki quickly backpedaled away from Kwan MandaKi, avoiding another slashing strike of the stone man's blade. Chaki continued moving backward, only stopping when his back slammed up against the far wall of the hallway. He glanced around the hallway. Chaki knew he could return down the steps behind him to the practice room, but there was no exit from the temple down there; he would just be trapped as much down there as he was up here. No, he needed to get past Kwan MandaKi and get out of the temple.

Kwan MandaKi stomped forward, his heavy stone feet plodding forward with echoing step after echoing step. The expression on the living stone face remained the same. Unsmiling and harsh.

"Run," Zhang Li whispered to the young girl. "Find my brother Chaki at the temple and tell him we need his help." Zhang Li released her grip on the girl's arm and rose back up to look out the front window of the school. Zhang Li was a petite woman with alabaster skin. She had hazel eyes, delicate rounded cheeks, and a soft rounded chin. Her black hair was cut short, very different from most of the other women in the village who let their hair grow well past their shoulders.

The demon strode towards the school. Zhang Li wasn't certain how she knew the man-shaped figure casually approaching wasn't human, but she knew. She could feel it immediately in her bones. This was a demon. A demon with dark intent heading towards the children under her charge.

Zhang Li glanced back down to see SuJin still standing next to her. The poor girl was terrified, but Zhang Li needed her to act. She bent down quickly next to SuJin. "You need to go SuJin. You need to go now." Zhang Li put an edge of harshness into her voice that she mostly used on the boys in the class when they were being rowdy and obnoxious. SuJin understood that tone. "Go out the back door," Zhang Li told her. "Go now!"

SuJin fought back tears, but she did as she was told. The young girl whirled away from her teacher and raced for the back door, her black school uniform skirt flaring up behind her as she ran. The other students watched her run past them, but said nothing.

Zhang Li turned back to face her classroom full of students. They ranged from five years old to ten years old, a dozen boys and fourteen girls. They were all dressed smartly in their new school uniforms, all of them wearing powder blue short-sleeve tops, while the girls had black skirts on and the boys wore black knickers. "Children, listen to me. I need you to be brave for me."

One of the boys immediately burst into tears.

Drog Kuhn noticed movement behind the school and saw a young girl race out from behind the building. She was probably no more than seven or eight years old, he surmised. Drog Kuhn reached out his hand and placed it against a tree trunk on one of the trees that lined the dirt road leading up to the school. He pushed some of his power into the tree, eyeing the gnarled trees in the area just ahead of where the girl was running towards.

The branches on one of the gnarled trees came alive, writhing and wriggling like snakes. The branches clutched at the girl, but she ducked just in time and the branches missed her. Another gnarled tree grabbed at her, but the young girl was quick and she evaded the snatching tree limb. A third tree managed to grab the young girl's left wrist, but the girl was surprisingly quick with her defensive strike. She brought her right fist down hard on the branch, snapping it in two with the quick strike, freeing herself from the gnarled tree's grasp. She managed to avoid two more of the gnarled trees, ducking beneath the grasping branch of one, and side-stepping the lunging branch of another. She raced off down the narrow path that led away from the school towards HungYao temple high on the hill in the distance.

No matter, Drog Kuhn thought as he watched her race away. She'll be in for a big surprise when she reaches the temple and no one there is left alive to help her. He smiled and turned his attention back to the school full of children before him.

Chaki charged at the approaching stone statue of

Kwan MandaKi. He hurled the torch at the stone statue's face and the burning stick hit the stone statue in the mouth. Sparks erupted from the collision of flaming wood and solid stone, the small bits of fire fanning out in all directions.

Chaki continued to rush closer to Kwan MandaKi, and then he threw himself feet first into a slide. The floor was slick with his brother monk's blood so Chaki slid fast and smooth across the tiles. He went straight through between the legs of Kwan MandaKi. Chaki hooked his arm around one of Kwan MandaKi's stone legs and pulled with all his might as he slid past, timing his effort with one of Kwan MandaKi's lumbering steps. The speed of his slide and the strength of his pull was enough. His effort caused Kwan MandaKi to stumble and take a misstep that sent the now off-balance stone statue teetering and then toppling to the ground. Kwan MandaKi twisted as he fell, landing on his back. The stone statue's arms and legs moved back and forth like a baby kicking and flailing at the air in its crib.

Chaki, still on the floor, stared at the fallen stone statue. Kwan MandaKi looked like a turtle that had been flipped over on its back and was unable to right itself.

Chaki got back to his feet, now soaked in the blood of his brother monks. He stood near Kwan MandaKi, staring down at the stone man, careful to stay out of the range of the statue's flailing arms and legs. Blood dripped down from Chaki's clothes. His once-white headband was now smeared with blood, the redness nearly covering the entire circle of cloth.

Chaki felt a presence behind him and turned to see a bronze dragon sitting on its haunches at the end of the hallway, blocking the only exit out of the temple. It was Firelord. Firelord was somehow alive, just as Kwan MandaKi's statue had been brought to life. A few stray beams of sunlight coming in from the windows positioned high up on the hallway walls illuminated the dragon. The dragon's body gleamed with a wetness and Chaki knew it wasn't rainwater that coated its metallic skin. It was more blood. The blood of his brother monks. The dragon had a long, sinewy body, a snake-like body, its metallic skin scaly with ridges. It had a set of small wings jutting out from its body about a quarter of the way down its length. Chaki wondered if the dragon could actually fly with those small wings, and then realized it most assuredly would be able to fly. Firelord was now some kind of demonic creature with powers beyond any normal understanding.

This was supposed to be a joyous week, a week filled with love and the hope of new life for his sister and her husband. Now, it was only filled with terror and the end of life. Chaki clenched his jaw tight. He would find who was responsible for all this horror and he would make them pay.

Now all he had to do was find a way past a bronze dragon covered in blood. Or did he? Maybe there was another way to get out of the temple. Chaki glanced up. There were small glass-covered windows positioned high up in the hallway walls to his right. He knew he could squeeze through a window if he could reach it, but reaching a window was another problem altogether. About half a dozen of these windows dotted the corridor walls, but they were dozens of feet off the ground, situated far up the walls, well out of his reach. Stronger rays of sunlight

245

were now visible, the beams streaming through several of the windows as the stormy weather outside continued to lessen.

Chaki suddenly came up with a plan.

Drog Kuhn stood at the head of the class. The pretty young teacher sat at a desk in the front row, her slender body looking much too big for the small desk she now sat in. She didn't have much fear in her eyes, only anger and hate. Drog Kuhn looked at the soft pale skin of the young teacher. Drog Kuhn didn't find much joy in the pleasures of the flesh, but on occasion he did find some. He was pretty certain today would be one of those occasions. If he couldn't scare the teacher with threats of torturing the children in her charge, then a little bit of physical activity might bring about some terror in that stoic face of hers. He knew she was just being strong for her children, and for a brief moment he respected that strength. He was still going to fuck her bloody, but he at least gave her a few second's thought of admiration.

He surveyed the students sitting quietly in their seats. He gently stroked one of his earlobes as he studied them. Oh, some of them were whimpering, and one young boy in the back row of seats wouldn't stop sobbing, but for the most part they were all very well behaved. Drog Kuhn had a delicious decision to make. Whose scream would he eat first?

"Chaki!"

Chaki froze when he heard his name being cried out. The sound had come from outside the hallway, past the bronze dragon who was still sitting in front of the hallway doorway blocking his exit.

"Chaki!"

Chaki looked over to Firelord. A young girl suddenly appeared in the hall, moving around a narrow gap between the hallway wall and one of Firelord's bronze legs. Chaki recognized her. She was SuJin, a girl from Zhang Li's class. She was dressed in her school uniform. What was she doing here?

Chaki didn't have time to ask her because he was too busy watching the bronze dragon open its mouth. Chaki shouted at SuJin, pointing above her at the dragon. "SuJin, look out!"

SuJin froze for a moment, then glanced up. The dragon lowered its open mouth, enveloping her in the dark hole within. Firelord closed its mouth, muffling SuJin's scream. The bronze dragon lifted its head back up and started to make chewing sounds. The faint screaming coming from within its closed mouth quickly stopped. Blood oozed out of both sides of the dragon's mouth, the dark liquid sliding down its metal skin.

Chaki stared with hopeless anger at the spot where the young school girl had been standing. SuJin was gone. Just like that in an instant. Devoured by Firelord. Chaki immediately wondered what she was doing here. She had been dressed in her school uniform, and she had been shouting his name. SuJin had been looking for him. Why? And then he felt a tightness grip his neck. Chaki feared he knew why. His sister Zhang Li must have sent her. And she wouldn't have sent a young girl off alone like that unless she was in trouble. Desperate trouble.

Chaki stared at all the dead bodies littering the corridor floor. The stone statue of Kwan MandaKi still lay on its back on the floor, kicking uselessly at the air, but he feared the stone man could right himself at any moment. He had to put his plan into action. And he had to do it now.

Drog Kuhn ate the pretty young teacher's scream first. She held out for a long time, but that did not surprise him. He had hoped for such a show of silent defiance. It made that first scream of hers so much more satisfying. It was a deep, long scream, too. Coming up from the bottom of her lungs and bursting forth from her pretty mouth in a screeching, shrieking wail.

Drog Kuhn stared down at the student he clutched by the neck. The boy was dangling a few feet of the ground, his legs no longer kicking. Drog Kuhn knew sticking one of his clawed fingernails slowly into the student's eye would make his teacher scream. And he had been right.

Many of the other students screamed as well. Drog Kuhn snatched their cries out of the air, the tiny tendrils from his ears weaving and snaking all about the room, plucking the sounds out of the air, pulling them back into his ears so he could feed upon them.

The demon released his grip on the boy and the boy's body dropped to the school house floor in a heap.

The bronze dragon just watched him. Chaki forced himself not to keep looking at the metal beast. Firelord still sat at the entrance to the hallway, guarding it, blocking it. Chaki had no idea when, or even if, the dragon would come charging at him, so he continued with his work.

There were five bodies piled atop each other now, pushed tight against the hallway wall beneath one of the small windows high above. Chaki felt guilty using the bodies of his dead brother monks in this fashion, but he had no other plan. He needed to reach one of the windows to escape.

Chaki lifted the half-body of Brother Chupang and struggled with his weight, awkwardly putting him into place atop the upper torso of Brother NiJow. He had saved the bodies of Brother Chupang and Brother NiJow for last since their sliced-in-half bodies were lighter than the others. Chaki glanced down at Brother Hammo. He was the fattest brother monk so Chaki had used him as the base of his dead flesh ladder, but now he wasn't so sure that was a good idea. Brother Hammo's fat protruding belly made the entire structure unsteady.

Chaki looked up at Brother Chupang. Brother Chupang stared at him with glassy eyes. A crushing sadness threatened to paralyze Chaki, but he forced the feeling away. There was no time for grief, no time for sorrow, and certainly no time for self-pity. Chaki reached up and gently closed Brother Chupang's eyelids. Chaki looked away from the dead brother monk's face, returning his gaze to the top of the pile of bodies. Chaki didn't think he would be able to hoist another body onto the pile. The stack of bodies was as high as he was going to be able to make it. He glanced up at the window, mentally gauging the distance from the top of the pile of bodies to the window. It would still be out of arm's reach, but he was convinced he could still grab the window ledge if he made a solid jump.

Chaki glanced over at the bronze dragon. Firelord still just stared at him. Then the dragon lowered its head towards a nearby dead brother monk and scooped the corpse into its mouth to feed. Chaki wondered why a dragon made of metal would need to feed on human flesh, but he had no idea how dark magic worked so he just accepted what his eyes told him.

Chaki turned back to his flesh ladder and started to climb.

Drog Kuhn could still feel the delightful tingle flowing through his dark veins. He was full. At least for now. The school full of children had been a feast for his ears. A fucking feast. They had taken hours to die. All that screaming. All that wailing. It was quite intoxicating.

He looked at the two remaining children sitting quietly at their desks. He was just too full to continue. He had taken in all the sounds of pain, the wailing, the crying, the shrieking, the screaming, the begging, and absorbed them into his system, digested them, but now he felt bloated. He had already urinated several times, but he still felt an uncomfortable weight inside him. He needed to release some of the fullness he felt. Drog Kuhn grunted and pushed out the unwanted remains of his feast from his anus. But all that was left of the sounds he had feasted upon was silence; his demon body had already extracted everything it needed.

The two children sitting at their desks wrinkled their noses in disgust and their faces scrunched up as the sour stench of the demon's silent waste reached them. Drog Kuhn's noxious cloud of death surrounded them, and the two children started to gag as they began to choke to death. The demon just watched them, letting their gurgling, gasping noises fade away, the sounds of their misery uneaten.

Drog Kuhn knew he would be hungry again soon. Soon he would need to feed. The deathly cries of one victim was no longer enough to appease him. He needed more. So much more. The school full of screaming children had given him a satisfaction that he had never felt before. He had finally felt full. Truly and completely full. It was a deeply satisfying feeling. It was a soothingly satiating feeling he knew he would want to experience again and again.

But now he just needed a nap.

Chaki stood on Brother Chupang's chest. His hands were wet, slick with blood. He tried to wipe them dry on his pants, but those were also soaked with blood so that did not help. The tower of flesh was somewhat steady, but Chaki could feel it give under his weight. He wasn't sure how long the pile of dead bodies would hold up. He looked up at the window. The ledge was out of arm's reach, a few feet beyond his outstretched fingers. He crouched down, readying himself for the jump. He knew he would probably only have one chance at this, so he took a deep breath as he bent his knees. And then he jumped, pushing up fast and hard off the chest of Brother Chupang. His groping fingers grabbed at the window ledge, but there was nothing to hold onto. Chaki clawed at the window ledge with desperate fingers, but his fingers were too slick with blood to get any kind of grip. He felt himself falling. His bloody fingers scraped helplessly at the wall as he plummeted back down. He hit the stack of corpses with a grunt and the entire tower of flesh came crashing down all around him.

Chaki lay motionless amidst the dead bodies of his brother monks, breathing heavily. He crawled away from the bodies and collapsed flat to the hallway tiles, splashing up crimson liquid as he fell into a pool of blood on the floor. There was no spot on the floor that wasn't covered in blood. Chaki lifted a weary head and glanced up at the bronze dragon. The dragon just stared at him.

On the floor behind Chaki, the overturned stone statue of Kwan MandaKi still kicked its legs and flailed its arms. The stone man was still on his back, unable to right himself.

Chaki heard a coughing noise near him and he quickly turned his head to see Brother Geo staring at him with eyes that still held life. "Brother Geo," Chaki said and quickly crawled over to him. He put his arm on Brother Geo's chest in a comforting gesture. Brother Geo was one of the older monks in the temple. He had a thin white beard, peppered with a hint of the black hair he had in his younger days. Rumor had it that Brother Geo hadn't left the temple for years, not even to go to the village, nor did he even go outside in the gardens or to the outdoor practice fields. He just wandered the halls of the temple talking to brother monks (or to himself), or read scrolls in the temple library. Or painted. He was quite a skilled artist, especially when it came to painting portraits of his fellow brother monks. Chaki was supposed to get his portrait done in a few weeks, but Chaki knew Brother Geo wouldn't be painting any more portraits any time soon, if ever.

"Chaki..." Brother Geo said his name in a long, slow exhale.

"You'll be okay," Chaki said. He sat upright next to Brother Geo's prone body, keeping his hand splayed comfortingly on the gravely wounded monk's chest.

Brother Geo slowly turned his head back and forth in his best effort of shaking his head in denial. "No... no..." he groaned. He raised a shaking hand; his fingers were drenched in his own blood and the blood of other brother monks. "It was a demon," Brother Geo managed to utter. "I saw him."

Chaki clutched at Brother Geo's hand, holding it tight.

Suddenly, Brother Geo bolted upright into a sitting position and looked wide-eyed at Chaki. "It was Drog Kuhn. He is heading for the village. You have to save them, Chaki!" And then Brother Geo collapsed back to the ground, panting like a dog on a blistering hot day, as if that last outburst used up whatever energy reserves he still had left. He stared up at the ceiling, his breath gushing in and out of his mouth in short little bursts.

Chaki stared down at Brother Geo, still clutching his bloody hand in his. Drog Kuhn. A demon. Chaki knew the name immediately. They had studied the demons in the temple library. Every brother monk had to recite the names of the thirteen demon lords. Their village and temple had been blessed as no demon had come calling on them for generations, but now their blessed days were no more. A demon had come to Fallen Rocks. Chaki clenched his jaw. A demon had come and they had not been ready for him. Despite all their training, they still had not been ready for him. He thought of all the people in the village and his blood ran cold. His sister Zhang Li was in the village. The school was near the village. Chaki knew he had to get there. He had to get to the village now.

Chaki looked to the bronze dragon guarding the doorway. Brother Geo coughed and sputtered, spitting up blood. Chaki glanced down at him, then looked back up at the dragon's mouth.

❦

Drog Kuhn awoke from his nap, feeling refreshed. He looked down at his bulging erection and sighed. He glanced up in the direction of the village. There was some fucking that needed to be done.

❦

Chaki pushed Brother Geo's body along the floor. The body of the gravely wounded brother monk slid easily through the blood that coated the tiled floor.

Brother Geo struggled to lift his head to look at Chaki. "What are you doing?" he managed to ask, his words coming out in halting gasps.

Chaki didn't answer. He continued pushing

Brother Geo's body along the floor, moving Brother Geo closer to the bronze dragon.

Brother Geo turned his head in the direction Chaki was pushing him. He quickly turned back to look at Chaki. "No," he said. "No, Chaki. Please, no."

Chaki didn't respond. He kept his gaze locked on Firelord.

Firelord watched him push the body closer. The dragon's long tail was curved around the front of its body and it flicked ever so slightly as the body of the bleeding monk moved closer and closer.

Chaki stopped pushing. Brother Geo's body was still out of reach of the dragon. Brother Geo looked at Chaki, looked at the dragon, then turned back to look beseechingly at Chaki. "Don't do this, Chaki."

Chaki finally looked down at Brother Geo. "What would you have me do? I have to get to the village." He looked up at Firelord, then back down to Brother Geo. "I have to get past him."

Brother Geo spit up a mouthful of blood, turning his head to let it drain out of his mouth so he didn't choke on it. The elderly monk closed his eyes for a moment, then slowly opened them to look up at Chaki. Brother Geo nodded.

Chaki squeezed his shoulder reassuringly. "I will avenge all of us," he said to Brother Geo. "I swear it."

Brother Geo made a motion to raise his hand, but he couldn't do it. His fingers just trembled. He nodded again, ever so slightly, but the movement was there.

Chaki pushed the body of Brother Geo closer towards Firelord.

Drog Kuhn pushed the woman's face closer to the hot coals as he drove his cock deeper into her anus. She was very tight and very dry, so he had to thrust with extra effort to bury his length all the way inside her. She shrieked in pain. He wasn't quite certain if the woman was screaming from his cock being shoved all the way up her ass, or if it was because of the hot coals searing the flesh of her cheek. He mentally shrugged. Probably both. She screamed and he fed.

The dead blacksmith lay on the ground nearby, his apprentice also dead a few feet away. Both of them had their throats slit and their bellies carved open. Two resurrected skeletons stood nearby, each one gripping a long curved sword. The blades were smeared with blood; some of the blood streaks were already dry, some of the smears still freshly wet.

Beyond the blacksmith's shop, more dead bodies lay strewn in the streets. Several skeletons could be seen in the distance, moving through the village, hunting down anyone who moved. One of the skeletons had a flower garland wrapped around its body, somehow picked up as it moved through the wedding preparations that had been taking place in the village, but it paid that decoration no heed as it hacked at an old woman cowering on the ground.

Chaki waited. Brother Geo lay gasping on the ground, a few dozen feet away from Firelord. Brother Geo's body was just out of reach of the dragon, so Firelord would have to move if it wanted to feed on the dying brother monk. But for now the bronze dragon only stared at the twitching body just out of its reach. Chaki again wondered why a dragon made out of metal would need to eat human flesh, but he had seen Firelord eating another brother monk (and the poor little school girl SuJin) so he assumed it would eventually want more. Maybe eating human flesh was what kept Firelord in its new animated state. Chaki didn't know. He just knew he had to try something to get past the bronze beast and get to the village.

A trickle of blood dripped down Chaki's forehead from his blood-soaked headband. Chaki pulled the cloth off his head, tossing it to the hallway floor. The cloth hit the floor near a dead brother monk whom Chaki recognized immediately, despite the monk's face being smeared with blood and his jaw being nearly sliced completely off his face. It was Brother Tong. Chaki glanced at the mutilated corpse of Brother Tong. His mentor. He remembered the first day he had come to the temple and Brother Tong had greeted him with wide open arms and a cheerful smile. Chaki had been in grave trouble in the village. Again. He had stolen some chickens from a family in the village and then tried to re-sell them in the marketplace. He hadn't realized the chickens had been branded with a tiny mark under their wings to signify their owners, and a group of men rightfully accused him of being a thief. He had to fight his way out of that one. Chaki had broken a few limbs, crunched a few noses, and busted several lips before they had taken him down and bound his arms behind his back with rope. After the fight was over, Chaki had looked down to see that one of the men he had struck was an old man. He had broken the old man's arm and busted up his lip. In the blind rage of his violence, he hadn't realized it was his own father. Chaki remembered staring at his father laying curled up on the ground. His father clutched at his arm, tears streaming down his face. Chaki had never seen him cry before. It was a very sobering sight. At that moment, Chaki knew he was out of control. He knew he needed help. He went to the temple the next day. The village elders had let him go. They knew the brother monks would help him far more than sitting alone in a solitary cell ever would.

Chaki had been living in the temple with the brother monks ever since. He remembered what Brother Tong had said to him on his first day. "The man who strikes first admits that his ideas have given out." And Chaki knew Brother Tong had been right. He had given up on trying to reason things out in a calm, rational manner. He had resorted to using his fists and his feet to resolve everything. And had nearly crippled his own father.

Chaki frowned at the thought of his father. His father never visited him at the temple. That made Chaki sad, but he understood. Chaki wasn't even quite sure where his father was.

And then Firelord moved, drawing Chaki back to the present. The bronze dragon creeped forward, its snout sniffing the air before it as it neared the wriggling human on the floor.

Chaki saw his chance. There was a narrow opening between the dragon's body and the corridor wall, just enough room for him to get past the beast. Chaki bolted for the opening, charging across the room.

Firelord turned its head towards the racing Chaki and lunged for him, its jaws opening wide.

Chaki dove for the narrow gap, his arms outstretched in front of him as he flew through the air.

Firelord snapped its metal jaws shut with a tremendous clank, just narrowly missing taking a chunk of flesh and bone out of Chaki's foot.

Chaki soared past the dragon, moving through the narrow gap between the dragon's body and the temple wall, and out into the corridor beyond. He hit the ground on his shoulder, rolled right to his feet, and kept on running without even looking back.

Drog Kuhn watched with wry amusement as his skeleton army continued to move through the village, hacking and biting and kicking and punching their way past any villager unlucky enough to be caught in their path. He saw one skeleton with a spear stab the weapon straight through an old man, lifting the hapless villager up off the ground on the end of the spear. The old man's scream got cut off by a pool of blood filling his mouth, so Drog Kuhn turned away with disinterest. Two skeletons had another man trapped in a corner and they took turns kicking and punching at him. The man was quiet as he fought for his life, so again Drog Kuhn lost interest quickly.

Then a group of women burst out of a building, numerous skeletons in hot pursuit. They raced towards the pink pagoda that had been set up for the wedding on a platform in the middle of the village square, as if that feeble structure would offer them some protection, but none of the women made it. The skeletons grabbed at the long hair of the women, all four of the skeletons each managing to curl their bony fingers into the dark mass of hair of a woman. The skeletons tugged sharply on their prey, all of them viciously whipping the women about by their hair.

Drog Kuhn finally smiled. The air was now thick with screams, his demon eyes seeing the sounds mingling with all the decorative paper lanterns that had been festooned on strings throughout the village. The demon snatched a few cries down from the air as they floated past him, his tendrils snaking out of his ears to grab them as the sounds drew close to him.

Soon, the village was quiet. Soon, Drog Kuhn was feeling full again.

Chaki stood in a cluster of thick trees near the village graveyard, just off to the side of the dirt road that led to the village from the temple. He had started to race past the cemetery, but then had to stop after what he had seen behind the low metal fence that marked off the boundary of the village's graveyard. He fought to catch his breath. He was in excellent shape, but running all the way from the temple to the village cemetery was still something that took a lot of energy. He leaned against a tree, breathing hard.

The graveyard had clearly been disturbed. Upended mounds of dirt were scattered everywhere, and deep holes dotted the cemetery. Holes that once housed the dead. Chaki stared at the deep, empty graves. Piles of ragged dirt and mud were splashed across the ground around each of the grave sites, as if something had dug itself out of each one. A stone statue and a bronze dragon had come to life, so why not the bones of the dead? Chaki smiled a tight smile. His mind was primed for vengeance, and his body was aching for a fight. He was determined to stop the cause of this madness and bloodshed.

One of the graves was very small, small enough to hold an infant. Chaki clenched his jaw and his tight smile vanished. He knew whose grave that was. It was his son's. It was the grave of the bastard child he had with Wei Lin. The boy had come into the world sickly and unwell. He had died within hours of being born. It was one of the things that had set Chaki off on his self-destructive rampage before he turned to the brother monks and the temple for salvation. He stared at the small patch of disrupted earth. They had never even given the tiny infant a name.

Chaki forced himself to look away from the small grave. There were dozens of other disrupted graves all throughout the cemetery. He could see the trails their former occupants left in the dirt. He looked up, following one muddy trail across the ground, a trail that headed straight for the village.

He moved through the graveyard, walking amongst the trees that dotted the cemetery, glancing into the open graves as he passed by them. Chaki thought about who else was buried in the village cemetery. There were some famous warriors buried here. Would their bones remember the fighting skills their owners had obtained during their lives? He scoffed at himself. Of course they would. That's how his luck was going today.

Chaki turned to look back towards the village and saw a skeleton standing in his path. The creature stood motionless, staring at him with dark empty sockets. Its bones were an off-white color, with a hint of a very slight pale brown texture coating their surface. The skeleton clutched a curved sword in its bony fingers. Chaki knew who the bones belonged to. He recognized the sword the skeleton was gripping. They had buried the blade with the man when he had died. It was one of the first burial ceremonies Chaki had attended as a child, so he vividly remembered the huge gathering of mourners who had come to pay their final respects to the recently deceased man. The skeleton was the remains of HongHui, a renowned swordsman.

Chaki glanced around the ground near him and spotted a fallen tree branch. He quickly snatched it from the ground and clutched it like a club. Then he spotted a large stone cross thrust into the ground near an open grave and tossed the branch to the ground. He grabbed at the cross, exerting his strength as he pulled at it, jerking it back and forth to loosen its hold in the earth, then yanked it out of the ground with a strong tug. He lifted the cross and clutched it tight. He stood before the skeleton warrior, ready for a fight. The stone cross was much heavier than a sword, but Chaki felt confident he could wield it effectively as a weapon.

Then something brushed across his bare toes. Chaki glanced down to see an infant's skeleton clutching at him, the tiny skeletal fingers trying to grip his toes. The baby's skull shifted as it lifted its head to raise its tiny empty eye sockets up towards Chaki.

Chaki stomped on the tiny head, but he didn't crush the skull with the first blow because he was too hesitant. He stomped again and again and again, finally crushing the small skull with a heart-wrenching crack, then continued to stomp the rest of the skeleton to shattered shards of bone. He tightened his fingers around the stone cross he held in his hand, clenching his other hand tight into a fist against his side. He stared down at the smashed infant's skeleton. A darkness crossed over Chaki's eyes. Some would call it a veil of madness. He looked up at all the empty graves all around him, then looked left towards the school, then looked in the direction of the main village square to his right, then back down to the shattered bones of his dead bastard son, then over to the sword-wielding skeleton standing before him. A chortling snort burst forth from Chaki's lips. It was turning out to be a hell of a day indeed.

And then Chaki attacked, swinging the cross with a savage fury, striking out against the skeleton with a two-fisted grip on the stone cross. The skeleton tried to block and parry, but the undead stack of bones had no chance against the unrelenting onslaught of Chaki To. Chaki cracked the edge of the cross hard against the skeleton's ribs, cracking the curved bones, knocking two of them completely out of the skeleton's frame. Chaki reversed his swing and knocked out a few rib bones from the other side of the skeleton's body. The skeleton swung his curved sword at Chaki, but Chaki ducked under the slashing blade and struck again, cracking the skeleton's knee with a tremendous blow that shattered more bone. The skeleton stumbled, its body drooping to the side. Chaki struck again, viciously swinging the edge of the cross to connect solidly with the skeleton's skull, cracking the empty braincase with the force of his blow.

Chaki swung again and again, sending chips of

bone flying off from the skeleton's skull as he battered it and shattered it into a dozen pieces. The skull was empty; there were no brains directing the skeleton's movement. There was no real life emanating from the skeleton. It was a grotesque puppet, its strings being pulled by some demonic force. Chaki smiled grimly at that thought, laughing with a grunted laugh. He was fighting some cursed puppet.

With a final effort, the skeleton raised its sword and Chaki smashed its fingers, crushing them, shattering the bones with the edge of the cross. The curved sword the skeleton had been holding dropped to the earth. Chaki stared down at the tangled mass of bones. The skeleton of HongHui lay motionless on the ground. Chaki kicked at the remaining bones, sending the skeleton tumbling into an open grave. He made an effort to wipe the sweat from his brow, sliding the back of his forearm across his forehead, but that just smeared the blood on his arm across his forehead. He tossed the stone cross to the ground.

Chaki grabbed the curved sword the skeleton had been holding and stood indecisively for a long moment, again looking to the left in the direction of the school, then looking right towards the village. He knew the skeletons were headed for the village, and were probably already in the village causing chaos and death, but he also knew everyone at the school was in dire danger. He took one last look toward the village, then headed for the school, quickening his pace.

Chaki quickly moved along the road, heading for

the school in the near distance, darting his gaze about, continually surveying his surroundings. He re-gripped the curved sword, tightening his fingers around the handle of the blade.

The school was quiet. It was the most terrifying silence Chaki had ever heard. The school should not have been quiet. It should have been filled with the noise of children. Then he heard the sounds of sobbing, the very unnatural sounds of a man crying noisily. The memory of his father laying on the ground, crying as he clutched at his broken arm, flashed through Chaki's head. He wondered if his father was still in the village somewhere. He knew he didn't have time to think of that now, so he pushed that thought away. Chaki moved around the corner of the school building and saw his old friend Savio Grilleti on his knees on the ground.

Savio's parents were not natives of the village, which is why Savio had such an odd last name. And that was why he physically looked different than everyone else in the village. He had naturally paler skin, blond hair, a longer nose, and a much more angular face than everyone else. His parents had traveled from some faraway place called Italirio. They had visited Fallen Rocks on some kind of religious pilgrimage, seeking some kind of mystical enlightenment that they soon realized didn't exist anywhere but in their own minds. They had enjoyed the simple lifestyle of the villagers who lived in Fallen Rocks so much that they had decided to stay and make Fallen Rocks their new home. Savio had been born in the village years later, only a few weeks later than Chaki, and Chaki had become his friend when they were both four years old. They had been friends ever since. Savio had not been happy when Chaki had decided to go live with the brother monks in HungYao Temple, but Savio married young and he had his own family now, so his unhappiness with Chaki's decision didn't have much time to linger in his mind before family duties absorbed all his attention.

Chaki stared at his friend. A child was cradled in Savio's lap. A motionless child. Chaki recognized the child. She was Savio's daughter Gianna.

Chaki hurried over to Savio, scanning his surroundings as he neared his friend, but he saw no other movement in the nearby area.

Savio rocked Gianna slowly in his lap.

"Savio," Chaki said, his voice barely above a whisper.

Savio looked up at him and Chaki felt his heart breaking. Savio's pale face was covered with tears, his eyes blistering red with grief. Savio said nothing.

"What happened?" Chaki asked.

"It was Drog Kuhn. He has come for our village."

So Brother Geo had been right, Chaki thought. Drog Kuhn has come to Fallen Rocks. The demon was in their midst. Chaki looked up the dirt road that led to the heart of the village. It was quiet and empty, the trees lining the road stiff and unmoving in the still air. He knew he would find chaos at the end of that road. He looked back down to Savio. "Where is he? Did you see him?"

Savio shook his head. "I don't know. I think he's probably somewhere in the village still." He continued to rock Gianna in his arms.

Chaki looked at the school building. "Did you— did you go inside?"

Savio nodded. "You don't want to go in there, Chaki."

"Is Zhang Li in there?"

Savio nodded. Chaki started to move towards the building, but Savio suddenly shot out his hand and clutched desperately at Chaki's wrist, startling him, nearly causing him to drop the sword. "You don't want to go in there, Chaki."

Chaki glanced down to where Savio gripped him. He tried to ease his arm away from his friend, but Savio wouldn't release his hold. Chaki reached down and gently pried Savio's fingers away from his wrist. "I have to."

"No! No, you don't! Don't go in there!"

Chaki was taken aback by the desperate cry in Savio's voice. He couldn't recall Savio ever raising his voice in his entire life, even when he was angry at his children.

"Savio, I have to. I have to find my sister." Chaki started to move towards the school.

Suddenly, Savio was on his feet, grabbing at Chaki, tugging at his arm. Chaki turned to see Savio looking at him with the most anguished, sorrow-filled face he had ever seen. His eyes were awash with tears, his expression full of torment. "No!" Savio shouted, his voice nearly a scream.

Chaki looked down to see Savio's dead child sprawled awkwardly in the dirt at their feet, and he felt an awkward flush of embarrassment for his friend and a deep sadness for the child Savio had just dumped to the dirt in his desperation to stop him. He looked back up to Savio. "Savio, let go." Chaki put his hand on Savio's fingers where his friend gripped his arm, but Chaki did not pull on them.

Savio shook his head. "Just burn it, Chaki. I'll help you. We'll just burn it."

Chaki tore Savio's fingers away from his arm, pushing his friend's hand away sharply. "No!" He frowned at Savio. "No." He started back towards the school, but Savio quickly moved in front of him, putting his hands on Chaki's chest. Then Savio withdrew his hands away from Chaki and stared down at his now blood-soaked fingers. He looked back up at Chaki and seemed to just notice for the first time that Chaki was covered in blood. He raised his hands up to block Chaki again, but he did not touch Chaki's chest. "No, Chaki," Savio said, shaking his head.

Chaki felt his ire rising, but he did not want to yell at his friend. "Savio, take care of Gianna," Chaki looked down to the ground where the child lay. Savio followed Chaki's gaze and saw his dead child laying in a heap in the dirt. Savio burst into a fresh round of tears and he let his arms fall down defeatedly to his sides. Chaki slowly stepped around him and continued towards the school, raising the curved sword before him as he neared the building.

Savio had been right. He should not have gone into the school. Zhang Li lay flat on a table in the center of the room. She was clearly dead. She looked like she had been dissected. Her midsection was carved open and her insides laid bare, her intestines dangling down the side of the table like twisted coils of rope. Blood pooled on the floor beneath the table, spread out in a wide circle. Nearby, a child hung from the ceiling, a rope made of intestines tied around his neck. His body was battered and bruised from head to toe, as if he had been used as a human piñata.

Chaki vomited.

Drog Kuhn stared down at the naked men on the table. Disturbingly, one of the men had an erection and Drog Kuhn shook his head disapprovingly. The man was probably some kind of sick pervert. There were four men laid out in front of him, all of them flat on their backs on the big table. They were bound tightly with ropes, the bindings wrapped around their naked torsos and shoulders, keeping their arms tightly pinned to their sides. Their ankles were bound with ropes as well. A metal horseshoe was hammered into the table around each of their necks like a collar, keeping their heads pressed down tight against the table. They were laid flat on the table like slabs of steak laying on a grill waiting to be cooked. But he wasn't going to cook them. Drog Kuhn was going to play them. He was going to make music with their screams. Sweet, delicious music.

Two naked women were positioned nearby, one on either side of the table, both standing. They were tied upright to posts. One of the women was young and pretty, her breasts full and perky. The other woman was old; her tanned weathered skin was flabby, her breasts were flabby, her belly was flabby. Drog Kuhn stroked the old woman's face and she glared back at him. He smiled at her. She would make good music. It might take a little bit of extra effort on his part, but she would sing for him. He glanced over at the younger woman. She was clearly terrified. She would sing, of that he was certain. The question was how loud and for how long. There was only one way to find out.

Drog Kuhn raised a sharp fingernail over the naked body of one man and slowly started to insert the tip of his fingernail into the man's chest. The man screamed immediately. So much for stoic resistance, Drog Kuhn mused. His ears pulsed and glowed a soft red.

And then he began to play, moving quickly from man to man, inserting a fingernail here, cutting flesh there, using the entirety of their exposed flesh, their arms, their legs, their chests, their faces, their thighs, their shoulders, their scrotums, their cocks, cutting, slashing, piercing, penetrating. The air filled with notes that only Drog Kuhn could see. Both of his ears throbbed and lit up a deep red. The thin tendrils from his ears danced and weaved, snatching the sounds out of the air and pulling them into his ears. Drog Kuhn threw his head back and closed his eyes as he continued to play his grotesque symphony of screams.

Drog Kuhn moved down the row of naked men, stabbing, poking, cutting, slashing. Blood covered the men now, running down the sides of their bodies, dripping to the table, oozing along its surface, then dropping to the floor with soft splashes. He reached the last man on the table and did a pirouette, his robes flaring out majestically as he twirled. As he came out of his spin with a wild flourish, Drog Kuhn shoved four sharp fingernails deep into the gut of the young naked woman tied upright to the post. The young woman screamed a most delicious scream.

Drog Kuhn smiled a rapturous smile as he continued to play. He fed and he fed and he fed.

※──◀◎▶──※

"Are you sure?" Chaki asked. He cradled the lifeless body of Savio's daughter in his blood-stained arms.

Savio nodded his head. "She loved her classmates. It's okay. I think she would want to be with them." Savio clutched a burning torch in his hand, holding it slightly away from his head. He clutched the curved sword Chaki had taken from the skeleton of HongHui in his other hand.

Chaki nodded. He carried Gianna into the school, then quickly came back out to stand at Savio's side. Savio wordlessly handed the sword back to Chaki, then moved up to the school to set it ablaze. Once the wooden exterior walls started to burn, Savio hurled the torch into the building and returned to Chaki's side. They watched the school burn in silence.

The sour taste of vomit still burned in Chaki's mouth as he watched the school his sister had worked so hard to build blacken and begin to turn to ash. The burn on his cheek flared with pain.

"This is all your fault, you know."

Chaki stopped breathing. He looked incredulously at Savio. His friend had said it so casually, so matter-of-factly as if the point could not be argued. "What?"

Savio nodded. "You and those damned monks."

Chaki could think of nothing to say to that.

Savio waved his hand in the air, motioning towards the temple in the far distance. "You go and hide in the temple and mutter your prayers and practice your kung fu to keep your body and spirit strong, when you should all be here guarding and protecting the village. You think peace and prayer will drive Drog Kuhn away? You think even a million brother monks humming in meditation will make him just disappear?"

Chaki just stared in silence.

"The monks made you soft. You gave up the way of violence. You were afraid to use your strength for your own gain. You gave up who you really are." Savio looked at him. "You really think you were being strong by going to the temple? You think you were being strong by resisting your urges?"

Chaki said nothing.

"You were being weak," Savio said. "You turned away from what you are. You turned away from *who* you are."

"Is that what you really think?" Chaki dropped to the ground and did a one finger push up. He raced towards a tree, leaped towards it feet first, raced up the trunk a few feet, then did a backwards flip and landed solidly on his feet. He moved back to Savio and flexed his well-defined muscles.

"You idiot." Savio thumped his own chest. "I am not talking about here." Savio tapped at his own forehead. "I am talking about here."

Chaki was quiet for a long time.

"Would you even be able to kill Drog Kuhn if you had the chance?" Savio asked. "Or would the monk's teachings of peace stop you, make you hesitate before you deliver the killing blow? It is as my grandfather used to say. Man who places head in sand will get kicked in the end."

"I—" Chaki couldn't find the words to continue.

Usually Savio's silly proverbs made him laugh, but not today. Finally, he looked up at Savio, feeling a sense of defeat enshroud him like a blanket wound tight about a newborn babe, rendering him immobile. No words came. A dark seriousness came over Chaki's face. "We need to stop him."

Savio looked at Chaki squarely. "The damage has already been done. There was no one here to stop him." Savio paused for a moment. "Drog Kuhn will eventually tire of our village and move on."

"He will kill everyone!" Chaki exclaimed.

Savio shook his head. "Drog Kuhn won't kill everyone. He is not a fool. Would a poulterer kill all his ducks in one season? Would a pig farmer kill all his pigs and leave none to create more pigs for the next season?" Savio shook his head. "No, he won't kill everyone. He will leave some of us alive so he can return in a generation's time and feed again." Savio put his arm on Chaki's shoulder. "Go back to your temple. Say some more prayers. Maybe that will work."

Chaki brusquely shrugged Savio's hand away from his shoulder. "There is no more temple to go back to. It is destroyed. All the brother monks are dead."

Savio left his hand hanging in mid-air for a long moment, then slowly lowered his arm to his side. "I am sorry, Chaki."

A wrenching scream exploded out of the village, the sound racing up the road like a roaring wind.

Chaki reached the edge of the village and turned down a side street, racing between the rice ball seller and the noodle maker's shop. He quickly skidded to a stop. Both shops were empty, the street devoid of people.

Savio, huffing and puffing, finally caught up to Chaki. He bent over, clutching at his side, his blond hair covering his face. "I'm really out of shape," he panted.

Chaki said nothing. He gripped the sword tightly.

Savio continued to pant, struggling to catch his breath. He looked up at Chaki. "Chaki—" but then closed his mouth as he saw the intent look carved into Chaki's face. He followed Chaki's gaze.

A group of five skeletons standing in the middle of the street blocked their path. One of the skeletons held a severed human arm as a weapon, an arm the skeleton had most likely just ripped right out of its victim's socket because it was still dripping with blood. Three of the skeletons had no weapons, but Chaki could see they had obviously used their bony fingers, feet, and even their skeletal jaws as implements of destruction; all of those parts were stained with blood. The fifth skeleton did have a weapon clutched in its skeletal hand, a long straight sword.

Chaki tightened his grip on his curved sword. He had to get past them. He had to find the source of that terrified scream. Terror clutched at Chaki's heart because he was afraid he knew that screaming voice. Even though he had never heard her shriek like that before, he feared that screaming voice had belonged to Wei Lin. "Savio," Chaki said. "Get behind me."

Savio slowly moved behind Chaki, peering out from behind him at the skeletons before them. Savio then quickly glanced around the area, scanning the surroundings for a weapon, but he saw nothing that he could use.

A stray paper lantern floated down between the group of skeletons and the two men. The small pink globe drifted slowly towards the ground, then lightly touched the earth. As if that was their cue, the skeletons attacked, surging forward with dark intent. They had but one objective: to destroy every human they came across.

Chaki stepped forward, moving towards the skeleton with the straight sword, immediately engaging it. Their metal blades crossed with a heavy clang. The ringing sounds of sword strikes and parries filled the street as the two combatants dueled with their blades.

The skeleton with the severed arm swung the bloody appendage at Savio, sweeping the severed arm across its body, aiming for Savio's chest area. Savio tried to jump back out of the way, but he was too slow. The severed arm hit him hard in the chest and he grunted under the force of the blow. One of the unarmed skeletons charged straight at Savio, wrapping its bony arms around him, tackling Savio to the ground. "Chaki!" Savio cried out.

Chaki looked back over his shoulder at the sound of Savio's cry and nearly had his head taken off by the straight sword. Chaki ducked just in time as the skeleton's blade sliced through the air where his neck had been a second earlier. He turned his attention back to the skeleton battling him. The skeleton was clearly experienced with wielding a blade from its prior human life and Chaki knew he had to keep his focus on his attacker if he had any hope of beating it. Chaki swung low, aiming for the skeleton's thigh bone. The skeleton blocked the strike and Chaki quickly countered with a strike to the skeleton's shoulder as the creature bent to block his attack. The skeleton wasn't fast enough to parry Chaki's blow and Chaki's curved blade chipped off a big chunk of the skeleton's shoulder bone.

Then Chaki felt something bite down hard on his shoulder and he glanced quickly to his left to see one of the other skeletons biting at the back of his shoulder. He twisted his body sharply, trying to maneuver away from the skeleton. The biting skeleton held on tight and Chaki felt pain searing through him; he could feel blood dripping down his back as the skeleton's clamping jaw broke through his flesh. Chaki backpedaled, moving quickly backward, ramming the biting skeleton hard into the stone wall of one of the buildings that lined the street in an effort to dislodge the creature. That did no good. That action only dug the skeleton's hard bones into Chaki's back. Chaki grimaced and twisted, contorting his body, trying to shake the biting skeleton off his body.

Then the sounds of loud commotion filled the street. Chaki turned to see his future brother-in-law Shan Xun had joined the fray, along with two other men. Brother-in-law. The thought filled Chaki with dismay. The image of his sister Zhang Li laying on the table in the school, cut open like a dissected frog for study, flashed into Chaki's head. He quickly remembered with a tightening ball in his stomach that Shan Xun would never be his brother-in-law. Shan Xun and the two other men with him engaged the skeletons in battle.

One of the men with Shan Xun clutched a staff.

The man was quite skilled with the weapon and he wielded the dense wooden pole with great precision. He managed to get the biting skeleton off of Chaki's back and quickly engaged the undead creature. The man with the staff thrust the end of the shaft into the gap between two ribs of the biting skeleton, then jerked the shaft sharply to the side, snapping the skeleton's rib.

One of the other men with Shan Xun was not quite so skilled. He had a hoe for a weapon, but the thin edge of the farming implement got caught between the ribs of another skeleton and the man lost his grip on the weapon as the skeleton jerked away from his attack. The skeleton yanked the hoe from his rib cage and then proceeded to use it on the man who attacked him with it. The hoe sunk deep into the man's neck and blood spurted everywhere. The man went down and twitched horrifically in the street.

Chaki kicked at the skeleton with the long sword, pushing the skeleton back away, giving Chaki a chance to get over to Savio. Chaki lopped off the head of the skeleton that had Savio pinned to the ground, but he didn't wait around to see Savio shove the skeleton away and clamber to his feet. Chaki immediately turned his attention to another skeleton, also lopping the head off of this puppet of bones. He wasn't sure why severing their heads stopped the skeletons, but it did. The forces that commanded dark magic were beyond his grasp.

A man grunted hard and Chaki spun to see the man with the staff go down. The skeleton with the long sword withdrew his blade from the man's belly as the man sunk to the ground. Shan Xun grabbed the fallen staff and struck out at the skeleton's legs, swiping the hard pole against the skeleton's shin bones. The skeleton staggered and Chaki attacked, swinging his curved blade with precise strikes, cutting through the skeleton's neck bone with a hard, fast hit. The skeleton fell to the street and lay unmoving, its decapitated skull resting a half dozen feet away.

Savio hobbled over to Chaki and stood at his side, panting heavily, staring at the carnage before them.

The two men who had been with Shan Xun were dead. The five skeletons no longer had heads and lay in crumpled heaps of bones in the street. Shan Xun was also breathing very hard, nearly panting as loudly as Savio. He looked over to Chaki. "Have you seen your sister? I need to find Zhang Li."

Chaki thought of telling Shan Xun about Zhang Li, but now didn't seem to be the time. He just shook his head. Chaki looked back up the street towards the village square. He breathed slowly in and out. There were pools of blood everywhere, corpses, body parts. There was chaos and destruction and death everywhere he looked. "We need to find this demon. We need to find Drog Kuhn and stop him. But first I need to find Wei Lin." Chaki looked over to Shan Xun. "Have you seen Wei Lin?"

Shan Xun started to shake his head, but his motion was interrupted by someone yelling.

"Get me out of here!" a voice shouted.

The three men turned in the direction of the voice. It sounded as if it had come from a building nearby. Chaki stared at the small stone structure at the end of the street. Chaki knew the building. He had spent many nights there during his rebellious youth and during what he now called his angry days. It was the village jail.

"Get me out of here!" the voice said.

Chaki looked at Savio and Shan Xun, then walked towards the jail.

The building that housed the village jail was small, only consisting of a main outer room and three small, steel-barred cells. The outer room contained a small table and two chairs. The jail guard was gone, probably out fighting skeletons somewhere, or already dead. A weapons rack lined one of the outer room walls, containing a few spears, half a dozen swords, two bows, and a few quivers filled with arrows.

Two of the cells were vacant, their cots empty of any sheets or pillows as they awaited prisoners to fill them. The third cell was not empty. It was occupied by a man. He paced back and forth behind the bars like a wild animal in a cage, muttering to himself. He stopped and laughed, then continued pacing back and forth, continuing to mutter. The man stopped and stared at the wall. "Get me out of here!" he shouted at the bricks. Then he resumed his pacing, walking half a dozen steps in the cell, then whirling around to pace back the other way.

Chaki frowned at the pacing man. Shan Xun stepped up beside Chaki. "His name is JaLee. He is mad."

"Why is he in jail?" Chaki asked.

"He's a thief and a murderer. He killed four people before they caught him."

Chaki watched JaLee pace the small cell. "Does he even see us?"

Shan Xun shrugged. "He lives in a different world

than we do." Shan Xun tapped at his own head. "He drank some water from a dirty pond a few weeks ago and they say he swallowed a spirit."

"He is possessed?" Chaki asked.

Again, Shan Xun shrugged. "He is dangerous."

"We can use him," Savio said.

Chaki turned to look curiously at Savio.

Savio now had one of the bows in his hand, a quiver full of arrows clutched in the other. "We need to draw Drog Kuhn out. Set up some kind of trap or something," Savio said. "We can't beat him on his terms. We need to take the offensive."

"What are you saying?" Chaki asked.

"He's a condemned man, Chaki. He's going to hang in two weeks anyway," Savio said.

Shan Xun nodded. "Let's put him to good use."

Savio nodded. "It is no good going to the river just wanting to catch a fish; you have to take a net as well." Savio looked at JaLee. "Or some bait."

"He's still a human being," Chaki said.

"Is he?" Shan Xun asked. "You didn't see what he did to that old man and his wife." He paused. "I did. I don't think anyone still human could do something like that."

Savio looked over at Chaki. "Maybe the gods brought us to him for a reason? Maybe he has a purpose and we didn't know it until now."

"To be a sacrifice?" Chaki asked. He immediately thought of Brother Geo, of what he himself had done to a brother monk, and realized how hypocritical his question was.

"Get me out of here!"

They looked over to see JaLee gripping the cell bars, his face pressed up tight against the thick metal poles. "I thought I smelled cock." He sniffed grotesquely towards Chaki. "Or is that monk pussy?" JaLee shook the prison cell bars. "I'm going to fuck your mouth!" he shouted. "I am going to gut you like a pig and fuck the holes I make in your belly!" He shook the bars some more.

Chaki walked over to the weapons rack and grabbed the other bow, hooking it over his shoulder. He grabbed the remaining quiver of arrows and looped the leather strap over his other shoulder. Chaki looked at Savio. "Let's do this."

JaLee tried to bite back the scream that begged to come out from behind his lips. But eventually it had to come out. He opened his mouth and howled in agony.

Drog Kuhn looked up and turned his head toward the delicious source of the noise in the distance. He felt his ears tingling. He rose up and headed for the tasty sound.

Drog Kuhn appeared in the market square a short time after JaLee started to howl. The demon took a moment to glance around the area, quickly assessing his surroundings. He looked up at the man hanging from the hook. The hook was lodged deep into the man's back. A rope was attached to the top of the hook and the rope was looped around a high thick branch on a nearby tree, keeping the man aloft. The man couldn't reach the hook, but he kept trying, twisting his hands behind him as far as he could. The man swayed as he struggled futilely to free himself. The man groaned loudly in pain and Drog Kuhn smiled. It was a delicious little bite of sound. A pleasing appetizer before the next main course.

Chaki felt a stabbing pain of shame in his heart as he watched JaLee dangle helplessly from the hook. Chaki, Savio, and Shan Xun were hidden nearby, watching their bait wriggle on its hook from a safe distance behind a row of parked wagons. What they had done to the man was vicious and cruel, but JaLee was sentenced to die anyway. Chaki knew that wouldn't really alleviate the remorse, but he forced himself to retain that thought. It was the only thing he could hold on to that didn't drive himself mad with guilt. He again thought of Brother Geo and how he had fed him to Firelord to escape the temple. What was he doing? What kind of man was he becoming? He thought of racing over to JaLee and letting him down, but now the demon Drog Kuhn was here and there was no time.

It was the first time Chaki had seen the demon. Drog Kuhn wasn't the terrifying ogre he had first envisioned. His garish robe was a bit outlandish, and his fingernails were obscenely long and looked to be very sharp, but he still looked very much like a man, a tall man, but still a man.

Chaki let the first arrow loose with a well-practiced hand. He had practiced his archery skills three days a week in the temple and had become quite proficient with the bow. Chaki's arrow sliced through Drog Kuhn's garish robe, sinking deep into the demon's back, right between his shoulder blades. Drog Kuhn did not move; he just froze in place.

Shan Xun gripped a spear, watching. He had taken the weapon from the weapons rack in the village jail. He was crouched on the opposite side of Chaki from Savio. "He didn't even move," Shan Xun whispered with just a touch of trepidation creeping into his voice.

Savio, on the other hand, was not so skillful with the bow. Savio's arrow missed Drog Kuhn. But the errant arrow did not miss JaLee. The sharp arrow head thunked into JaLee's chest, right below his drooping chin. JaLee threw his head up and howled in agony.

"It was the wind," Savio said immediately. "The wind took it."

Chaki glanced up at the deathly still branches in the trees near them, but said nothing. He nocked another arrow and let it fly. His second arrow lodged into Drog Kuhn's back, just below and to the left of his first arrow strike. Drog Kuhn still did not move. He wasn't reacting to the arrows at all. Chaki had no idea if the arrows had any effect on the demon at all. He had no idea how to kill a demon. They all had assumed they could kill Drog Kuhn with conventional weapons, but that was clearly not going to be the case.

Savio fired another arrow and this one hit the demon in the leg, penetrating the back of Drog Kuhn's left calf. Still, the demon did not move. Drog Kuhn stood frozen in place, making no motion at all, not with his head, not with his hands, not with his feet. Nothing. He stood absolutely still, his big body facing away from them.

Chaki sunk another arrow into the demon's back, this one hitting Drog Kuhn in the upper left shoulder.

"Does he even feel them?" Shan Xun asked. "How do we stop a demon who feels no pain?"

Savio let another arrow loose and again missed Drog Kuhn. This arrow sailed past the demon and sliced through JaLee's inner thigh, cutting him with a ragged gash. JaLee again howled in pain, wriggling and writhing in agony on the hook.

⊰⊱⊰⊰❀⊱⊰⊱

To Drog Kuhn, the arrows were nothing but the annoyance of an insect pinching at his skin. A minor annoyance to be dealt with in time. The screams coming from the dangling man were too tasty to be ignored. He would deal with his attackers in due time.

⊰⊱⊰⊰❀⊱⊰⊱

"Does he even feel them?" Savio asked, whispering to Chaki, mirroring Shan Xun's earlier question. "I don't see any blood."

Chaki lowered his bow after sinking another arrow into Drog Kuhn. He kept his stare on the demon in the garish robes. "I don't know." Chaki studied the scene, moving his gaze to JaLee. The man still writhed on the hook, screaming and shrieking. Blood dripped from the arrow sunk into JaLee's chest and more blood streamed out of the cut in his inner thigh.

"I think he is feeding on JaLee," Shan Xun said. "He is not touching him, but I think he is feeding on him somehow."

Chaki nocked another arrow, aimed, and let the arrow fly. The arrow sunk deep into JaLee's screaming mouth. JaLee's screams abruptly stopped and a still silence spread out over the village.

Drog Kuhn snatched the fading sounds out of the air with his tendrils and pulled them into his ears. His ears pulsed, but the light was very faint, a very pale red. Feeding time was over. For now. The arrows in his back itched him. He did not bleed. He had no blood running through him as humans did. When he was younger, he had found that to be quite curious. The first time he had been cut, he had expected a flowing river of red fluid to pour out of him, but nothing had come out. He remembered peeling back the cut skin and staring at some thick mass of black goo that lay beneath. He had no idea what it was. He shrugged and put the skin flap back in place. The skin quickly healed itself and the cut was gone. That is just how the universe made him. Who was he to question what he was made of?

Drog Kuhn reached down behind him and plucked the arrow out of his calf, dropping the arrow to the dirt. He reached behind himself and plucked two of the arrows out of his back. He couldn't reach a third arrow lodged slightly lower down his back and this annoyed him greatly. He turned to face his attackers.

But they were no longer behind him.

Chaki, Savio, and Shan Xun had moved to a new position, moving very quietly and with great stealth to avoid being heard. They were hiding behind stacks of bagged rice, the bags reaching seven bags high, offering them enough shelter to hide behind without being seen.

Chaki slowly rose up behind the bags —

— and stared straight into the face of the demon Drog Kuhn.

Chaki started, drawing back, stumbling awkwardly, falling to the ground on his buttocks.

Savio yelped and jumped backwards as he rose up, hitting his back against the support beam of the building near them. He tried to push himself through the wall of the building, his feet churning on the ground, but the wooden wall would not let him pass through it.

"I can hear you breathing," Drog Kuhn stated calmly. "There is no sense in hiding." He sighed. "But then you humans often do things that make no sense."

Shan Xun slowly rose to his feet, keeping his gazed locked on Drog Kuhn as he got up. He gripped his spear with both hands as he rose.

Drog Kuhn turned around, then glanced back down over his shoulder at the arrow lodged in his back that he could not reach. He looked over to Chaki. "I need you to remove that arrow from my back."

Chaki hesitated. He stared up at Drog Kuhn from his position on the ground.

Drog Kuhn made an insistent gesture with his eyes, looking at Chaki, then looking abruptly at the arrow, then back to Chaki.

Chaki climbed to his feet, brushing his hands off on his pants. His bow lay on the ground nearby. He moved around the bags of rice and hesitantly moved closer to Drog Kuhn.

Drog Kuhn nodded, again looking at the arrow, then back up to Chaki.

Chaki paused as he reached the demon. He raised a hesitant hand, then grabbed the arrow shaft and tugged. The arrow remained lodged in the demon's back.

"Go on," Drog Kuhn said, his tone full of encouragement. "Just yank it out."

Chaki grabbed the arrow shaft with both hands. He yanked hard on the arrow and it came out of the demon's back with a soft slurping, sucking sound. Chaki stared at the tip of the arrow. There was no red smear on it, no red wetness. In fact, the arrow head was mostly clean. There was a tiny smear of some black substance near the base of the arrow head where it was connected to the shaft, but that was it. Chaki continued to stare at the arrow.

"Expecting blood?" Drog Kuhn asked.

Chaki looked up at the demon, but his mouth was too dry to reply.

Suddenly, Savio came charging at Drog Kuhn, clutching an arrow.

Drog Kuhn reacted quickly, thrusting his right arm straight out towards the charging Savio. Savio ran straight into the demon's large hand. Drog Kuhn's fingers wrapped around Savio's face, stopping Savio's momentum dead. Savio swung the arrow futilely before him, missing the demon.

Drog Kuhn snatched the arrow out of Savio's hand and immediately shoved the arrow into Savio's gut. Drog Kuhn was quite familiar with the structure and workings of the human body, so it was easy for him to miss any vital organs. There was no pleasure in rushing the death of his victims when he could feed on the sounds of their dying agony.

Savio looked down at the arrow embedded in his gut. Blood oozed out from around the edges of the arrow shaft that protruded from his belly. Savio looked over to Chaki, and then he smiled. He smiled a big, fat smile. And then he laughed. A deep and hearty laugh. Savio gripped the arrow and shoved it deeper into his own belly. His laughter intensified.

Drog Kuhn released his grip on the arrow as if the arrow had suddenly turned flaming red hot in his hand. The demon stepped away from Savio, clearly disturbed by Savio's actions.

Chaki moved over to Savio, grabbing his friend as he started to fall. "It's okay, Chaki," Savio said. "I'm going to be with Gianna." Chaki gently eased Savio to a sitting position on the ground. "I'm going to be with Gianna." Savio laughed again. "It's turning out to be a good day after all," Savio said with a fat grin. He grabbed Chaki's hair and pulled Chaki close. Chaki winced, but he did not try to take Savio's hand away from where he yanked on his hair. "Kill me, Chaki," he whispered. "Kill me before I stop laughing and start crying." Chaki tried to pull away, but Savio kept him close. "Do it," Savio said in an urgent, whispered voice.

Chaki took Savio's head in his hands and twisted his head sharply. Chaki felt, and heard, Savio's neck snap with the violent movement.

Drog Kuhn gasped a delighted gasp at the sound of Savio's neck breaking, but then frowned as he knew that particular would-be-feast was not going to happen as planned.

Chaki gently lowered his friend's dead body to the ground.

"What is that?"

Chaki looked up to follow Shan Xun's pointing spear. Chaki immediately recognized the huge shape flying in the sky. It was Firelord, the bronze dragon. And the living stone statue of Kwan MandaKi rode atop the dragon's back. Chaki looked over to Shan Xun. "Run."

Chaki and Shan Xun raced into the building and they both froze when they saw the bloodied bodies. They were in the room where Drog Kuhn had set up his twisted symphony of screams. The four men were still strapped to the table, all of them silent and unmoving. The two women were still tied upright to the posts on either side of the table. There was blood everywhere, covering the bodies, the table, the floor. A brazier filled with hot coals sat off to the side of the table, the coals white and still glowing red with heat. The older woman was clearly dead, but Chaki was astonished to see the younger woman shift her head, trying to lift it, but clearly too weak to do so.

"Wei Lin!" Chaki started towards the young woman, but a bloody hand grabbed his wrist. Chaki looked down to see one of the men on the table was also still alive. The man's naked body was criss-crossed with cuts and gouges and deep grooves sliced into his flesh. Chaki tugged at his wrist, but the man would not let go.

Shan Xun hurried towards Wei Lin and started to untie her from the pole.

Chaki tugged his arm, trying to wrench it free from the man's tight grasp.

"Chaki…" the man holding Chaki's arm said, the word coming out in a slow, pain-filled grunt.

Chaki froze. He recognized that voice. He looked away from Shan Xun and Wei Lin, lowering his gaze down to the man strapped to the table. Chaki looked closer at the man's blood-stained face. The layer of red coating the man's face was thick, obscuring his features behind the liquid as if he were wearing a mask of blood. But Chaki could see his father's eyes beneath the gory splash of red fluid that coated his face.

"Chaki…" his father said, slowly grunting out his name again. He looked at Chaki with pain-filled eyes, his face contorted in agony.

A huge thundering crash from above made Chaki whip his head up towards the tremendous splintering sound.

Firelord came crashing down through the wooden ceiling, cracking beams with its heavy bronze body as the beast descended hard into the room. The dragon landed right where Shan Xun was standing trying to get Wei Lin free, smashing him and Wei Lin beneath its massive metallic bulk.

Chaki stared at the spot where Wei Lin and Shan Xun had been standing. Sunlight streamed in from the jagged hole in the ceiling, illuminating the dragon, making its bronze body gleam. Just like that, Shan Xun and Wei Lin were obliterated from the earth. Chaki stared blankly, trying to absorb what was happening. The man who was going to be his brother-in-law was now smashed to a pulp. Wei Lin was gone; his secret lover was dead. And the father who shunned him lay strapped to a table covered in a shroud made from his own blood. And a dragon powered by dark magic glared at him with malicious intent, the beast's long, sinewy body dancing in the air like a cobra listening to music only it could hear. And then he just laughed. Chaki threw back his head and laughed and laughed. The veil of madness layered another coating of lunacy over Chaki's eyes. The madness clawed its way deeper into his mind.

The dragon craned its neck to look closer at him. Kwan MandaKi was no longer mounted on the dragon, but Chaki had no time to figure out where the living stone statue might be.

Chaki wrenched his hand free from the grip of his dying father, and grabbed the leather handle of a metal poker from the burning brazier that was positioned near the table, withdrawing the poker from where it rested amongst the still-burning hot coals. The leather was warm in his hand; the tip of the metal glowed a bright red. Chaki thrust the poker at the dragon, jabbing the hot red tip into the dragon's right eye. The dragon howled and withdrew, shaking its head madly back and forth as if the poker had actually burned it. There was a slight smell of molten metal in the air. Chaki stared at the yowling dragon. Maybe he had actually hurt the creature. He smiled darkly at the thought.

The dragon twisted its neck to look at him and Chaki could see that one of its eyes was now gone, replaced by a clustered mass of molten metal. It turned its head to look at him with its other eye. How could it see in the first place? It was made of metal. It had no real eyeballs. Chaki didn't know the answer to that. He didn't know how the arcane magic of living metal dragons worked. He just knew Firelord now seemed to be blind in one eye.

The dragon roared at him, screeching with a wild fury. Chaki quickly moved to his left, dancing with quick steps, keeping himself towards the side of the dragon's burnt-out eye. The dragon snapped at the air, missing him by a wide margin. Chaki looked over at the burning coals in the wide pan of the brazier. He moved over towards the brazier, skirting back around the table where the dead men still lay. He chanced a quick glance down at his father, but his father's eyes were now frozen open, his stare glassy. Chaki felt a pang of regret and remorse at his father's death, but he had no time to reflect on such things now.

Chaki moved near the brazier and ducked behind it, using it as a shield. He could feel the heat of the metal pan radiating towards him as he crouched near the brazier.

Firelord eyed him warily with its one good eye, keeping its distance from the hot coals. Chaki laughed at the beast. A dragon afraid of fire. Chaki shoved the brazier over, spilling the hot coals towards the dragon, then turned and raced out of the building.

<hr />

Chaki ran down the street, heading towards the one way out of the village. Everyone he knew was dead. Maybe he could reach another village and get help, maybe Whispering Trees near the bend in the river, or maybe even SnowDrop higher in the mountains to the east. He knew he could never rid

Fallen Rocks of the demon Drog Kuhn all by himself. He turned onto the main street and skidded to a stop, nearly stumbling in the dirt.

Kwan MandaKi stood silently in the street, clutching his sword, just watching, and waiting. The stone man guarded the only exit from the village. Four skeletons flanked Kwan MandaKi, two on each side of him, standing like silent guard dogs by their master's side.

And then the skeletons attacked, all of them charging Chaki at once.

Chaki only hesitated a second before charging right at them. He singled out the skeleton on his right as he sped towards the attacking group of living bones. It looked to be a skeleton of a young boy or girl, so it was smaller than the others. It carried a spear. Chaki wanted that spear. He timed his charge so that he was near the wall of a building as they drew closer. He leaped onto the wall, using his momentum to continue moving along the wall, to continue moving past the skeleton attackers, up and around them. As he passed over the small skeleton and started to move back down the wall towards the ground, Chaki grabbed its head and tugged it sharply, jerking the young skeleton down onto its back. Chaki grabbed the spear and twisted sharply, jarring the weapon out of the small skeleton's hands.

Chaki expertly wielded the spear, striking his opponents with great precision and skill. He knocked out ribs, picked away at pieces of the skeletons, plucking them apart. He shoved the spear through the jaw of one skeleton, then used the spear as a leverage tool to whip the skeleton about, smashing its bones against a nearby wall.

Soon, only two skeletons remained. One of the undead skinless corpses raised its sword towards Chaki. Chaki threw the spear and pinned the skeleton to the wooden wall behind it, sinking the spear through the skeleton's mouth. The skeleton gripped the shaft of the spear and pulled itself along the wooden shaft in an effort to free itself. Chaki used a loose brick he picked up off the ground to smash its skull into a dozen shards of bone before it could get fully free of the spear.

Suddenly huge stone hands gripped Chaki's shoulders and he felt himself being lifted off the ground. He was in the clutches of Kwan MandaKi and there was no way he was going to be able to shake himself loose from that grip. The stone fingers were tightly clamped around his shoulders. Kwan MandaKi held Chaki in the air, presenting him to Drog Kuhn as the demon approached.

Drog Kuhn stepped up to Chaki and looked at him. "You have proven to be quite a nuisance," Drog Kuhn said.

"You have proven to be quite an asshole," Chaki said in reply.

Drog Kuhn extended a single bony finger towards Chaki, his long sharp fingernail inching towards Chaki's chest.

Chaki watched the sharp nail get closer.

Drog Kuhn pushed the tip of the nail into Chaki's flesh, drawing blood. Chaki looked up at Drog Kuhn and smiled. "That tickles."

A dark shadow swooped down towards them and Chaki looked up to see Firelord careening towards them. There was something about its erratic movements that made Chaki think of an intoxicated fool who had drunk too much rice wine. The dragon's one-eyed vision was clearly throwing off its depth perception and its balance. The looming form of the wildly swaying dragon quickly drew closer. Drog Kuhn sighed and took a few steps away from Chaki, casually stepping back from him.

And then Firelord crashed into Kwan MandaKi with a heavy thud. The dragon's wing nearly sliced Chaki's head off, but he dipped his head just in time and the edge of the metal wing sailed past his head and struck Kwan MandaKi hard with a tremendous thud. The stone statue lost his grip on Chaki and Chaki fell to the ground, rolling along the street. Kwan MandaKi toppled to the ground, unable to keep his balance. Kwan MandaKi floundered on the ground, kicking his feet and arms wildly, again stuck like a turtle on its back, unable to turn over. A skeleton was caught beneath the fallen body of Kwan MandaKi and all Chaki could see was its bony legs flailing about. Chaki laughed a very hearty laugh. It was the funniest thing he had ever seen.

Drog Kuhn frowned at the foul sound coming from the man. He scowled at the one-eyed dragon and motioned angrily at the beast to go and right Kwan MandaKi. Firelord shuffled its heavy body over to the flailing stone statue and pushed Kwan MandaKi over onto his stomach with its snout. Kwan MandaKi struggled to get to his feet, smashing another skeleton beneath the weight of his stone arm as he tried to rise up.

Another wave of laughter burst out from Chaki's lips, a deep belly laugh. He thought of his dead brother monks, the mutilated school children, Brother Hammo, Brother Chupang, his dead sister, his dead father, his dead friend Savio, Wei Lin. It was too much for him to absorb. It was all too much. The mad laughter continued to pour out of his mouth.

Drog Kuhn turned his attention back to the man sitting in the street. There were snippets of sound floating about the man's body. He knew they were laughter, but he had never tasted the sounds of laughter before. Perhaps they would prove just as satisfying as screams. Drog Kuhn extended a tendril from his ear and pulled in a sound. He immediately scowled and made a puckered face. The sound of the man's laughter was bitter, sour, and quite unpleasant. It was truly foul. Most distasteful. He left the remaining swarm of sounds floating about in the air above the man untouched. The demon felt as if he had just ingested poison. He needed to get away from this man, from this place, and find a quiet place to rest.

Drog Kuhn turned away from the laughing Chaki, feeling a disturbing queasiness spread through him. He moved over to Firelord and climbed atop the dragon, mounting the beast. Firelord rose up into the sky, its small wings beating the air.

Kwan MandaKi stomped away down the dirt street, following his master and the one-eyed dragon.

Firelord careened again like a drunk bird, hitting the roof of a building nearby, nearly dislodging Drog Kuhn from his perch atop the dragon's back. The wall of the building collapsed. Firelord regained its balance and rose higher into the air.

The last remaining skeleton fighters trailed the stone statue of Kwan MandaKi, fading into the distance as they moved away from the village of Fallen Rocks.

Chaki sat in the dirt and just continued to laugh and laugh.

A NOTE FROM JACK O'DONNELL

Thanks for reading this fourth collection of my Land of Fright™ tales of terror. I hope you continue to journey with me deeper into the Land of Fright™.

I grew up in the suburbs of Illinois on a steady diet of comic books, Creature Features, WWII movies, Hammer horror movies, used paperbacks, James Bond, Edgar Rice Burroughs, the Don Pendleton Executioner series, Andre Norton science fiction, and kung-fu movies. And yes, it's true, when I was growing up we never even locked our doors at night.

My one claim to fame (so far) is that I co-wrote and co-produced the movie Stephen King's The Night Flier, based on his short story.

I'm a huge fan of graphic novels and would love to turn my Land of Fright™ series into a set of comic books, but I can barely draw stick figures, so if any artist is out there listening…

Visit www.landoffright.com and subscribe to stay up-to-date on the latest new stories in the Land of Fright™ series of horror short stories.

Or visit my author page on Amazon at www.amazon.com/author/jodonnell to see the newest releases in the Land of Fright™ series.

-JACK

MORE LAND OF FRIGHT™ COLLECTIONS ARE AVAILABLE NOW!

Turn the page and step into fear!

Land of Fright™ terrorstories contained in Collection I:

#1 - Whirring Blades: A simple late-night trip to the mall for a father and his son turns into a struggle for survival when they are attacked by a deadly swarm of toy helicopters.

#2 - The Big Leagues: A scorned young baseball player shows his teammates he really knows how to play ball with the best of them.

#3 - Snowflakes: In the land of Frawst, special snowflakes are a gift from the gods, capable of transferring the knowledge of the Ancients. A young woman searches the skies with breathless anticipation for her snowflake, but finds something far more dark and dangerous instead.

#4 - End of the Rainbow: In Medieval England, a warrior and his woman find the end of a massive rainbow that has filled the sky and discover the dark secret of its power.

#5 - Trophy Wives: An enigmatic sculptor meets a beautiful woman whom he vows will be his next subject. But things may not turn out the way he plans...

#6 - Die-orama: A petty thief finds out that a WWII model diorama in his local hobby shop holds much more than just plastic vehicles and plastic soldiers.

#7 - Creature in the Creek: A lonely young woman finds her favorite secluded spot inhabited by a monster from her past.

#8 - The Emperor of Fear: In ancient Rome, two coliseum workers encounter a mysterious crate containing an unearthly creature. Just in time for the next gladiator games...

#9 - The Towers That Fell From The Sky: Two analysts race to uncover the secret purpose of the giant alien towers that have thundered down out of the skies.

#10 - God Save The Queen: An exterminator piloting an ant-sized robot comes face to face with the queen of a nest he has been assigned to destroy.

Land of Fright™ terrorstories contained in Collection II:

#11 - Special Announcement: A fraud investigator discovers the disturbing truth behind the messages on a community announcement board.

#12 - Poisoned Land: Savage hunters patrol the Poisoned Lands, demanding appeasement from the three survivors trapped in a surrounded building. How far will each one of them go to survive?

#13 - Pool of Light: A mysterious wave of dark energy from space washes over the Earth, trapping a woman and her friends in pools of light. Beyond the edges of the light, deep pockets of darkness hold much more than just empty blackness.

#14 - Ghosts of Pompeii: A woman on a tour of Italy with her son unwittingly awakens the ghosts of Pompeii.

#15 - Sparklers: A child's sparkler opens a doorway to another dimension and a father must enter it to save his family and his neighborhood from the ominous threat that lays beyond.

#16 - The Grid: An interstellar salvage crew activates a mysterious grid on an abandoned vessel floating in space, unleashing a deadly force.

#17 - The Barn: An empty barn beckons an amateur photographer to step through its dark entrance, whispering promises of a once-in-a-lifetime shoot.

#18 - Sands of the Colosseum: A businessman in Rome gets to experience the dream of a lifetime when he visits the great Colosseum — until he finds himself standing on the arena floor.

#19 - Flipbook: A man sees a dark future of his family in jeopardy when he watches the tiny animations of a flipbook play out in his hand.

#20 - Day of the Hoppers: Two boys flee for their lives when their friendly neighborhood grasshoppers turn into deadly projectiles.

Land of Fright™ terrorstories contained in Collection III:

#21 - The Prospector: In the 1800's, a lonely prospector finds the body parts of a woman as he pans for gold in the wilds of California.

#22 - The Boy In The Yearbook: Two middle-aged women are tormented by a mysterious photograph in their high school yearbook.

#23 - Shot Glass: A man discovers the shot glasses in his great-grandfather's collection can do much more than just hold a mouthful of liquor.

#24 - The Champion: An actor in a medieval renaissance re-enactment show becomes the unbeatable champion he has longed to be.

#25 - Hitler's Graveyard: American soldiers in WWII uncover a nefarious Nazi plan to resurrect their dead heroes so they can rejoin the war.

#26 - Out of Ink: Colonists on a remote planet resort to desperate measures to ward off an attack from wild alien animals.

#27 - Dung Beetles: Mutant dung beetles attack a family on a remote Pennsylvania highway. Yes, it's as disgusting as it sounds.

#28 - The Tinies: A beleaguered office worker encounters a strange alien armada in the sub-basement of his office building.

#29 - Hammer of Charon: In ancient Rome, it is the duty of a special man to make sure gravely wounded gladiators are given a quick death after a gladiator fight. He serves his position quietly with honor. Until they try to take his hammer away from him…

#30 - Pharaoh's Cat: In ancient Egypt, the pharaoh is dying. His trusted advisors want his favorite cat to be buried with him. The cat has other plans…

Land of Fright™ terrorstories contained in Collection V:

#41 - The Hatchlings: A peaceful barbecue turns into an afternoon of terror for a suburban man when the charcoal briquets start to hatch!

#42 - Virgin Sacrifice: A professor of archaeology is determined to set the world right again using the ancient power of Aztec sacrifice rituals.

#43 - Smog Monsters: The heavily contaminated air in Beijing turns even deadlier when unearthly creatures form within the dense poison of its thick pollution.

#44 - Benders of Space-Time: A young interstellar traveler discovers the uncomfortable truth about the Benders, the creatures who power starships with their ability to fold space-time.

#45 - The Picture: A young soldier in World War II shows his fellow soldiers a picture of his beautiful fiancé during the lulls in battle. But this seemingly harmless gesture is far from innocent…

#46 - Black Ice: A vicious dragon is offered a great gift — a block of black ice to soothe the fire that burns its throat and roars in its belly. Too bad the dragon has never heard of a Trojan dwarf…

#47 - Artist Alley: At a comic book convention, a seedy comic book publisher sees himself depicted in a disturbing series of artist drawings.

#48 - Dead Zone: A yacht gets caught adrift in the dead zone in the Gulf of Mexico, trapped in an area of the sea that contains no life. What comes aboard the yacht from the depths of this dead zone in search of food cannot really be considered alive…

#49 - Cemetery Dance: A suicidal madman afraid to take his own life attempts to torment a devout Christian man into killing him.

#50 - The King Who Owned the World: A bored barbarian king demands he be brought a new challenger. But who can you find to battle a king who owns the world?

Land of Fright™ terrorstories contained in Collection VI:

#51 - Zombie Carnival: Two couples stumble upon a zombie-themed carnival and decide to join the fun.

#52 - Going Green: Drug runners trying to double cross their boss get a taste of strong voodoo magic.

#53 - Message In A Bottle: A bottle floats onto the beach of a private secluded island with an unnerving message trapped inside.

#54 - The Chase: In 18th century England, a desperate chase is on as a monstrous beast charges after a fleeing wagon, a wagon occupied by too many people...

#55 - Who's Your Daddy?: A lonely schoolteacher is disturbed by how much all of the students in her class look alike. A visit by a mysterious man sheds some light on the curious situation.

#56 - Beheaded: In 14th century England, a daughter vows revenge upon those who beheaded her father. She partners with a lascivious young warlock to restore her family's honor.

#57 - Hold Your Breath: A divorced mother of one confronts the horrible truth behind the myth of holding one's breath when driving past a cemetery.

#58 - Viral: What makes a civilization fall? Volcanoes, earthquakes, or other forces of nature? Barbarous invasions or assaults from hostile forces? Decline from within due to decadence and moral decay? Or could it be something more insidious?

#59 - Top Secret: A special forces agent confronts the villainous characters from his past, but discovers something even more dangerous.

#60 - Immortals Must Die: There is no more life force left in the universe. The attainment of immortality has depleted the world of available souls. So what do you do if you are desperate to have a child?

AND LOOK FOR EVEN MORE
LAND OF FRIGHT™ TALES
COMING SOON!

THANKS AGAIN FOR READING.

Visit www.landoffright.com

Made in the USA
Las Vegas, NV
03 March 2023

68475738R00184